GIRL IN A G(

GH00866460

Lucy Branch lives in North London with her husband and three children. She is a restorer of public sculpture and historic features and has worked on some of the UK's most well known monuments including Eros, Cleopatra's Needle and Nelson's Column. The passion she has for her work inspires her writing.

Also by Lucy Branch: A Rarer Gift Than Gold.

ABL Press 2016

Copyright © Lucy Branch 2016

Cover illustration by Debbie Cassidy
Logo illustration by Florence Boyd

First edition

The author asserts the moral right under the Copyright, Designs and Patents Act 1988 to be identified as the author of this work.

All rights reserved. No part of this publication may be reproduced, stored in a retrieval system or transmitted, in any form or by any means without the prior consent of the author, nor be otherwise circulated in any form of binding or cover other than that which it is published and without a similar condition being imposed on the subsequent purchaser.

This book is a work of fiction. The characters, incidents and dialogue are drawn from the author's imagination and not to be construed as real. Any resemblance to actual events or persons, living or dead, is fictionalised or coincidental.

GIRL IN A
GOLDEN CAGE

LUCY BRANCH

ABL Press

Chapter 1

The first scream felt like splinters being pushed under my nails. The sound echoed around the high ceilings of my room and blended with an eerie after-tone of glass droplets chiming. The vast chandelier hanging down the centre of the open staircase always had something to say about the comings and goings of those staying in its mansion. The second scream was more primal: one soul begging another for help. My own soul responded, but my body would not. I couldn't have helped, or even stood up to investigate what sounded like a murder in my father's hallway. I was about nine hours into a migraine which, for anyone who has never battled with one, is a place where you have nothing left to give.

The migraine had begun that morning in the taxi on the way to Heathrow Airport. Tiny dots of white light began to move in figures of eight at the edges of my vision. Hiding a lie from my mother, a woman whose profession it was to sift for truth, had taken its toll. I hadn't anticipated how hard it would be. I'd managed fine with my secret for about eight months, but it was a lot easier with two hundred miles between us. This migraine was a protest at the stress of the last few days added to the anxiety that always cropped up before I went to stay in Milan with my father. I felt like a pet goldfish dropped into a lake for a couple of months each year before being fished out again. It wasn't that the luxury of a real lake was anything to complain about, but what was familiar was my little glass tank with its variety of small plastic plants.

I pulled my sunglasses out of my handbag and took a deep breath. I'd be okay; we were almost there. The taxi was moving through the entrance into Heathrow. I tried to ignore the numbness creeping through my fingers on my right hand. Closing my eyes, I could hear my mum's voice in my head saying, 'Take a pill, *now,*' irritation making her voice razor edged.

These days, my mum *loved* the drugs she'd fought so hard to veto. I'd been diagnosed with infant migraine when I was three years old. Mum had been relieved. She'd thought I had some kind of bone cancer because I would wake in acute pain most nights. I found sleep to be a portal into a land of pain where my bones were snapped and my stomach was booted by someone with enormous feet. Her response was to find a gentle, natural solution: piercing my tender pre-school skin with lots of sharp pins was *gentle*, as was the bitter bathwater of brown herbs fed to me in endless spoonfuls matched only in number by my tears. She tried just about anything to avoid the use of what she termed 'the dreaded drug route'. Incidentally, we had now rechristened the phrase 'the awesome drugs route'. None of the alternative practices made the slightest bit of difference. All that happened was my baby migraines grew into great strapping ones: migraines with auras!

The taxi stopped. The driver got out of the car to get my luggage. I pulled out my purse and slipped a small white pill into my mouth from the packet I kept in there. It was anyone's guess whether it would work at this stage. Hitting it early was the key and I'd been too frantic this morning to pay attention to small symptoms. It could go either way: slope off like it never had any intention of attacking me or go psycho.

The driver stood at the car door with my pull-along case, waiting for me to get out. I tried, but my right arm had gone sulky and was flatly ignoring anything I was telling it to do. With the driver watching me, I felt self-conscious as I twisted my body so that my left hand could take hold of the handle. He could see I was having some difficulty and pulled the door wide for me.

In my head, I said, 'Thank you,' but it came out, 'Zoofidd golltigger.'

The taxi driver looked at me, his eyebrows furrowing.

I smiled, rubbed my forehead, and tried again, 'Skelden glooo.'

Then he gave me *the look*, the one I always get when this completely inexplicable language tips out of my mouth. It's a combination of concern and incredulity. I could see the thoughts tick across his face: was I playing a prank on him? Did I not speak English? Or was I mentally challenged in some way? Auras are like added-value migraines. You get all the fun of the migraine with an appetiser of other symptoms that just *freak-people-out*.

Fortunately, I'd prepaid so I only had to give him a courteous nod, but saying goodbye was so natural I forgot I couldn't speak.

'Noot noot,' I said as I left.

Noot noot? Embarrassment flooded my body as I

walked away. I had to concentrate. The key to getting on this plane would be to not speak a word to anyone and to try not to behave more strangely than was absolutely necessary. Otherwise, I would end up sitting with St John Ambulance staff, unable to explain that I was not having a stroke.

Once inside the terminal, I tried to focus on dealing with the departures desk. The problem was that when I'm at this stage of a migraine, it's like being in a Hall of Mirrors at the House of *No* Fun. Everything seems exaggerated – noise particularly, but also people's faces, their words and space around them. Simple tasks, like laying my passport on the desk, take on a level of complexity only neurosurgeons should have to contend with.

'First class, Miss?'

I smiled. I could see my mum's face grimacing if she knew Dad had sent me these tickets. Born in Scotland, she had refined her accent while rising through the ranks as a police officer in London before securing the role she was made for: Chief Detective Inspector. These days she reserved the chords of her native Glaswegian for adding colour when swearing, or uttering words like *first class*. My dad might have done it on purpose – he liked nothing more than baiting her staunch socialist principles.

Check-in over, I went to the first class lounge to see if I could score some ice and make a cold compress for my head. This simple remedy was about the best temporary relief I could hope for. I managed to find a quiet, cool corner to sit in but, annoyingly, there wasn't a single traveller in a sufficiently celebratory mood to order champagne. I'd been hoping to plunder their bucket for the ice rather than having to interact with a waiter. I closed my eyes and my mind drifted to the possibilities that the summer might bring.

4

Usually, it took a similar form: I stayed in my dad's house for a fortnight full of parties. Dad took great pleasure in introducing me to people who would make my jaw hit the floor in a perfect cartoon characterisation.

'Chris, have you met my daughter, Francesca? She lives not far from your house in North London.' Suddenly, I'm chatting with Chris Martin from Coldplay about how great Hampstead Heath is. Yes, really, I am…

Or, 'Oh, Francesca, have you met Bill? He's staying with the host. Francesca went to see the Giotto frescoes at Padua yesterday, have you seen them?' Yep, suddenly I'm chit-chatting to *Bill Clinton* about the bulky figures and drapery of a Renaissance genius.

August was likely to involve being flown off in Dad's private jet to a Caribbean island to stay somewhere ultra-luxurious and ultra-lonely. Dad pays a lot of money for total isolation. Not a bad problem to have, I admit, and nice to have a father who wants to spend quality time with me, but despite all of that time we've spent together over the years, all the witty speeches I've heard, he is not an easy man to know. The same magnetic presence that has people flocking to be close to his energy, he uses to repel anyone who comes too close, which is my theory as to why he's never married or had a steady partner.

This year, I had a lot of work to do on our dream holiday, wherever that might be. This would be the setting where I'd reveal to my dad that I'd dropped out of medical school, twenty days after starting the course, and had been working on the till at a bookshop for three terms.

My migraine flexed its muscles. Ouch, a jab to the stomach which made bile rise to my throat. The aura stage was annoying, but not painful. Now, the beast was waking up and so would begin many hours of vicious battle. I planned to make my revelation after Dad had

5

enjoyed a lazy day swimming in a crystal clear sea, his tension rubbed away by a luxurious masseuse who made Naomi Campbell look like a frump. Just at the moment when he was enjoying his first whisky soda of the evening, I'd hit him with it.

The next part of the plan was negotiating his assistance in telling my mother, and then getting him on board with helping me to become a professional artist – the career I've wanted since I could hold a pencil. It sounded so straightforward. If only I was a bit ballsier. Then, maybe, I wouldn't be battling a migraine that was threatening to rival the wrath of the gods.

These thoughts circled my head like wary sparring partners until our flight was called. First class was quite full and hot, which didn't help my head much. As the engines revved for take-off, the pain ignited: small fires were lit all over my brain, and then the surrounding areas caught too. I began to feel almost desperate to get off the plane and the journey had only just begun. When we took off, the change in cabin pressure took me to a whole new realm of agony, but today, I felt like I deserved the pain I was in. I should have been honest with my mum two years ago when she was writing my university application forms for me, but that would have required breaking her heart. She was so desperate for me to become a doctor like her father.

The aeroplane's ascent seemed to be unending. I dropped my head into my hands. I've found when I'm like this the best thing I can do is try to slow my breathing and imagine dialling the pain down like I would the volume on a radio, but this is only possible to do if I am uninterrupted, which I most certainly wasn't.

I happened to score the most irritating air hostess in history. I tried hard to be patient with her, but I was raw from the pain. She buzzed about me ceaselessly like a merry mosquito, speaking in a voice so squeaky that nails on a blackboard would have sounded sweeter. I lay with my coat over my eyes to block out some light. She actually lifted my coat around nine times in an hour to ask something inane, and each time she led with, 'Coo*oeeeeee.*' Only an elderly grandparent can pull that off.

I ended up going to sit in the toilet for much of the journey to escape her. Splashing my face with tepid water, I looked at myself in the mirror. My hair's new colour was muted with sweat, and I'd taken such trouble to make the cut look perfect before I left. My shaggy ponytail had been lopped off by a hairdresser who was unaware of the bond he was severing to my childhood. My natural ash colouring had been upscaled to white blonde, cut to graze my collar bone in a blunt style and dried poker straight. My skin was red, the foundation incapable of holding up to the times that I'd rubbed my head and massaged my face. My jaw was clenched; my expression was that of someone clinging on to a cliff's edge.

Coming through arrivals, I must have looked like a drunk. I had one focus which was to get to a dark, quiet room. Dad had told me that his new assistant, Lorin, would be waiting for me. Focusing on the relative bliss of a quiet air-conditioned car, I swayed towards a man holding up a board with my name on it. He lowered the board.

Just when I thought it couldn't get any worse, Lorin turned out to be completely gorgeous: tall with dark hair and serious eyes, and I had to meet him for the first time in this state. I managed a nod of acknowledgment at him just as my legs seemed to stall. They stopped lifting on command and I looked down at them, confused, like I might find them stuck in some mysterious airport glue. That's when Lorin vaulted the barrier, because anyone who looked so much like a James Bond character would never be been seen ducking under it. Victorian as it sounds, I gave way into his strong arms as soon as he had hold of me.

It seemed no task at all for him to hold me steady and slip a phone from his pocket. He made a quick call, and within a few minutes, a porter appeared and took my bags. Lorin walked through the terminal carrying me, childlike, in his arms. The car was brought round to us. Thankfully, it wasn't one of Dad's collection of souped-up sports cars where I wouldn't have been able to take possession of a back seat, but a more sensible silver Jaguar. This seamlessness was how my dad's world worked all the time, all accomplished by pots of money and an army of staff. Yes, my father had staff – lots of them.

Lorin laid me across the back seat of the car and, with my face pressed against the leather, I tried to breathe slowly. He didn't speak to me on the journey, but he threw nervous glances over his shoulder every minute or so. The only problem was that I was beginning to feel nauseous.

'I need you to stop. Please, stop,' I burbled, too late. I was already retching with spittle dropping from my lips.

Lorin took the executive decision to get me home as fast as possible and to hell with the car. My father would probably buy another one rather than clean it. I retched repeatedly; tears were pushed from my eyes, doubtless carrying mascara with them. I thought how ironic it was that I'd made such an effort with my appearance that morning. My Italian father enjoyed making jibes about English women – he felt they were ungroomed, had poor dress sense, and didn't pay enough attention to detail, unlike French or Italian women. My mother was Scottish so he considered her outside of the category. I hadn't wanted to pour fuel onto his opinion; now all I could do was hope that he wouldn't be in when I arrived – I doubted there was any excuse big enough to justify my inelegance to him.

Fortunately, I didn't see my dad as Lorin carried me up to my room. He left a glass of water by my bed and an enquiry about getting more pills.

***

When the screaming began, I thought it was in my head. I thought my migraine was screaming at me with a girl's voice. It was only when I heard my father shouting that I realised something was going on downstairs. I made a vague attempt to move, but immediately encountered the *elephant-on-my-head* phase. This is where it feels like my head weighs about ten tonnes and, for that reason, I can't move around.

I closed my eyes again, but another scream soared right through me, operatic in its volume. *What was going on down there? Had one of the staff trapped their hand in a door? Had someone called an ambulance?* Another door slammed; another scream – this time further away. Then quiet again, like silence had gobbled up the noise.

I slid back towards oblivion. On the fringe of my consciousness, a note in that scream replayed. I knew pain better than most and would have recognised its call, but this was something else.

Fear.

Chapter 2

I woke the next morning in deep darkness. The windows had ultra-high spec blinds to ensure that not a single dot of light could penetrate. Stretching out, I smiled gratefully: back to normal.

My tongue was like leather left in the sun. I sat up slowly and took a drink from the glass of water Lorin had left me several hours ago. Getting out of bed, I pushed a button to begin what was a massive feat of engineering involving several blinds rolling, windows sliding, shutters falling back to reveal the early morning light which surged in to greet me. I revelled in its touch, though only a few hours ago it would have been so hurtful. The air was already warm and sweet.

Walking into my dressing room, I couldn't avoid a pause for admiration. Whereas many of my friends had enviable bedrooms, perhaps even with en suite bathrooms, no-one could outdo my walk-in wardrobe. It was the size of my whole bedroom back in London, with added conveniences such as a mini-bar and range of beauty products, and was filled each year with new clothes and shoes chosen for me by Dad's stylist.

Extracting a bottle of ice-cold mineral water from the fridge, I walked back into the bedroom and over to the window which opened onto a small stone balcony with table and chairs. Letting myself out, I looked over a wide and very pretty courtyard with an elegant fountain in the centre. The courtyard walls were filled with trailing pink, purple and white flowers: cascades of clematis, jasmine and bougainvillea. There were several seating areas; my favourite had large sofa-style furniture, a pergola laden with vines above it and troughs of lavender at each side. This space was designed and kept to perfection by my father's full-time gardener.

This room had been my own since my first visit when I was about eight years old. It was updated in some way every year, and it was always exciting to see what changes my father had thought to add. When I was eight, I had a bunk bed, rocking horse, dolls house and mini-trampoline. By the time I was twelve, I had a sleigh bed, a double seat swing, a nail varnish bar and games console. This year, the room looked much more grown-up: there was a laptop only slightly thicker than a piece of card, and a couple of sculptures on the mantelpiece that I was sure were by Giacometti. The walls were a mint green and had a silky texture to them which made me want to stroke them. A book corner had been created with tall shelves and dozens of brand new novels. An over-sized armchair had been upholstered in contemporary silver-grey velvet with matching footstool, and to one side, there was a small table with a collection of glossy magazines fanned out.

Fortunately, my drawing table was untouched, except there were fresh supplies. A huge blank page was laid out invitingly on the sleek walnut surface which was tilted at the perfect angle. It had a shelf which pivoted out, holding all my pencils and a lamp on an extendable arm for drawing at night. The window above the desk had its own remote control to alter the amount of tint in the glass. I could darken or lighten it by degrees or even add a colour filter if I chose to.

I could never admit to my mum how much fun it was to come to Milan each year because I got to live a completely different life to the one I had back in London. She did not believe in spoiling me; she had achieved success in her career through hard work, and she wanted me to have what she called a 'positive work ethic'. I'm pretty sure that if my mum had asked my dad for a house in Chelsea, a car, three ponies and five holidays abroad each year, he would have said, 'Fine, *va bene!'* Instead, she asked only for help with my school fees. I had attended a boarding school in Sussex since I was seven as my mum's job required very long hours and was absolutely not something that could be done part-time, she often told me. Boarding school had been the only answer for her as a single parent.

In London, we lived in a terraced house close to Alexandra Palace. It had three bedrooms, a quaint, aka pokey, kitchen-diner and one reception room. In my opinion, the house had too many tatty musical instruments and too few flat screen TVs, although it did have a lot of charm with some beautiful Edwardian features. My mum had invested considerable time in restoring them.

Visiting Dad, I was propelled into the stratosphere of the mega-rich, and it was all the sweeter for not being the norm. The house was not what you would call homely, but it made a spectacular impression, which was always my father's intention.

When you compared my parents' triangles of background, lifestyle and temperament, it was amazing to me that I'd ever come about. When I asked my mum, she'd always wave away the question with the same phrase: 'It was a long time ago'. I could only deduce from titbits the pair occasionally dropped that Mum had been very young and they'd collided like two meteorites on their own trajectories, for a short time orbiting one another, fascinated by the alien-ness of the experience.

I threw off the crumpled clothes that I'd travelled and slept in and walked into my wet room, tiled floor to ceiling with tiny diamond-shaped porcelain tiles. Some were finished in a high-gloss glaze while others were sandblasted matte. They were laid in geometric patterns across the floor and along the walls. In the centre of the bathroom the floor fell away, providing a wide sunken bath like something Cleopatra would have approved of. It looked amazing, but took so long to fill up that I would lose the will to live before it was half ready.

I preferred the shower: the strong, massaging jets were just what I needed to rid me of the residual tension from yesterday's journey. There were no towels in this house. Once the shower was turned off then, at the press of another button, it became a full body drier: jets of warm air blasted every inch of my skin.

There didn't seem much point in going down to breakfast yet. My father was unlikely to be up and I wasn't hungry. I toyed with the idea of going up to the roof to swim in the blissful infinity pool that was hardly ever used. The pool gave the illusion you could swim off the end of the building.

Perhaps later, but right now my drawing table called to me; the sketch of the annoying airline hostess who had plagued me so much yesterday begged to be drawn. Caricature was my passion. I had a quick and merciless eye which I hoped – no, prayed – would enable me to become a commercial artist, though I should add the caveat 'over my mother's dead body'. Part of my mum's problem with my style was that it wasn't serious enough for her taste. She might have got behind me if I'd wanted to become a history painter, producing emotional and eloquent scenes like Goya or Delacroix. In my mum's eyes, my kind of art was rude and shallow; she was probably right. People laughed or gasped when they saw what I'd drawn, and the more outrageous I was, the better they liked it, my father in particular. Since my first visit thirteen years ago, when I'd drawn one of his visitors as a rat-about-town with hair greased back, tight navy suit and tapping out a text on his phone with his tail, my father had been my biggest fan. He'd framed that sketch and showed everyone who had visited the house that summer, even, to my embarrassment, the subject.

When I'd been at school, people had asked me how I did it. This question never made me feel like a talented artist, but more like a cheat because it was so easy. It was like being born flexible: people who could hardly bend enough to touch their knees, let alone their toes, marvelled at the ease with which looser limbed people could slide into the splits, but it was just their anatomy, not an innate talent. The image of the merry-mosquito air hostess was so crystal clear in my mind that all I had to do was copy it. I made her hover slightly off the plane's floor. There was a bob of curly hair; I used her antennae as a hair band. Two curls at the front fell into a parting above her big bug eyes; their sweep echoed the curl of her eyelashes. Her long insect nose quivered with anticipation. She wore a fixed purse-lipped smile, but her little tongue darted out of the side of her mouth and a drip of drool fell as she anticipated the juiciness of her next passenger. Her wings whirred out of the back of her uniform, which was bursting around her chest and sizeable rear end.

I finished and leaned over for my phone, snapped a photo and uploaded it to Instagram. For a minute, I considered tweeting it to British Airways, but decided that would be too mean.

I slipped into a new grey-green top and cotton skirt and left my room. Walking down the galleried staircase was so much less fun than sliding down the generous curves of the banister, which seemed to go on endlessly. A contemporary chandelier, with a drop of around twenty metres, hung down the stairwell, throwing scattered light onto the dark twists of iron balustrade. There were freshly-cut flowers selected for their sculptural silhouettes in a fairy-tale Murano glass vase on the hall table. The breakfast room was off the hall on the ground floor. The intricately carved door was ajar, and I could hear an animated discussion taking place in Italian.

'There must be something I could help with,' said a young man's voice, sounding like my half-brother Blake.

'There's nothing to do. Lorin has been planning it for weeks. It's what he's paid for,' said my dad, a note of irritation in his voice.

'I'd really like to be...'

Dad cut Blake off as I entered the room by standing and throwing his arms open. Blake's eyes never left Dad as he fussed over me.

'*La mia Giraffa!* Your poor head, how are you?' He clasped me to his chest as if trying to absorb any residual pain that might be in my body.

'I'm fine, Dad. All better.'

Just to be sure, he twirled me around like a ballerina: a tradition from my junior days. Giraffe was a fairly apt likeness for me, as I had been all legs and neck until I'd grown into myself. He gave a sigh and took a moment for his eyes to drink in all the changes the last few months had made.

'The hair looks so sophisticated; blonde suits you. I

can see that this summer I will have to find you a chaperone. Maybe, Blake?' He turned to my brother, who made a face in horror. 'You do look very like your mother.' He sighed, shaking his head. 'How is she? Still locking up bad guys?' He gave the last phrase an American twang and laughed, showing a wide set of perfectly white straight teeth.

I'd forgotten how bright this room was. I lifted my hand to guard my eyes, which were super-sensitive post-migraine. The room had tall ceilings, its walls were clad in pale yellow silk and there was half-height wooden panelling painted out in a soft eggshell-grey. The sun blazed through long windows that ran the length of the room, and at the far end a whole wall of glass doors was folded back to bring the most exquisite Italian courtyard and summer planting inside.

Blake stepped forward, giving me an affectionate hug and kissing me on both cheeks. He had Dad's eyes, but not his build, being taller and more willowy. Dad was as stocky as a bull and not tall, standing just below five foot eight inches; I'd shot past his height before I hit four-teen. I thanked my lucky stars that I hadn't inherited his figure, and had dodged the Roman-nose bullet.

Each of Blake's features was more elegant than Dad's, but the totality was a little bland, whereas my father was all spice. It was the combination of icy blue eyes, which danced with humour, and his thick, rippling platinum hair, but his best feature, everyone agreed, was his sixty-five metre yacht named *Orion*. I'd inherited his eyes and Mum's nose, which was as concave as my dad's was convex. No-one knew where the giraffe genes came from.

We sat down. I gave Paolo a little wave. He had been making the most magnificent blends of coffee for my dad and his guests ever since I could remember. He was at his usual post, which was a fine industrial-sized coffee machine behind a small marble bar area in the corner of the room, and gave me a captain's salute.

A young woman, working alongside him, came to the table.

'Alice, we need some breakfast tea, fresh pancakes and strawberries for my daughter,' my dad said in Italian. 'Oh, forgive me for forgetting to ask how your father's recuperation is proceeding.'

She was around my age, had a neat pixie haircut and was smartly dressed in a dark pencil skirt and white shirt cinched at the waist. She looked more like a secretary than a waitress. I didn't recognise her from previous years.

Alice looked at my dad with shiny eyes. 'He's improved so much since your physiotherapist has been involved. I can't thank you enough.' Her voice disappeared in her throat. She turned her head towards me. 'I'll get your tea,' she croaked.

I raised my eyebrows to Dad, encouraging him to elaborate.

'Her father had a stroke. He is only forty-seven, poor man. I've been sending Phillipe to work with him.'

'Dad, last night I'm sure I heard someone screaming in the hall – was there an accident? It sounded like a girl.'

Blake raised his eyebrows. Dad rubbed his temple and forehead with one hand and then laid it back down on the perfectly white tablecloth. His eyes met mine and his own were soft.

'I'm so glad you didn't have to see that. It was truly awful.' He breathed out slowly before continuing. 'You remember Marco, my nephew?'

I nodded.

'He has a close friend who has been very ill since last year.' He tapped one of his temples. Blake folded his arms and leaned forward a little.

'She attempted to take her own life several times and was institutionalised for a number of months. Marco had been visiting her regularly and noted that she was always heavily medicated. The hospital did not seem to prioritise rehabilitation. After several months of little change, he came and begged for my help. He asked if she could be brought here and assessed by new doctors with the hope that some better approach could be put in place for her.'

'That's a big ask,' I said.

Dad nodded. 'I have to admit – I wanted to help, and I think a great deal of young Marco. She is very important to him and he cannot have her at his own place; they have a young child and it is likely she may attempt to hurt herself again.'

'What about her own family?'

'They are at a loss. My sister-in-law is the closest of friends with the girl's mother. The family are devastated and do not know what to do. They were happy for me to intervene. When she arrived, she was wild. The doctors had to sedate her, but we hope this will be temporary until she settles. I would be surprised if they ever get her back on track.'

'How awful: she did sound terrified,' I said, shaking my head.

Dad nodded. 'I just thank God it's not you with such an *illness,* Francesca. Physical things we can treat, but even in this age, the mind is unknown territory.'

Blake cleared his throat and checked his phone.

Alice brought a pot of tea to the table. 'I think, this summer, we must stay more in Milano than usual because of the girl. I do not want to be away for too long. I hope that is satisfactory? In August, we can take some trips to Capri or Elba on *Orion.*'

'That sounds fine by me.' I smiled, but it felt stiff. I was thinking how much less palatable my revelation would be without the top-model masseuse and the snow-white beach backdrop. He leaned in and gave me a kiss on the cheek. There was a pause in the conversation as we seemed incapable of thinking about anything other than the unhappiness of the fragile girl. The happy mood that had swum around us with my arrival began to dissipate.

The delivery of the pancake banquet brought the distraction we all needed. There were half a dozen varieties of pancake with accompanying pots of syrups and jams. Slivers of fruit, cut by a chef who should have been an artist, decorated the edges of the display. My admiration of the food jump-started the conversation again.

'This is a new table, isn't it, Dad? How lovely.' You couldn't ignore it. It was an eerie black wood, satiny soft with a dappled patina, and where cracks in the planks had been, the makers had poured in cast brass which made it look like a static lightning bolt in the dark.

My dad's voice was heavy with pride as he caressed its surface with his thumb and fingertips. 'It is unique. It has been submerged in a bog under water for 8,000 years in the Czech Republic. Isn't that remarkable?'

'Wow, that's special,' I agreed, not daring to imagine what that kind of history must cost.

'How's medical school?' Blake spoke perfect English. Though my father had paid for private Italian lessons for me since I was three, it wasn't uncommon that I spoke less Italian in Italy than in England.

'Fine,' I said, giving him a forced smile. Blake nodded, but I felt him reading my eyes and forced them down, feeling shame splashed across them. I'd always liked Blake, but we weren't particularly close because our paths seldom crossed. We usually met for only a few days each summer, and the rest of the time he would be in Calabria with his mum's family. I saw snippets of his life on Instagram. He lived in Milan with his mother so he saw Dad regularly.

Dad stood and touched me on the shoulder. 'I need to make a few phone calls in my office. Let's meet in the courtyard in an hour to catch up a little more, and I need to tell you about the wonderful celebrations I have planned tonight for my birthday. It was such a good thing that we didn't arrange it for last night. I didn't want to disturb you – Lorin told me how much pain you were in, *povera*.'

I looked up at him – a rare perspective for me, given our different heights.

'But, your birthday was three months ago!'

'I postponed it,' he said with a slight roll of his shoulders like he was the master of time. 'This year, I have something special planned and I wanted us to celebrate together.' He looked at me and then Blake, who gave a forced smile. 'It's good to have you back home, *Giraffa*.'

He nodded to Blake as he left the room. I continued with my breakfast, adding fruit to my plate and a petite *pain au chocolat*.

'Well, if you believe that, you'll believe anything,' Blake said, smiling in a superior way as the door closed.

'Sorry?'

'Papa and his sincerity act: holding your hand, looking into your eyes. *I'm so glad you didn't have to see it.*' He mimicked Dad's voice, lengthening the vowels and infusing his voice with deep concern.

'What?' I challenged. 'It sounded disturbing, and why should he lie?'

'Hmm – why indeed? Probably the same reasons as you are lying about university. You just never know with people,' he said, pushing back his chair and standing up. 'Am I right?'

The feeling of being seen through was about as unpleasant as having cold soup dropped down my back.

'You can't leave now you've said that. Sit down and dish the dirt on Dad – if you have any. It sounded like a reasonable explanation to me. What other good reason could there be for a girl to be screaming in our hallway at night?'

'I have things to do, little sister, and I don't know any more than you do. That's the point – no-one does.'

'That's not fair. He's just told us he's helping out his friend.'

'No. He told you what he wants you to hear.'

'You're paranoid,' I said, shaking my head and taking the last mini *pain au chocolat*.

'And you're greedy,' he said with warmth in his eyes, but a condescending smile as he leaned across the table and swiped my delicious pastry.

Chapter 3

Pushing my earphones into my ears, I hit play. I was listening to a lot of Florence and the Machine, a band beloved of my best friend, Kristin. I hadn't seen her since February as we were at different universities and I missed her, so listening to them made me feel a little less far from her.

I stretched out on one of the wide grey sofa-sleighs in the courtyard to wait for my dad and looked up through the canopy of foliage and flowers to the towering walls of the house above. I bounced my eye from window to window, wondering which one the girl was in, allowing myself to be distracted by the light which was trickling through the vines above my head, highlighting segments of every leaf. The desire to draw the pattern appeared from nowhere and became unbearable in an instant. The compulsion was such that taking an extra three seconds to put on my flip-flops was out of the question.

I ran barefoot harum-scarum up the stairs to fetch my sketchbook. My mum would usually yell at me when the desperation to draw gripped me like this; she didn't like its hold over me and felt my behaviour was too like that of an addict. It was certainly safer than drugs, but as with any addiction, the more I drew, the more I wanted to draw. I suspected if I'd had the same kind of need to solve quadratic equations, she wouldn't have yelled quite so loud.

Wrenching out the top drawer of my desk, I used it as a tray. Ramming an A3 pad under my arm, I dropped a collection of pencils, pastels and charcoals into the drawer. In went a jar of brass powder and a can of fixative – something to set the powdery materials in place.

I was panting by the time I settled back down on the sofa in the courtyard. The vine was at an awkward angle to draw, being above my head. First, I tried to take a photo on my phone so that I didn't have to look up continually, but through the lens, it didn't look right.

'Euh!' I yelled in frustration and propelled myself off the sofa in a giant leap. I managed two bounding strides at top speed before smashing into Lorin, who'd been coming in the opposite direction. Being only slightly smaller than him, my head came up and hit him just under the chin like a boxer's upper-cut. I saw, in horror, his head hinge backwards awkwardly and heard his jaws snap together. He staggered a couple of steps and swore in Italian.

'I'm so sorry! I didn't see you at all.' The first Italian I'd used since I'd arrived. 'Oh, that must have hurt!'

He gave me a look which I read as *ya-ha!*

In my state yesterday, and what with all his James Bond-style vaulting barriers, I hadn't taken him in properly: he was quite spectacular. His hair was dark, almost black, and cut quite short to keep it in order, but it had a natural curl which defied his attempt at control. Tanned olive skin led to dark stubble around his mouth and chin. His eyes were a wolfish grey-blue, completely out of character with the rest of his complexion. I guessed he must be around twenty-seven, much younger than my dad's previous assistant.

Rubbing his chin and moving his jaw from side-to-side, he nodded. 'Were you stung by something?' he said in English.

'Only frustration,' I said, shaking my head.

'I'll remember to look both ways before crossing the courtyard next time in case any runaway trains are passing through.' There was a flicker of humour in his eyes, but it didn't change his serious expression.

Once Lorin had made it safely out of the courtyard, I continued on up to my room in a slightly less frantic way. Retrieving the small art-deco mirror that I had hanging on one wall, I finally had all I needed. Back downstairs, I lay the mirror between my legs in a position that could not be described as modest, but perfectly captured the view of the vine I wanted.

Within what felt like seconds of starting the first leaf's curve, I left the courtyard behind completely and went into a space in my head which was all about me and the vine. In this place, I could see much more than I had been able to ten minutes ago. I stopped seeing the vine as it actually was and saw something completely new. This was the place I craved being in; it wasn't exactly my imagination because it was quieter and less cluttered than I envisaged that would be. It was a hybrid zone. Occasionally, it crossed my mind that the migraines were the price I had to pay for being allowed access to this strange place. Most people seemed to be able to dip in and out of it when they were dreaming, or see things in an out-of-focus kind of way, but I could spend hours here, and the reward for time invested seemed to be special privileges. Perhaps my brain felt overused, under-appreciated. The migraines did have a protest vibe to them.

I drew rapidly, allowing the pencil to suggest the patterns rather than define them. I smudged the highlights with the brass powder and found unexpectedly that I could see each leaf was a character in itself, some sweet and angelic and kind, others sinister, predatory and cruel. As I drew on, it became more a tangle of faces, and the original subject of the vine began to be almost lost.

'*Fantastico!*' My father interrupted my pencil. 'Your style is evolving,' he said, moving the drawer of materials over and sitting down. I could no longer see the vine with a thousand faces. I had been hauled out of whatever that place was, and now I could only see a vine with highlights and lowlights once again.

He took the sketchbook and I stretched my arms above my head. My hand felt stiff. I looked over at my work. Every inch of the A3 paper was filled with charcoal and brass dust. It still had the flavour of a caricature, but there was something grittier to it.

'This would make a magnificent mural. Shall I have the ballroom ceiling whitewashed?' He chuckled, his eyes crinkling with humour. I smiled too.

'A great compliment, Dad, but I think the Baroque fresco works well in there.'

'Yes, true.' He nodded and turned his mouth down at the corners as if he was slightly regretful of the fact. 'Alice, iced tea, please.'

I hadn't noticed her standing just inside the breakfast room. 'It's like living in Italian *Downton Abbey* here, Dad. You should get Alice to call you "Milord".'

'Not enough Labradors here for that,' he said, giving his eyebrows a little flick as he always did when he made a joke. 'I want you to show this to Sergio. He's already late, but that's no surprise.'

My heart gave a little skip. I had not grown up at all. Sergio Rudolpho was a highly successful sculptor whom I'd known about four years. My father's business partner, Pierro Ricco, had discovered him, and between them they had helped him rise to huge fame in the art world – and had profited greatly through his success.

When I was fourteen, Sergio had been my first proper crush. In fact, I'd been crushed in every way because I was soon told that he was gay. So smitten was I that, despite this key information and our difference in age, one day, I'd tried to kiss him. The resulting embarrass-ment was so acute on my part that I could hardly look at him for at least a month, though I still worshipped his feet which was as high as my eyes dared to rise.

In my defence, he was ridiculously easy to fall in love with. He was young, perhaps twenty at the time, and very, *very* good looking: lean, chiselled, tanned with ash blond hair short, but messy. In fact, he was better looking than anyone I'd ever seen in a magazine, let alone in real life. Critically, because of who my dad was, he was always nice to me, and that cemented my feelings for him. What had my father been thinking, allowing this God-like creature to hang around his life when I had very little to do all summer?

At the end of that painful summer, I received a short, sharp shock which put things into better perspective and helped me move on a bit. It was at a party; I was due to fly home the next day. It was getting towards eleven o'clock in the evening and I'd been looking everywhere for Sergio.

I discovered him on this very sofa in the courtyard, lying in the darkness in the arms of another man. They were passing a hand-rolled cigarette between one another, trading a few words back and forth and laugh-ing at each other's responses. Just as I was about to

26

reach them, Sergio lifted himself on to one elbow and kissed the other man intensely, roughly. The spark between them frightened me, but I had a moment of clarity. Young as I was, I recognised need when I saw it. Sergio needed what this man could give him.

It was a painful lesson, and it was my drawings that eventually founded our real friendship. I ridiculed him, my father and Pierro mercilessly with my pencil, and this secured me a genuine place in his affections somewhere between little sister, fellow artist and friend. I took tonnes of photos of us together and put them on Facebook and Instagram without telling my friends the key details; I continued to indulge in daydreams where I was older, about the age I am now, and he would realise that he was not gay after all. Of course, in this scenario, I had become a Victoria Secret model and he suddenly couldn't resist my allure. Although these unconfessed fantasies did continue, in general, when I was around him I had become relaxed and could be myself.

'*Grazie*, Alice.' My father's voice broke my train of thought. Alice slid a tray with a jug of iced tea, glasses and some fresh blueberries on ice in a bowl on to the side table.

I took back the sketchbook from my father and smudged some lines. This seemed like the perfect time to admit to him that I'd dropped out of medical school, but I felt my stomach clench when I thought of the histrionics to come when my mum found out. I felt like a worm. I hadn't failed with a brave attempt; I had failed because I had made no attempt.

'Did you know Sergio would make it the first time you looked at his work?' I asked as casually as possible. I knew my dad had cultivated Sergio, and I wanted him to bristle at the idea that Sergio could have done it without him.

It worked. He poured us both a glass of iced tea and,

reclining back on the sofa adjacent to mine, put his feet up.

'Talent doesn't get you very far in the world, and even less far in Italy. Without Pierro and myself, Sergio would never have done more than studied at art school. He was fortunate that with a father as wealthy as Crassus, he would not have needed to anyway.'

'So why did you make it happen for him?'

'Art is a business the same as any other. I invested because I could see the return would be significant. Handsome, educated, a little wild, which you need to ramp up your PR, and talented enough. His art fetches some of the highest prices for contemporary art in the world, and that's because he is part of an experienced team and he does what they tell him to do.'

My heartbeat was accelerating; I needed to execute the next question perfectly. I ran it through in my head. It wasn't difficult. I just had to say, 'Would you do the same for me?'

My mouth dried. I opened it and Lorin appeared.

'Sir, Mr Regno has been trying to reach you on your mobile without success. He asks if you could come to the phone in the office,' he said in Italian.

My dad looked up at the sky theatrically and at me apologetically. 'I'm sorry, *principessa*. I'll return.'

'Damn it!' I yelled as he exited the courtyard. I hurled my sketchbook on to the floor. As if on purpose to really annoy me, I noticed a hazy dazzling gather on the periphery of my vision.

'Perfect!' I needed to go and get a pill as swiftly as possible. Also, if the dazzling had started, I should sit inside which I really didn't want to do on my first day in a sunny climate, but then again, I didn't want to miss the party that night.

I stood up. The haziness hovered. This dazzling wasn't quite like my usual symptoms. Its colour was slightly off, more golden than white and rather more shards of opaque light than the angry dots that usually dogged me. Grabbing my phone, I headed upstairs.

Typically, by the time I arrived in my room, the dazzling had gone, but so it sometimes was with migraines. I didn't want to take any chances so I took a pill and lay on the crisp white cotton sheets on my bed, which had been made perfectly since this morning. My bag had been unpacked and put away, and the air conditioning had been set to a blissful cool.

I wanted to Skype Kristin, who was travelling to Barcelona today, but she would still be in the air. She and about half of our old class were having a reunion holiday. I had consumed the bitter pill of not being able to join them several months ago when the trip had been planned, but the aftertaste had stayed with me. They were renting two flats and spending a few weeks there. They would be having such fun. I'd tried to persuade them to holiday in Milan instead, but several of the other girls didn't fancy it.

'*Bella, Francesca, dove sei?*' Sergio's boyish call arrived before he did. 'Hey!' he shouted, diving from the doorway of my calm room on to the bed, which was quite far away. He almost missed and fudged the landing. I threw my arms out to stop him falling. He clambered up and gave me two kisses and a bear hug with real affection before holding me at arm's length for an assessment.

'Blonde hair, I like it. You look *adult*.' He said the last word in a way that made it sound sleazy.

Positioning himself on the bed, he put one arm around me. I dropped my head onto his chest and nestled into him, sighing like a puppy reunited with its master. Just for a minute, I let myself go to that place where I was always in his arms.

My dad must have followed Sergio upstairs, though

at a slightly more leisurely pace. The corridor, being carpeted, gave no warning of his coming, and so when he entered the room, his eyes swept our intimate position. He made a hissing noise like a cat when its claws are drawn and gestured for Sergio to get off the bed with a single stroke of his finger.

'Ahh, how cruel you are, Domenico. I'm not even allowed a hug with your little girl,' Sergio said, sloping over to the window and leaning against it.

'Not so little anymore,' my dad replied, settling on my drawing stool. I suspected he didn't take the over-sized armchair as it would have minimised what height he did have.

Sergio was one of the only people who ever spoke to me in Italian here, though his English was near perfect. He ignored my dad's presence and wolf-whistled.

'So what's with the cute hair?'

I flung a nervous glance at my dad. Sergio's natural flirtatiousness felt excruciating with him looking on.

'Your dad is trying to make me have a meeting, Francesca, isn't that cruel? I don't want to work on a day like this. In fact, that's why I became an artist. I don't want to have serious meetings about things. Talk to me, Francesca, or better still, show me a funny sketch.'

'I like this one,' my dad said, passing him the one I'd done that morning of the air hostess.

'Oo, that's good!' Sergio smiled like he was enjoying the first lick of an ice-cream.

I saw an opportunity to move back towards my summer agenda. 'Dad, will I see Pierro Ricco tonight? I'd like to show him some of my work from this year.'

At Pierro's name, there was an instant change of atmosphere in the room. Dad stood up and paced a little. Sergio stood up straight, but wouldn't meet my eye.

My dad cleared his throat. 'Pierro has ... disappeared. The police think he might have been murdered.'

'What? How?' I tried to catch my dad's eye, but he was fiddling with the sculpture on the mantelpiece. I looked at Sergio; he looked down at his hands. I had known Pierro ever since I'd been coming to Milan. Dad had a close business relationship with him. Murdered? It seemed so unlikely. Pierro had been a tall, fit kind of man, not the type who would easily have been taken advantage of. Like my father, he gave the impression of being a man who could take care of himself.

'I can't believe it,' I mumbled.

'He's been gone several months now,' my dad added, shaking his head. 'Come on, Sergio,' he said gruffly. 'The others will be downstairs waiting for us by now. Francesca, I will see you tonight.'

I nodded and he left the room.

Sergio slid back over to the bed. 'I suppose I had better go,' he said, looking as though he had about as much enthusiasm for it as drinking sea-water. 'Perhaps you need company? Can't *you* ask Daddy-dear to leave me out of the meeting?'

'No, Sergio. He'd kill you.'

Sergio's mocking eyes grew wide. I clapped my hands over my mouth, realising what I'd said, and then we both started to laugh. He fell back flat on the bed again and I lay next to him, the laughter rippling between us.

'I've missed you, Sergio.'

'And me,' he said, squeezing my hand.

Chapter 4

I started getting ready around six o'clock. There was a timid tap on my door and a girl entered. She said, in Italian, that her name was Sylvia, she had finished my father's hair and nails and would I like mine done? This made me laugh. Though my father spoke English probably better than I did, he was so un-English in other ways. I couldn't imagine Bill, my mother's partner, having his hair set and nails done before he went out. It was a sketch too good to miss.

'If you'd prefer, you could come to the salon room. It's likely to be more comfortable in there.' Sylvia smiled. She was in her early twenties, tall with long, curly brown hair and deep chestnut-coloured eyes. I could imagine my father enjoyed being preened by her.

When I'd been a child, I'd taken up any excuse to go into the salon room. I'd loved pretending to style all my soft toys professionally in there, although many came out looking much worse than they had when they'd gone in.

'If you don't mind, I'd rather stay here. Could you please wait a few minutes?'

She nodded and started to set up while I grabbed a piece of paper and sketched out my father reclining on a chaise longue, wearing his Armani suit, with his hair in large rollers. His forehead was exposed, and I drew his nose even rounder than normal, making him look like an elephant seal. Sylvia, the hairdresser, I drew with no tweaks, concentrating as she painted his finger and toe nails. I grabbed a red pencil to add a dash of crimson to the nails. I couldn't bear to be torn away from this delicious image, and so I sprint-sketched for the last minute, aware that I was keeping her waiting too long. She glimpsed the picture and a smile passed between us, but no words.

When she was doing my nails, my mum FaceTimed me and I told her about the horror of the journey. She asked if I'd gone to the hairdressers *again* and was slightly horrified when I got Sylvia to wave to her on the screen.

'Well, don't get too used to it,' she said, frostily. 'When you're back at university, there'll be no-one other than yourself brushing your hair.' I felt the guilt of not telling the truth thrust and twist its knife.

I dressed in a glitzy cocktail dress which, I assume, my father's personal shopper must have selected. It had delicate straps across my shoulders, quite a low shapely neckline and fell in a simple way to the knee. It was heavy, with sequins running in a diagonal pattern. They began in silver along the neckline, gradually becoming darker as they went lower and ending in black at the hem. With each step I took down the dramatic staircase in my Sergio Rossi stilettos, the excitement bounced higher and higher in my stomach.

Blake was at the bottom of the stairs in a tux. I smiled.

'You look very Zac Efron.'

'You look very Scarlett Johansson, so that's worked out well.' He offered me his arm and we glided through tall wooden doors, inlaid with the most exquisite leaf pattern.

The party was to take place in our very own ballroom which was exactly as grand as the name suggested. Its ceiling was several storeys high and decorated with a mural of semi-naked gods and goddesses enjoying leisurely pursuits, all in an ultra-theatrical Baroque style. In case the theme of the ceiling wasn't sugary enough, a decorative plaster frieze of *putti*, fruits and vines had been piped around the scene like whipped cream on top of cheesecake.

There was a large marble fireplace with the kind of pattern that looked like a snapshot had been taken of a cocktail mid-shake, carved to twist and turn like a tendril of a woman's hair. Above the fireplace was a portrait of the Pope sitting in state. Its frame was highly decorative and gilded for good measure. On one side of the room, every segment of the wall was covered in paintings or tall mirrors. Nothing, it seemed, could be perfect without a little added gilding. The other side of the room had elegantly dressed windows which opened onto small stone balconies overlooking the city. Each window was dressed in an excess of cascading fabric referencing the pink colour of the marble columns.

Some guests had arrived already. Keen waiters stood tall, ready to charge forward and fill champagne flutes at the slightest indication. My father was chatting with a curvaceous, attractive woman in her forties. Her hair was particularly lovely: snaky russet curls bounced softly on her shoulders, complementing a few bronzy freckles on her nose. Blake introduced his mother, Vero. Dad twirled me round and Vero admired.

'Beautiful, beautiful,' she complimented, 'and hand-some too, of course,' she added, looking at her son with pride.

I chatted politely to Vero for a short while, and then, as the room began to fill, moved over to Blake who had found Sergio. Blake was scowling. They were both sitting on an enormous cushioned and, of course, gilded sofa. I squashed myself between the two of them, shoving them apart.

'What was that for?' Sergio huffed. 'I was just enjoying sitting next to your tempestuous brother. There's nothing as sexy as a brooding youth.'

'Why is he brooding? And hands off my brother!'

'Jealous?' Sergio teased and put his lips together, pouting at me.

'Yes, very,' I said truthfully. 'I forbid you to fall in love with my brother. That would make the situation much worse. Me in love with you, you in love with him, and him in love with someone else – I imagine.'

'Good guess,' said Blake. My suppressed feelings for Sergio had become something of an ongoing joke between us. It was good, in some way, that we could laugh about it – though in truth it still smarted.

'So why are we brooding?' I asked Sergio rather than Blake.

'His girlfriend isn't here,' Sergio said, whispering flirtatiously into my ear.

'Why didn't *we* invite her?'

'I am here, you know,' Blake said, clenching his jaw. 'Papa didn't invite her. He is not interested in her.'

'That should be a good thing,' said Sergio, elbowing me. I giggled, but Blake didn't.

'Tonight he'll introduce me to at least four carefully selected girls. If I dance and flirt with one, he'll reward me. It's about the only time he sees the point in me,' he said in a low tone brimming with bitterness. 'They will be connected to someone he's doing business with or wants to get closer to. The worst of it is I'll probably do it – to please him. I'm pathetic.'

'No more pathetic than anyone else in his circle. We'd all jump through fire to please your father,' said Sergio, taking a slug of champagne with his eyes on my dad.

'The problem is, I really like Antonella and I feel like I'm cheating on her.'

'Are you cheating on her?' I asked.

'Yes, sometimes.'

'Well, that would be why then.' I couldn't quite keep the contempt out of my voice.

Sergio shook his head at me in disapproval, but patted my leg, leaving his hand just above my knee.

'You know, I think I've figured out why he's never married,' said Blake. 'His criteria for dating is *what use is this person to me*?'

My dad must have sensed that he was the topic of our conversation. He glanced over at the three of us, and seeing where Sergio's hand was situated, he scowled. I nudged Sergio, who seemed completely oblivious to the bad vibe being projected towards him. Dad stood by the grand fireplace, talking to a woman who was wearing a lot of make-up and seemed to be comfortable invading his space. A young man stood next to her who wasn't a lot older than me, but my eyes glided past them both and settled on Lorin who was on the fringe of their group.

As the waiter passed, Sergio dived at the tray of champagne like a viper striking. He swapped his empty glass and relieved the waiter of three full ones. I didn't want more, so he drank two and passed one to Blake.

'I must say, I do approve of your dad's choice of assistant. The other one was so creepy,' he said, staring at Lorin like he was a cream-cake.

'He's not very chatty,' I added.

'Who wants to chat? Though I bet I could get him talking,' said Sergio.

'Bet you can't,' I challenged.

'Are we in competition?' he said with interest in his voice. 'A little old for you, isn't he?'

'I'm nearly twenty. I'm no longer gaol-bait.'

'If your father finds out, he'll be lucky to end up in gaol.'

'Besides, you can't play. You aren't a free agent. What about darling-devoted-Luca, *your boyfriend*, pining away for you back home in Florence?'

I knew this would needle him.

'Oo, I like grown-up-Frankie. A worthy rival who isn't afraid to fight dirty,' he said, putting his arm around my shoulder and drawing me in to kiss my temple.

My dad beckoned to me. I stood up.

'Back in a minute.'

Sergio grabbed my hand before I managed to take a step and held it for a second. I turned to look at his beautiful chiselled face. He kissed my hand slowly in a courtly way. His eyes glittered.

'Enjoy being pimped,' he said with a teasing smile. I snatched my hand back.

'I need another drink,' said Blake in a grey voice.

***

The band played after dinner. Blake and I were dancing with partners that my father had introduced us to. Mine wasn't too awful a job: I was enjoying the company of Kit, the son of a lady who ran several companies located in a business park my dad owned. This was fresh news – I had no idea he owned a business park. As we danced, Kit told me it was on the outskirts of Milan and offered to drive me over there to take a look – apparently, it was the largest of its kind in the region. He was a nice boy a couple of years older than me, studying history that autumn in Bologna.

Sergio had annexed Lorin. They were both sitting on one of several deep silk sofas and Sergio was lounging across it diagonally, almost touching Lorin's feet. Though Sergio was talking, it wasn't obvious whether Lorin was listening. He had the type of expression that you might see if someone was enduring root-canal treatment. When he caught me staring at him, instead of looking away, as was my usual instinct at being rumbled, I held his gaze for a moment and tried a slight smile.

He didn't break eye contact immediately, and this time I smiled to myself. He had given me more than he had Sergio.

On the edge of my vision, the dazzling that had begun earlier that day reappeared. I rubbed my head.

'I'm sorry, I'm feeling tired. Do you mind if I sit down?' I said to Kit, who was very gracious.

I moved across to Lorin and Sergio. Sitting on a chair, I laid my head on the arm of the sofa. Sergio stroked my hair.

'We were just talking about my statue which is arriving tomorrow,' he said.

'Another migraine?' Lorin enquired with a note of concern in his voice.

'She's always had them, poor thing.' Sergio was being more caring than usual. I suspected his motives. 'She'll probably be speaking in tongues in half an hour – now *that* is worth hearing.'

The lights went off, except for one illuminating my father who was holding a microphone. The band stopped playing, and Blake drifted over and stood behind our sofa. My father lifted his glass and cleared his throat.

'I would like to thank you all for coming to my birthday party this evening. It's wonderful to see so many good friends here and, of course, my family.'

He lifted a glass towards Blake and me.

'Your invitations asked that you were not to bring a present this evening. It is not that I am embracing self-denial.' There was a blast of laughter. 'I am hoping that you will give me the best present I could hope for by contributing to a cause very close to my heart. The Milliardo Foundation, which I set up almost five years ago, is working in partnership with the Bill and Melinda Gates Foundation. Our aims are ambitious: we want to help the world's poorest people lift themselves out of hunger and poverty through health initiatives, science, technology and education. There are golden envelopes around the room. I hope you might pledge funds towards our mission and ensure we leave this world a better place than we found it.'

There was a thunderous round of applause. Dad lifted his hands, gave a broad smile and shook his head to quieten everyone.

'But, I will not deny myself cake!' He turned to the door and clapped as a trolley was wheeled into the ballroom carrying a mountain of cupcakes that must have been painstakingly constructed. Each cupcake held a sparkler and a blazing candle. The overall effect was dazzling, and whooping, loud gasps and shouts punctuated more clapping.

'My chef has prepared these especially for the evening and tells me that each cake is completely unique. I hope they will bring some sparkle to the event, as will the fireworks a little later. Thank you for coming and have a spectacular evening.'

My father lifted his glass in a toast. There was a roaring cheer and one or two lights came back on. I was proud of the fact I'd kept up so well with the Italian. The waiters ran forward to divide up the masterpiece and carry it round to the guests. The sparklers were out by now and some of the candles had gone out too. We all took a cake when they came round, but I was distracted by the migraine dazzling. It was definitely different to my familiar symptoms.

In the ballroom's soft light, this was more of a golden haze like a fine cloud of shimmering dust, stretching from the floor upwards to a height of between one and a half and two metres. Another oddity was that it seemed to be moving around the room rather than being on the periphery of my vision: migraine dazzling wasn't normally so pedestrian.

I took a large bite of my cake while concentrating on the dazzling and was poked in the back of the throat by the sparkler which I had not removed. I gagged and crunched down on it. A gritty burned taste filled my mouth. I held it there and glanced both ways to see if anyone had noticed. I really didn't want to spit it all over the place.

Lorin looked at me and said, without humour, 'You've just eaten your sparkler, haven't you?'

Sergio and Blake burst out laughing. My mouth was still full so I just nodded, feeling ridiculous. Colour burned in my cheeks, though it was too dark for them to see that. I stood up, trying to be controlled, and was about to depart to the nearest bathroom when the dazzling moved unexpectedly into the middle of the dance floor, passing a few feet away from our sofa.

I spat the cake out into my napkin. My breath caught in my throat and I felt a sharp spike of fear.

Feeling the ash clinging to my tongue, I tried to wipe it with my napkin.

'Smooth and *very* sexy,' Sergio said between gasps of laughter. Blake's eyes were actually watering.

'Did you see that?'

I pointed. Both of them paused for a second.

'Don't try that old distraction tactic on us,' Blake

said, leaning on the sofa for support.

'Those lights that just went past.' I pointed again, looking at Lorin as he was the only one whom I might get some sense from. He raised his eyebrows and looked into the space I was pointing at.

'Maybe it's the ghost of the sparkler you just ate.' Sergio roared again and beckoned to a waiter for more champagne.

'Can you still see it?' Lorin asked.

'It's by the door.' I looked at their faces, hoping one of them would be looking at it too, but they weren't.

'Shall I get your medicine?' Lorin offered, standing.

'No, I'll go,' I said, and then watched in utter amazement as the golden haze exited the room. 'I think I need to see a neurologist,' I said out loud, though I hadn't meant to. Dropping my napkin on a tray, I left the group without another word to follow my lights.

Outside the ballroom, the hallway was quiet and cool. There was a member of staff standing by the doorway with a table full of Tiffany boxes. These were the going home presents for each guest and I could imagine the kind of tasteful delights that would be inside. There were a few people standing together chatting, but the lights had gone.

I went to sit on one of the chairs that the hallway offered. The seat was opposite the galleried staircase, but no sooner had I descended into it than I was on my feet again. The lights were moving up the stairs. They didn't hover like a stereotypical ghost, but moved rhythmically forward and up. Now I knew for sure whatever it was had nothing to do with my migraines: no migraine used stairs. It moved unhurriedly up to the first floor and along the open gallery past my bedroom and to the next flight of stairs. I decided to follow, watching it all the time as it ascended.

It was darker at the top of the house and the dazzling

lights seemed brighter. I moved quickly to catch them up until I was just a few feet behind them. Up so close, I noticed something faint within them. It was hard to see – an outline? I stepped closer, almost into the light, and then the image sharpened: a girl. As if feeling the intrusion, she stopped abruptly and turned around. The image was definitely female, quite tall, her hair just below her collarbone, wearing jeans, a vest-top and, oddly, slim fingerless gloves.

I stood centimetres away from the figure, my breathing almost still. We stared directly into each other's faces. The girl looked completely terrified and the light suddenly broke up. It disintegrated around me, leaving me standing on the third floor alone in the darkness. I had no idea what I'd just seen, but I wasn't scared. She was too contemporary-looking to be a ghost.

I walked back down to the first floor and into my room. I moved over to my drawing table and turned on the light. Sitting at the desk, I drew the face I'd seen which was so clear in my head.

A knock disturbed me. Sergio put his head around the door.

'I told Lorin I'd check on you – just to impress him with my solicitous nature,' he said, making the word solicitous sound wicked. He was quite drunk.

'He's not into you.' I gave him my most pitying eyes.

He drifted from the door to hold himself up on the mantelpiece.

'Shhh. I'm reserving judgement on Lorin, he's not that easy to read.'

'I can read him.'

'You're such a baby, you can't read your ABCs.' He moved over to me so that he could see what I was drawing. Putting a hand on my shoulder, he leaned in, and then suddenly pulled away.

'Frankie, why are you drawing Abigail?'

'Who?' I had been adding some wisps to her hair, but spun to look at him.

'Abigail Argent.' He jabbed my pad with his finger.

A loud buzzer went off in the room and made us both jump. 'Internal phone,' I said, going over to it.

'Is Sergio in your room?' My dad's voice was icy with anger.

'Yes.'

'Well, he shouldn't be! Tell him to get-down-here-now!' He shouted this so loudly I took my ear away from the phone.

Hanging up, I mimicked, 'He says you are to get-down-there-now!'

Sergio nodded, threw another glance at my sketch and then obeyed orders. He pecked me on the cheek as he loped past.

'I don't know what's eating him at the moment. Or, maybe it's what he's eaten. Do you think he ate a sparkler too?'

He was almost out the door. I pulled him back.

'Sergio, who's Abigail?'

He fidgeted.

'I'll tell you tomorrow – gotta go. Don't want to up-set Milliardo too much on his birthday.'

Chapter 5

The next morning, I escaped the house for the first time since getting to Milan. It was another beautiful day, and stepping outside the cool, sheltered house into the baking street, I took a few minutes to adjust. Looking up at its huge white facade with Greek columns running parallel to one another and stretching away to the sky, I couldn't help wonder how my dad could have made quite so much money to own a house like this. My mum had a good job, by normal standards, and yet you could have fitted her house in London inside just one of its rooms. Dad's family were real Italian aristocracy, but only the eldest son had inherited the family assets.

There were two great arched entrances: one was for vehicles to pass in and out and the other, a grand entrance in the centre, was meant for people. The entrance was guarded by two huge limestone statues of Mars and Athena, God of War and Goddess of Art. I preferred to slip out, unnoticed, from the side door in the courtyard and hop through a small door cut out of the much larger wooden one which the cars moved through. Only someone like my father, or maybe Muhammad Ali, would have enough confidence to feel worthy of exiting something as grand as that main entrance.

Milan was a fun place to be, particularly if you had money. There were endless shops, though I'd always preferred being a tourist to shopping. This morning, I reckoned I had just over an hour before I should zoom back home to be around for the delivery of Sergio's statue, and I wanted to visit a couple of my favourite places. Our house was between the Duomo and Castello Sforzesco in the centre of the city, so it took less than ten minutes to walk to the Duomo. I adored the building, along with every tourist and resident of the city who has ever laid eyes on it. Stacked from top to toe in very serious-looking sculpture, it was so busy that it reminded me of a hive. For me, it was an endless source of inspiration as I found it impossible not to ridicule the statues. I drew the patriarchs and prophets, martyrs and saints as if they were off duty from their public roles. This might mean two were enjoying a chat over an espresso, another might be doing some stretches, another checking his watch; the variations were endless and I never grew tired of the theme. Though I wouldn't have wanted a priest to view them, they were indescribably fun to draw.

Facing the Duomo, I sat on the hard ground and pulled out my pencils and pad from my bag. Sitting with my back against the plinth of the equestrian statue in the square, I created the arches, slipping from the real world faster than a priest could say 'Amen'. The shadows were strong that morning and my interest was directed to them rather than the sculptures which I'd intended to draw. I pulled out some charcoal and formed abstract shapes in the shadows. They were divine to draw: arcs and angles, slopes and spheres. My fingers whizzed across the page, smudging and filling. I drew the towers as accurately as I could, not messing with their forms so that they contrasted with the unorthodox happenings elsewhere.

A shadow fell across my page and didn't seem in a hurry to leave. People often stared over my shoulder and I didn't mind; they usually moved off after a while. Seeing as shadows were the theme of the day, I traced the profile this one cast: a long, straight nose; lips that were all curls; a chin with its line softened by stubble.

'Hi, Lorin.' I turned my head and squinted up at him against the sun. He bent down and looked closer at my sketch. His face was inches from my own.

'You're really talented.'

I stared at his lips. I couldn't help it. They were so close.

'My mother always says, "There is nothing so common as unsuccessful men with talent."'

'Perhaps that's true, but that shouldn't lessen the fact,' he said.

The pins and needles in my feet and legs that I'd been oblivious to seconds before instantly became unbearable, and I realised that the pavement that I was sitting on was so hot I could fry an egg on it. I struggled up and he pulled me to my feet. I limped a couple of steps and looked up at him. He picked up my bag and sketchbook.

'Want to walk back together? I have to pop into Peck's; your dad asked me to pick something up for him.'

He passed my bag to me and we moved across the square together.

'Varied kind of job you have – chauffeur, administrator, errand boy.'

'I used to be in the army.'

Sergio was right: Lorin was too old for me. He'd already had a whole career before this one. To make matters worse, I was now picturing him with a tough-guy haircut in combats and chest bare. My lot in life, or at least in Italy, seemed to be being surrounded by men I couldn't have.

'Why did you leave?'

'I could have signed for longer, but it was time for a change. I really only joined to avoid the alternative. I'm ready for a different life now.'

'What was the alternative?'

'Family business.' I felt the full stop at the end of his answer. 'Your father said you are studying medicine?'

I made an incoherent sound in my throat.

'It's a complicated profession, I imagine,' he said, clearly feeling the need to fill the silence.

'It probably is, but the truth is I went to three lectures in a year then got a job at a bookshop. I dropped out.' Telling him was horrible and cathartic at the same time, like the way you feel after you've been sick.

'What happened?' His pace had slowed. 'Can't you talk to your mother?'

I laughed and banged my head with my hand. 'Duh! Why didn't I think of that?' He raised his eyebrows, not looking amused. 'I want to be an artist. I *really* want to be an artist.' I felt all the suppressed emotion that swirled around this issue tamper with my voice. I must keep a tight rein on it – I didn't want to blub in front of him.

'Surely that can be discussed. Working in art isn't such a terrible career. There's an enormous industry associated with it.'

'My mum doesn't see it that way and my dad has never interfered. I hope this summer I can talk Dad into helping me, but I will have burned my bridges with Mum, and in September I will be *persona non grata*.'

'Unlikely,' he said, shaking his head.

I sighed. 'She will be heartbroken.'

We'd reached Peck's, the most regal of Italian grocers' shops. Lorin turned before we entered and put a hand on my arm to stop me walking in. 'From what I've just seen of your drawings, I'd say you'd have made a terrible doctor.'

We looked at each other for a moment and then we both laughed.

'I'm sorry. That sounded so much better in my head – it was meant as a compliment,' he said, the broadest smile across his face. It was the most incredible thing, like the sun breaking out on a gloomy day. It lit up his face and I saw a different person emerge from the serious one who moved about our house with a monastic gait. It made him a million times more attractive. It might have been the laughter or it might have been his embarrassment that touched me, but I felt a jolt of attraction so strong it made me giddy, and my mood, which had been steadily dropping as I'd discussed the issues I had to face up to, soared.

He stepped inside the haven of all good things and I followed like a puppy with a new master. It was a good thing I didn't have a tail.

***

The sculpture had beaten me back to the house. It was already in the ballroom, which had been cleared and cleaned of every trace of the party since last night. The room was flooded with light coming in from the tall windows, giving it an entirely different feel to the previous night where, despite its size, it had seemed intimate. The sculpture was still in its timber crate and was standing upon a trolley. It looked very large.

I walked over to one of the window alcoves at the far end of the room, which didn't have a seat, to admire the view. It had been too dark to see the previous night. The window looked out over the Castello Sforzesco with its magnificent clock tower and old trees around it.

The rumble of several people walking and talking in the hallway caught my ears. I heard someone say, 'Drag her if you must.'

I stiffened. *What?* Without really thinking it through, I pressed myself against the alcove wall and slid towards the billowing fabric of the curtains. Most summers when I was younger, my father would hire a nanny to look after me. As a child, this had been one of my favourite places to hide when we played hide and seek as you could have hidden ten children in the excesses of the curtain fabric. I pulled the curtain from the wall a fraction and watched the group entering the ballroom. Two men were carrying drills, though they looked more like henchmen than workmen. I could see Sergio, my father and someone else I recognised instantly: the girl I'd seen in the lights last night.

My mouth dried. I'd known she wasn't a ghost yesterday, but it was entirely another thing to see her standing here so alive and real. Again she wore jeans and gloves, but she also had a largish leather bag with her which looked heavy. One of the men closed the main doors into the room and then they both unscrewed the crates with their electric drills. When the panels had been taken away, the statue still looked mummified as it was covered in a textile wrap. Sergio pulled this away.

It was marvellous. I had to inhibit the impulse to run to him and tell him how talented he was. The statue stood at twice life height. It was an angel with head thrown back, body arched and wing span wide. I couldn't see the face, but the figure looked sexier than any angel should be.

It seemed like the statue was unfinished compared to other pieces of his art that I'd seen. Last year, he had produced a collection of sculptures which the press and public alike had loved. They were the most incredible abstract pieces which had been coloured – or *patinated*, he'd called it – in a palette of wild and beautiful tones. This one looked pink, like the metal was bare.

The girl, Abigail, was looking at the sculpture, and I couldn't help liking her as I saw in her own eyes the admiration for Sergio that I felt was in mine. My dad circled the statue and threw Sergio some compliments. Then he began talking to the girl in a low voice. Her focus was taken away from the sculpture, and she stared at him in what looked like disbelief at whatever he was saying to her.

She was speaking in pleading tones, but I couldn't hear her until she raised her voice at the tail end of her last sentence.

'...not an alchemist!'

I could see my father was growing angrier and his voice carried more. 'This is not optional,' echoed across the ballroom. She looked to Sergio for support, but he had wandered away from the group and seemed to be examining my dad's display of ancient weaponry which was mounted on the wall close to the entrance doors. She shook her head.

I can't be certain what happened next, it was so odd. She seemed to be reaching for something inside her bag and half turned towards my father. In that instant, he reached inside his own suit jacket and pulled out a weapon, gun-like in shape but it was clad in black and yellow plastic. He pressed it against her chest. A strangled noise came from her throat and her body jolted. I saw pockets of dazzling lights propel out of her body, fly across the floor, and fall a few feet from the statue. Just like last night, the lights were akin to a migraine, but this time I was certain that they weren't one. For once, these lights were not of my making.

I watched as the cluster of dazzling lights rose up. I

couldn't see any outline in the haze, but I felt sure she was in there. I stared at my father and covered my mouth to stop the exclamation I could feel about to burst out. What I was seeing made no sense. At his feet, seemingly unconscious, lay the girl's physical body.

My dad and the rest of the group seemed completely unaware of the hovering lights that were only a few feet away from them. One of the men had gone to get some water and the other was trying to revive Abigail. Sergio edged away from the whole scene, and looked as if he was planning on getting out of the room altogether.

I turned my eyes back again to the lights and watched in horror as they moved slowly towards me. Seeing them creeping nearer, I wanted to scream and run, but the need to remain concealed pinned me down. I backed away from the curtains so that I stood against the panes of glass. Not being able to see the lights from here, I waited with my heart thudding against my chest and my breathing coming as fast as if I'd been running.

When the lights rounded the curtains, I actually felt like I might scream in terror, but as my eyes adjusted, I could see her face pinched with anxiety and this made my own nerves disintegrate. This time, it was she who came close to me, allowing the lights to envelop me. Inside the lights, I could feel her presence the way she must have felt mine last night. She tried to speak to me, but I could hear nothing. I felt thankful for this. Being caught spying would be mortifying, and I didn't really need volume to lip read the word *help.*

I shrugged at her. *How?* But she didn't get to reply as the lights broke up as if she was evaporating in front of my eyes. When I was sure she'd gone, I crept back to my curtain to stare at the men. They had revived her and she was sitting up on the floor, legs bent, leaning against her knees. She looked pale and disorientated, but she stared in my direction.

I stepped away from the curtain again, away from her gaze. What could I do to help her and why did she need my help? I was pretty sure I had just watched my dad taser her, though for what reason I could not fathom. To my relief, I heard them exiting the room, and after a few minutes, I felt safe enough to take a step out.

I moved quietly over to the main doors to check if they were still in the hall, but it sounded silent. I walked over to the sculpture. For a second, I was distracted from the scene I'd just witnessed. The angel's face was divine: classical features, but with a contemporary expression of ecstasy and exhilaration. Her hair rose around her face as if blown by the wind.

'Do you like her?' My dad's low voice made me jump. I suppressed the humiliation that I could feel scrambling up my skin – did he see me exit the window bay and know I'd been spying?

'She's magnificent. The best he's ever done, I think,' I said.

'He is talented, isn't he?' Pride rippled in my dad's voice. 'He's such a conundrum: spoiled, conceited. I don't like the way he fawns all over you!' He looked at me with a no-nonsense gaze. I was about to defend that part of Sergio's behaviour when he cut through my words. 'And then there is such depth here.' He stroked the statue's surface. 'He always surprises me. I really think he may be remembered as one of the *great* artists of our time, if he doesn't die young like many celebrities.'

This was probably the moment to bring my hopes into the conversation, but I had a million questions banging at my brain about what I'd just seen, though I couldn't ask any of them without revealing that I'd witnessed the whole scene.

'Why is she unfinished?' I asked, looking at the cold pink metal.

His phone rang. He took it from his pocket, made an apologetic face, and turned away from me. He spoke in rapid Italian and walked out of the ballroom towards his office.

I went up to my room and sat in the oversized arm-chair. Very odd things seemed to be going on. Somewhere in the house, there was a suicidal girl locked up. Was she Abigail, the girl in the haze? My dad's role in this was even more bizarre. Either he was in the habit of tasering argumentative contractors or he had just attacked an innocent, sick girl. The whole situation was confusing and sinister, and yet my father was one of the kindest people I knew.

Then Blake's teasing comments rattled in my head: '*You just never know with people*'.

Chapter 6

I needed to talk to someone. First, I tried calling Kristin. She didn't answer, but a text came back.

On beach, call ya later.

Mum would have been ideal. She was great at analysing facts and never indulged in guessing, plus she knew my dad's character better than me, but she wasn't answering her mobile and I knew she didn't like me calling her office unless it was an emergency.

I texted Blake and asked if he'd come over. I felt a bit guilty. It wasn't as if we were particularly close. He didn't reply and I began to feel sorry for myself. Homesickness was always something I had to work through in my first week of the holidays. Not having good friends on tap in Milan, or wherever Dad decided to drop me each summer, had always been a bit of an issue, particularly as I'd got older, but this was not just usual teenage stuff that needed dissecting with a sympathetic girlfriend. This was weird, scary, serious stuff!

Hearing the side door slam, I leaped off the bed and ran into the corridor. Laying my hands on the silky wood of the banister, I looked over into the hall below. Alice, in her black and white uniform, was crossing the chequerboard tiles of the hallway floor when Blake sauntered in. He looked up and waved.

'Wow, you really are eager to see me, little sis.'

He smiled and stopped Alice to make a request of her. I beckoned him. *Up here*.

Blake came up to my room and I closed the door. 'Why don't we go sit in the courtyard? Alice is bringing sandwiches,' he said.

I shook my head. 'It's more private in here.'

'How intriguing,' he said, moving towards the giant armchair. 'Love this!' He bounced up and down on it before settling himself. 'So why did I get the honour and not Sergio?'

'I just needed my big brother's advice.'

Blake looked sceptical. 'You only know two people in Milan. You and Sergio have the art stuff in common, and you do *lurve* him. He's the more obvious choice.'

'And yet I called you. This is about Dad and you know him better than Sergio does. And besides,' I said, feeling uncomfortable at the thought, 'Sergio is mixed up in what I want to talk to you about. Do you think Dad is an honourable man?'

Blake laughed aloud. 'What a medieval thing to ask. Do you need him to slay a dragon?'

'No, I realised today how little I know him. Secretive is the wrong word, but he's certainly not very open about himself.'

'Secretive is exactly the right word. If he was having a haircut, he wouldn't give you the information freely.'

I sat on the bed opposite him and took a deep breath. 'Okay, you're going to think I'm mad when I tell you this, but I'm, sort-of, *seeing* things.'

'What sort of things? Dead people?' He laughed, but when he saw I wasn't laughing, his face shifted to serious. 'Oh no, you're not, are you?'

'No, she's definitely alive, but...'

I started from the beginning, explaining about the dazzling all the way up to what I'd witnessed not an hour before. He got up and walked over to the window and didn't say anything. The sunlight cascaded over him and bleached out his skin colour. With his dark hair it made him look vampiric. I suddenly felt the strong tug of my pencil.

Later, I'll draw that later, I told myself. It was like trying to stop a cough that's desperate to come.

He was silent for a few beats longer than I could bear.

'What are you thinking?'

'I'm thinking that I don't really know you. You could be fanciful or one of those girls who enjoys creating a drama. Or, you might need some *real* help.' He shrugged. 'I'm just being honest.'

'People always say that when they're being rude. There is another *or* – I could be telling the truth!'

He walked over to the bed where I was perching and sat close, speaking with a soft voice.

'Have you ever *seen things* before, Frankie?'

'Not like this. With the migraines I often see lights, which are really similar, but these lights behaved in a human way, which was what made me suspicious.'

'It's a really good sign that you've asked for help. In fact, it's much worse if you let these things peak, believe me.'

This was not the kind of help I'd been looking for. I tried to speak in my most *together* tone.

'Blake, I'm not having a nervous breakdown. I'm telling the truth. I sought your help because I'm worried for the safety of this girl.'

He continued with the soft voice. 'But, if you *did* need help for yourself, I promise...'

I cut him off in exasperation. 'I don't need help, I need advice!' I said, moving off the bed and throwing myself down into the grey chair.

'I know a lot about this, Frankie.'

My heart thumped in excitement. 'Do you know about the girl?'

Blake shook his head and looked down at his feet. 'When I was about fourteen, I had what my mother calls my first episode. I began to find it hard to function in the realm of what other people describe as normal. My mood swung more dramatically than usual pubescent behaviour. It frightened my mum; I got quite violent at times, and very upset and depressed at others. I was disruptive with my teachers, and after a while even my friends stopped pretending I was okay. I was eventually given a diagnosis of bipolar and medicated.

'Papa wouldn't accept the diagnosis. At the time, he was sure my mum just couldn't control me and was pandering to my bad behaviour. He's never forgiven me for it really. I feel like he's still punishing me, even though I've been as stable as anyone else for at least eight years now. He still won't mentor me or consider my requests to work for him.'

'But you seem so close.'

There was a knock at the door. Blake was up in a trice. Alice brought in a tray of club sandwiches, a plate of cakes and a jug of fresh lemonade containing ice-cubes with mint leaves frozen inside. She laid them on my coffee table and Blake held the door for her and they exchanged a few words.

I stared into space for a moment, thinking over this revelation. *Poor Blake*. It seemed so incredible. If anything, my sense of Blake was that he projected a very balanced energy. Perhaps I'd mistaken balanced for controlled; maybe he held himself on a tight leash.

'Shall we have them on the terrace?' he said, picking up the tray. We took the refreshments outside and sat at the table flanked by the shapely weathered stone balustrades and looking over the flowered courtyard.

'I'm really sorry, Blake. He's probably not punishing you intentionally. He probably feels guilty that he kept you at a distance when you needed him.'

Blake poured us some lemonade and rolled his eyes. 'The best piece of advice I can give you is to talk to Dad about what you saw him do, but not to tell him about what you're seeing.'

I nodded. I did not relish that conversation: '*So, Dad, I saw you taser a girl when I was spying on you.*' I shrank from the idea of bringing that up. Blake interrupted my thoughts.

'Putting aside what you are seeing for a minute, have you tried looking for this girl?' he asked.

'Online do you mean?'

'No. In ... the ... house.'

'Well, no, the tasering thing only happened a short while ago. Before that, I didn't know what the lights were and had no reason to suspect anything.' Blake ate and I could tell he was thinking. 'That's probably somewhere to start.'

'Is there anything else that you haven't told me?'

I thought about it. 'If I heard correctly, I think she said "I'm not an alchemist," but I can't be sure. It was all so odd. Do you think he's part of the Mafia?'

Blake shrugged. I expected him to say I'd been watching too many American TV shows. 'Doubt you could be as successful as he is in Italy without being hand in glove, but this thing with the girl, it's not very Mafiaesque. Do you know my mum works for Papa?'

I shook my head.

'She is a curator of rare objects. She also locates and buys particularly unusual things for him. She told me something once – and this is top secret, by the way – that Papa is the head of an ancient guild.'

'Really? What kind?'

'An alchemist's guild.'

'No...' I looked at Blake in astonishment. 'Does that kind of thing really exist?'

'Probably, and if it does, it fits Papa's personality exactly. He would be at the front of the queue involving anything with secret handshakes and clandestine ceremonies.'

I laughed, mouthing *yep*.

'I think our best bet is Sergio. You say he's involved?'

'He was with Dad when he tasered the girl and he knew her from last year, he told me that.'

Blake nodded. 'I reckon we can crack him, no problem.'

'Now that's the kind of thinking I like, partner,' I said in my best wild-west accent, which was pretty poor so I added some gun fingers and a wink. Some references don't translate across cultures. He gave me the concerned expression again.

'Don't worry, I'm not going mad,' I said.

'Well, I will reserve judgement on that. At least I do know a good psychiatrist.'

***

Blake had gone to meet Antonella. She was finishing work early and they had plans, so there would be no wringing of truth from Sergio until the morning. When he left, I settled down to draw the vampire version of Blake, but the tasering of Abigail kept barging across my mind's eye and replaying.

I needed to look for her and establish, at the very least, that she was the girl who was supposed to be convalescing with us. I slipped out of my room and walked along my corridor on the first floor. Though I was certain she wasn't on my level, I still opened every door and took a peek inside the other immaculate guest bedrooms. I moved up the house, only checking bedrooms, but on reaching the final room on the fifth floor with no sign of her, I retraced my steps, adding in the less likely places like cinema rooms, the gym and even service cupboards. I was back down to the first floor with absolutely nothing to show for it within a quarter of an hour.

Continuing down to the courtyard, I sat on a chair beneath a pergola laden with jasmine and looked up at the windows that were on this side. *Where was she?*

Sergio sauntered out of the breakfast room holding a coffee. I jumped to my feet and felt butterflies scoot around my stomach. I couldn't seem to soften my expression; it felt stuck.

'What?' he said, raising his eyebrows.

'I didn't know you were still here. We hadn't expected to see you until tomorrow,' I blurted out.

He smiled a self-satisfied smile and stroked his hair away from his face. I could tell he was assuming my weird behaviour was due to his mega-appeal having its usual overpowering effect on me. He moved across to sit down on a seat close to me and put his feet up on my chair as a footrest.

'*We* hadn't made any arrangements for tomorrow,' he purred.

Where was Blake when I needed him? He was the one who was supposed to lead the questioning.

I swallowed. This was a good opportunity if I just calmed down a bit. Wasting it was stupid.

'Blake and I were chatting earlier about the drawing I

did after the party.'

Smirking, Sergio cut me off by holding a hand up.

'All I can remember about the party is you eating your candle. After that, it's all a blur.'

'It was a sparkler,' I corrected. *Like that was the point?*

He raised his self-assured eyebrows at me.

'You recognised the girl I was drawing. Abigail, you called her. I was wondering who she was.'

He made an irritated *tskk* sound and exhaled. 'I really don't remember.' Taking his feet down from next to my knees, he sat up straighter. He sighed and took a final swig of his coffee before setting the cup down on the floor, then he fake-smiled.

'What am I doing sitting here chatting to you? My darling Luca has arrived from Florence to spend the evening with me and is waiting for me at the flat this very moment.'

He stood up.

'Sergio!' I looked up at him, annoyed. 'Don't ignore me – answer the question.'

He emphasised his exhalation to be sure I knew I was being a pain. 'She's some boring girl that used to work for me, that's all. You probably saw her at one of the events last summer.'

'I wasn't here last summer. My mum had a...'

'So you've seen her somewhere else and your artist's eye dredged her out of your memory. Weren't you having a migraine last night? That must shake the brain up.'

'I wasn't having a migraine,' I said. He took this as his cue to start walking away. I was on my feet in an instant, bounding after him, grabbing his arm to stop him leaving – I had him on the line now and was prepared to yank. He spun, and from nowhere came a whoosh of anger that nearly seared my eyelashes.

'Back off, Francesca! I don't want to talk about her.'

I dropped his arm in surprise.

'But, why?'

Irritation was written across all of his features. 'She's dangerous – that's why,' he said, giving me a glare that said, '*No more,*' before continuing towards the courtyard exit.

I stayed where I was for a few minutes, trying to absorb his comment. Abigail was dangerous, but how? It hadn't sounded like he meant dangerous to herself.

I plodded back upstairs to my room, not knowing quite what to think. I had a message from Dad on my phone asking me to meet him for dinner at Terrazzo Triennale that evening and that Lorin would drop me there. The restaurant on the rooftop of the Triennale building had only recently opened, boasting great views over the city. I had a particular affection for the building because it housed cutting-edge exhibitions of contemporary and visual arts. Though my own work was very different from what was contained in its austere walls, I frequently found inspiration there in the fusions of installations, crafts, technology and architecture.

I sat down to the sketch of Blake that I'd started earlier and drew in his shock of blue-black hair which stood up like that of a Manga character. I wasn't sure which idea made me more nervous – an obvious opportunity to talk to Dad frankly or a ride with Lorin when I would look nice rather than vomiting all over the car. I simplified Blake's features down to just a few lines and let the two icicle-like canine teeth speak. The thought of bringing up this morning's situation did not appeal. As I added shadows, I considered how I would start the conversation.

'So, Dad, I notice you own a taser...'

Perhaps not.

'So, Dad, how about that taser technology, ever find

it useful?'

Probably not good either.

As I got deeper into the drawing, these thoughts slid further away until it was time to start getting ready for dinner.

Chapter 7

At 7.30pm, Lorin buzzed for me on the internal phone. He waited by the front door as I descended the stairs feeling super self-conscious. It was the theatrical sweeping staircase: it made me feel like I was going to a prom. I wore a pale yellow sixties-style summer dress which was quite short and high-heeled sandals the same colour as the dress.

I watched Lorin, and he watched me, or rather my legs.

When I got to the bottom of the stairs, he said, 'You look lovely,' very quietly.

I met his eyes. It was only there for a fraction of a second, but my artist's eye recognised desire.

'Would you like to choose what I'm driving tonight?'

'Sounds fun. What are the options?' I asked, unable to resist flirting with my eyes.

'Rather than tell you, let me show you.'

He led me through the scented courtyard, which was thick with floral flavours in the warm air, to the side door. Stepping on to the charming but uneven surface where the cars drove in, Lorin cupped my elbow, steadying me.

We walked into a generous sized car parking space with walls. I looked at Lorin in confusion and he removed a fob from his pocket, pressed the button and immediately the floor jolted and began to descend. In my high shoes, I fell forward onto him and he grasped me tight around the waist. His hand pressed firmly against me and I allowed myself the pleasure of leaning into him rather than righting myself as I could have done.

As we reached the basement level, I was forced back to reality as the platform stopped and Lorin turned me loose.

The lighting was bright and I had to strain my eyes after leaving the velvety darkness of the courtyard. At least thirty-five cars were parked in a basement that could accommodate many more.

I whistled. 'I've never seen this before,' I said, stepping into the main area.

'It was built about eighteen months ago to accommodate your dad's increasing collection.'

I walked the length of the car park, looking at elegantly shaped vehicles which I had no real knowledge about. Lorin guessed my predicament. He caught up with me, and as we passed the exhaust pipe of each vehicle, he recited names that I'd never heard of.

'Koenigsegg Regera, Lamborghini Aventador, Lamborghini Huracán, Bugatti Veyron, Ferrari 488 GTB, Porshe Boxster Spyder, and my personal favourite, Aston Martin DB10.'

'I may have to decide based on colour, I'm that much of a car philistine.' I laughed, but I wasn't joking.

'You can't really go wrong whatever you choose, but

as you are wearing yellow, I think we should take the Lamborghini Aventador,' said Lorin, walking to the far end of the car park and entering in a code on a panel. A safe was set into the wall. He placed his finger on a flat screen and the safe opened to reveal a small wardrobe of keys.

As we walked towards the car, the lights flashed.

'This is the fun part of the job.'

I couldn't resist. 'Taking me out or driving the car?'

'I don't think I should answer that,' he said, walking to my side of the car. He went to open the door for me. I put my hand out to stop him and misjudged it so that my hand closed over the top of his instead. Embarrassment flooded over me like a shower. With all the flirting, now it looked like I was making a pass at him, which I'd only been thinking about doing, not considering putting into practice. I pulled my hand away like I'd been burned by his touch.

'I'm sorry,' I gabbled at double speed. 'You don't have to do that kind of thing for me. It's different if my dad is in the car too.' I must have been so red I clashed with the car. Why couldn't I just have shrugged it off? A nonchalant *Oh, sorry* would have done fine.

We both climbed in simultaneously. My short dress lifted even higher and I felt Lorin's eyes brush my thighs. The seats were yellow and black and sculpted for support.

He started the engine, which roared like twenty angry lions, reversed out of the space and drove into the car lift, which brought us up to ground floor level. We didn't speak as he drove out of the courtyard. The nose of the car was so low to the ground and the stone sets were so bumpy that he was concentrating very hard. Waved through by the security guard on the gate, he instantly picked up speed.

What with the cool car and very handsome driver, I

felt my temperature rising.

'How is your holiday so far?' he said, seemingly unaware of the effect he was having on me.

'Oh, you know, bit quiet. It's amazing living in Dad's world, but I wish I had a friend in Milan. I did go swimming on the roof today which is always cool.'

'I've been thinking about what you told me about upsetting your mother.'

'Do you think I'm weak?' It was out of my mouth before I could stop myself. *Filter, Frankie, filter,* I snapped at myself.

He shook his head. 'I sympathise. When I told my father I was going into the army, he couldn't have been more scornful and that stayed with me for longer than it should have, but you learn to let it go. I was also going to say that if you are going to tell your mother, Milan is the perfect distance from London to do that.'

I smiled. He had a sense of humour. *Hmm, even more tempting.*

'Will you tell your father tonight?'

'My pencil is much better at explaining things than my mouth, which is very unreliable. Perhaps if I just drew the key scenes like wanting to blow my head off at the first lecture, then we wouldn't need to have the discussion.'

'When I did my law degree, I studied art history on the side.' The seat squeaked as my warm legs unstuck from the leather. I turned to face him, wanting to encourage him to share more of these personal details. He glanced at me, a touch of self-consciousness in his face. 'I was very young and fell in love with nearly every new artwork I came across, and every girl. Looking at what you drew at the Duomo reignited something which I thought had died out in me. I'd packed that part of myself away when I left for the army. There was no room for it there.'

We had arrived at the restaurant and he pulled the car up. I sat for a moment, thinking *How many girls did you fall in love with?*, which was not what I should have been thinking when he had just shared something intimate with me.

'Good luck tonight,' he said and was about to get out of the car before he stopped himself. 'You don't like it when I open doors, do you?'

I was thinking I'd like it if he kissed me. Instead, I hopped out and stood for a second leaning against the car, allowing my heartbeat to slow down. The light was changing. An invisible hand was adding indigo to the sky. I slipped across the street, a dash of yellow, but all the time I could feel the tug of Lorin's eyes upon me.

***

My dad was waiting for me at our table. He was sipping mineral water. The restaurant wasn't quite as I'd imagined it: we were inside, but the walls and ceiling were glass providing the illusion of being outdoors. Around the periphery, there were many plants in varying shades of green, with additional layers and textures coming from the backdrop of foliage provided by the tall trees in the gardens beyond. This gave the sense of experiencing a verdigris horizon. In the centre was a bar crammed with people along its length. We sat at the furthest corner of the terrace where there was a small island of space away from the rest of the tables. The regular seating area was overpopulated with parties of six huddling around tables made for four. People could hardly move their elbows without knocking into someone adjacent. The waiters slithered between tables like eels.

The waiters brought over menus as a woman approached our table from the bar area. I recognised Vero, Blake's mum. She had a walk that swayed, the type that leaves an S-pattern in the air. Dad stood up and kissed her on the mouth, sliding his hand around her waist as he did.

'I'm dining with my daughter, as you can see.' I stood and kissed her on both cheeks, thinking that the way Dad kissed her certainly wasn't the way he kissed my mother on the rare occasions they met. 'Join us for a glass of wine?'

'I'm with some colleagues from the office,' she said in Italian, glancing over at the bar, 'but I'm sure they'll understand I could not refuse an invitation from *the boss*.'

She said this looking up at him from under her lashes, then turned to me.

'Would I be interrupting you?'

'No, of course not,' I assured her.

She slipped past Dad to reach the empty chair between us and shimmied into place – I presumed to ensure that we'd noted her bouncy and ample top-half. Dad was admiring and his smile was self-satisfied.

The waiter brought wine, poured it. Vero tasted and approved it before the waiter took our order.

'Vero has excellent taste in all things,' Dad told me. A hint of colour rose in her skin at the compliment.

'And Blake tells me you are at medical school, Francesca?' she asked. Typical – the first proper conversation I'd had in Italian since I arrived, and this was the topic.

'End of her first year,' Dad answered with a dash of pride in his voice. They both looked at me expectantly. I looked over the view, wishing I could fly away from the discussion. I took two large mouthfuls of wine, and then I thought of Lorin. If I didn't go for it, he really would think I was weak.

I took a deep breath. 'Actually, I left university last October. I want to become an artist.'

There was a silence where other people's chatter and

clatter of cutlery filled our ears, then Vero chuckled.

'Oh, I do choose my moments well. Good for you, Francesca. Doctors are common enough, artists are rarer, and who appreciates that more than ourselves, Domenico?' She laid a hand with long fingers on my dad's arm and gave it a slight squeeze. Dad had a confused look on his face like he had ordered fish and been brought a steak.

'But you got in. You've started already,' he said as if that meant something.

'Dad, I didn't want to go. Mum chose the universities, she filled out all the forms and practically frog-marched me into every interview.'

'Why am I only hearing this now?' His voice was becoming more agitated. It was a reasonable question. Mostly, it was circumstance. During the year we never did much more than swap brief emails. He would often come to London on business trips, but he hadn't been to Leeds while I was supposed to be studying there. Last year had been an exception: the first summer in Italy I had missed in twelve years, and the first he hadn't visited the UK. Mum had needed two horrible operations on her foot involving breaking bones, and though she hadn't asked me to stay home, I'd overheard worried discussions between her and Bill about how she'd manage during the day when he was at work.

'I didn't get to see you last summer so I couldn't talk to you about it. Is it really such a surprise? I've always been ... an artist.' As I released the words from my mouth, I had a moment of clarity. I *had* always been an artist – how could I have even thought that I could pretend to be a doctor? It was like a giraffe trying to blend in with a herd of sheep; it was all wrong. I took another sip of my wine. My mum always said she had no imagination, but she'd managed to fantasise her giraffe into a sheep with proficiency.

'I don't understand,' my dad said, really looking like he didn't.

'Mum was so set upon it. I thought if it meant that much to her, I'd give it a try. I didn't take a gap year, so I figured if I hated it there would be nothing lost. I could apply to study something else. I knew at the first lecture that I could never be a doctor.'

'Domenico,' Vero squeezed his arm again, 'you've had it too easy all these years. This is a bit of real parenting. You should be there for her, support her, don't crush her with whys and wherefores. Let her study art.'

'You would say that,' Dad snapped, pursing his lips in disapproval, 'because you did.'

'Yes, and it was a wonderful experience. Does she have potential?' Vero leaned forward, giving my dad the full benefit of her splendid cleavage.

'A lot.' He drew his eyebrows down as if this was a fact for concern.

'Haven't you considered representing her? You're not usually one to miss an opportunity.'

'She's my daughter, not an opportunity.'

Vero tilted her head to one side and looked at Dad flirtatiously. 'Doesn't sound like you'd be taking advantage of her.' She turned to face me and smiled. 'I have a friend, Fennar, who owns one of the most successful contemporary art galleries in Milan. You should go and see him ... if your father won't help.'

I glanced at my dad. My heart was beginning to skip up and down. Dad made a grumbling noise.

'Thank you.'

I smiled. She leaned in conspiratorially.

'Fennar is your father's competitor so that's why he doesn't look very pleased. Tell me, what kind of art you do?'

'At the moment, mostly I draw.'

'There is less money in drawings than other types of art.'

'The market is saturated with other forms of art. I think there's a gap for an artist who can do large-scale drawings and marry other techniques in too.'

Vero laughed and glanced at my pad. 'Perhaps.'

'She's becoming a doctor,' Dad stated. Vero pouted at him, her heart shaped face mirrored by the squeeze of her lips. 'Why do you want to convince me that my daughter should be an artist?'

'It's what she wants. I'm all about helping our children get what they want,' she said, and suddenly I realised that this conversation was not about me.

The starter came: a mini-platter of rocket, parmesan, pear and walnuts, but my mouth had dried and the succulent salad became about as hard to swallow as brambles.

'It would cause a huge rift with her mother. You and I agreed years ago that I wouldn't interfere with the way you wanted to bring Blake up. I extended Francesca's mother the same courtesy.'

'That was about which brand of nappies I bought, not about their careers.' Vero dismissed that argument with a wave of her hand.

'I think Blake has an excellent eye for art. Why are you not encouraging him to study art too? He could work for Fennar in his gallery.' My dad had a teasing expression on his face.

'Blake wants to work for you. If he wanted to work for Fennar rather than you, he would be a fool.'

This woman was clever and she knew how to work my dad.

'Father-son dynamics never work in business. Blake is only a cub now, but he will grow into a lion and we will fight, and I'm not sure the pressure would be good for him.'

Dad gave Vero a meaningful look, but she ignored him.

'True, but I think you are referring to scenarios where the son is forced into the family business, which is not the case here. Besides, blood will keep your secrets better than Euros.' Dad watched her, half-admiring, half-annoyed. She added to me, 'If Fennar thinks you are good enough, he has the connections to make you very successful.'

'I don't know why we are talking about Fennar. If Francesca were to become an artist, it would be with me behind her, not that Mafia whipping boy.'

My breath caught in my throat. He'd said *if!*

Vero smiled broadly. Fish had arrived with a crusty herby topping and steaming boiled potatoes and green beans slathered in some garlic-tomato dressing which smelled divine, but my stomach felt too tight to consume any of it. I pushed it around my plate.

'You should bring me your work to look at,' said Vero, half-standing. 'I must return to my party, but before I go, a small toast.' With only a mouthful of wine in her glass, she said, 'To your daughter's dominance of the art world and my son joining the family business.'

Our glasses clinked together.

Chapter 8

At around 3am, I began to feel like I was burning up. I turned on to my front, trying to move the covers away, and light stung my eyes. I moved up on to my elbows and rubbed my eyelids, trying to open them again, but the light was too intense. I realised it was Abigail before I could see her. She was on my bed.

I jumped out of the bed like I'd been stung and ricocheted into a chest of drawers, banging my toe. Hopping about in pain, I was still freaked, though my eyes were beginning to adjust.

What the hell is she doing?

I could see her outline now. She was sitting watching me and had a slight smile on her face, as if my reaction was funny. I limped around my bed to the armchair and sat on its arm to rub my toe. She got up and moved to the other side of the bed. We looked each other over, slowly this time which, on both other occasions, had not been possible.

It was odd because the lights around her were just like those of a migraine, apart from the fact they moved with her rather than in a peripheral way. Then there was her outline, which pulsed. It looked strikingly clear one minute, and at another was hardly there at all. I wondered why I could see her, and without thinking asked the question out loud.

She indicated that she couldn't hear me. I'd read an article about astral projection a long time ago – the Chinese were reported to have used it for thousands of years to protect their borders from invaders. If I wasn't seeing her sitting on my bed, I would have said it was ridiculous. Having seen her hit with a taser earlier today, I wondered if this was happening because of some kind of psychic trauma.

As soon as the word trauma passed through my head, I knew that this was the girl who had been screaming the day I had arrived. This was the manifestation of that scream. This was the girl who had tried to commit suicide. I looked at her hands which were covered by gloves. No-one wore gloves in Milan in July. Again, I spoke without thinking.

'What's happened to you?'

She stood up and came closer to me; perhaps she thought I couldn't see her properly. I felt the uncomfortable prickly feeling of being inside her lights and it made me edgy. She lifted her hand and wrote in the air with her finger:

N-E-E-D – H-E-L-P

I nodded. Of course, I would help someone in trouble if I could, but this felt complicated on so many levels. My dad was involved. He must have his reasons, and I was sure he would not want me interfering. I had no idea who she was or what this entity of hers was; I didn't really know anything about her.

She started to finger-spell again and I halted her, jumping off my chair to grab a pencil and paper and put the bedside lamp on so that I had a little normal light. Positioning myself out of her migraine glow, I indicated for her to spell out for me again.

C-O-N-T-A-C-T – T-E-R-R-Y – G-E-R-R-A-R-D

T-E-L-L – H-I-M – I – A-M – H-E-R-E

Which Terry Gerrard? I wrote. She read what I'd written and was satisfied.

She walked across to my desk and pointed at it. Before going to bed, I had redrawn Sergio's angel bleeding from a gunshot wound. I followed her across and wrote, *Terry Gerrard had something to do with the sculpture?* She shook her head, spelled out:

A-R-T-I-S-T – E-N-G-L-I-S-H

L-I-V-E-S – V-E-N-I-C-E

She signalled a thumbs-up to my drawing. I smiled, but felt awful inside. I almost didn't want her to be nice. It would be easier if she wasn't because then I wouldn't feel so obliged. She didn't seem in any hurry to go, and I felt guilt prod me again when I considered why.

She wrote in the air M-O-R-E and looked at me expectantly. I pulled out my drawings from this morning at the Duomo. She leaned in close to them and turned to smile up at me occasionally, pointing and nodding with animate facial expressions. I went to pull out the thick sketchbook I had in a drawer under my bed containing sketches all based on the Duomo sculptures. She looked delighted and made me turn the pages at her command.

I was beginning to feel tired and couldn't help swaying a bit and yawning. She looked up and signalled for me to close the book, but she lingered, reluctant to go. Guilt battled with my fatigue, but the latter won. My last thought as I fell asleep was that she must be lonely.

***

Blake was keen to see Sergio and woke me at around 8.30am. As soon as I put my feet on the floor, I felt a migraine stir. Tiredness was often a trigger for me.

I slipped a pill into my mouth even before I'd brushed my teeth. As I dressed, my temples ached. Going to one of the drawers in my dressing room, I looked over a small shop's worth of designer sunglasses. I hadn't even heard of several of the brands, but their frames screamed luxury. I chose the darkest lenses.

'Have you ever heard of Terry Gerrard?' I asked Blake as we sat at the breakfast table and he ordered what seemed like an entire menu of food accompanied by coffee.

He shook his head. 'Should I have?'

'He's an artist, but I think he might be involved with the Abigail situation. Maybe you should ask Sergio about him.'

'Don't you mean *we* should ask him?' he said, and I saw the suspicion glint in his eyes as they narrowed.

I squirmed, but was saved by Alice who served Blake his bespoke breakfast of white truffle, scrambled eggs and smoked salmon with a small bowl of blueberries. The smell of everything seemed too strong, another sure sign of the head-banger that was coming.

Alice left me with the hot water with lemon that I'd asked for. I really wanted tea, but I knew to stay clear of stimulants at this stage as a migraine would use any weapon available to it to ramp up its torture.

'What did you do?' Blake asked swinging his silver knife back and forth as he said each word.

I told him about my exchange with Sergio in the courtyard after he'd left the previous day.

He threw the knife down so that it squelched into the scrambled egg and clattered on the rim of the elegant patterned plate.

'Damn, Frankie. Now you've put him on his guard and he'll be much harder to prise open.' He took a deep breath as if to start on the second verse of his tirade, but then stopped. 'Were you drinking last night? You look hungover,' he said. Picking up his knife and wiping it with his napkin, he dug into his eggs. My stomach turned.

'No, but my head is not good. Maybe I could lie down for a bit. I'm not so sure Sergio will be happy to see us.'

'No, you cannot lie down. He'll definitely be in at this time of day, and now you've told me about the *dangerous* part, there's no way we're not pursuing it. It's only about fifteen minutes' walk; you'll probably feel better once you get some air.'

I stood up. 'I'll catch you up. You'll probably do better with him without me there.' Giving Blake a pat on the shoulder, I ignored the disapproving sounds he was making.

Standing at the bottom of Dad's tiered staircase, I leaned against the scrolled handrail and put my head on my arm. Thank God and the housekeeper that the chandelier wasn't on. The staircase was perfectly symmetrical – it began as a single wide flight and then divided at a landing. The flights rose upwards in a generous arc until they reached the first floor, where they changed direction and swept up to the second floor in a counter arc. Of all the contemporary additions my father had made to this house, I couldn't imagine why he hadn't added a lift. Climbing to the first floor felt about as impossible as scaling Everest.

'The library is dark and quiet.' Lorin's voice echoed across the hallway. 'Or, I could carry you up?' His voice seemed to lose certainty towards the end of the suggestion, probably because of my scowl. I didn't want him seeing me like this *again*: a pathetic person who needed carrying about like an invalid.

'The library would be perfect.' I made the effort to smile, but it probably translated into a grimace.

Dad and I used the library mostly after dinner, particularly if I came to visit in winter as it had a fireplace so huge I could almost stand up inside it. The room was kept dark when not in use to prevent the light damaging the many first editions, rare volumes and drawings Dad had collected and displayed. As I stepped inside, the pain roared as it encountered Abigail's bright shards of light. I threw my arms up to block them and scurried over to the sofa which I collapsed onto, face down.

Lorin knelt down beside me. My hair had fallen across my face and he stroked it away. As his fingers touched my skin, the pain in my head receded at the joy of his caress, but then it rolled back when he lifted his hand away.

'What can I get you – water?'

I remained still; I didn't want to shake my head.

'No, thank you.'

'I'll go,' he said and began to rise. I didn't want him to leave. In fact, I wanted him to lie on the couch with his arms around me and protect me from the pain, but I didn't verbalise my thoughts. Instead, I reached out and grabbed at him, making contact with his knee. He did a little jumpy-skip thing.

'I'm sorry,' he said in an embarrassed voice. 'My knees are *solletico*.'

With my brain function down to around a quarter, it

was typical that his flawless English had failed now: *solletico* meant ticklish. Even in my situation, I felt laughter kindle. Lorin, the six foot plus army tough-guy had ticklish knees. It was fortunate for him that I wasn't in the mood to ridicule him.

He lowered himself towards the floor again and leaning forward, spread one hand along the length of my neck, and laid the other on the curve of my hip. I felt his lips touch my ear lobe. His voice was low and he dropped his words directly into my ear in a way that would have been incredibly intimate if I hadn't been having my brain lanced.

'Your father is waiting for me. I need to go, I'm sorry.'

My dad began to shout from the hallway for him at that very moment. I heard footsteps tap across the marble floor. Lorin jumped to his feet and moved towards the door.

Abigail approached as he departed. I turned my head away from her, closing my super-sensitive eyes. Then, the brain-grenades began going off. These are explosions of pain followed by lulls which make me feel sick, and they go off in a sequential way. Though I tried to keep my eyes closed, one grenade was so powerful that I sat up and opened them wide, gasping. As I did, she tried to get my attention by waving madly. She was very close to me and it was hard to ignore her. I closed my eyes partially, trying to let in as little light as possible, but even this was worse than severe toothache. She was tapping her temples and moving her hands away from her head without moving her lips.

She repeated the movement, temples and away, and continued to do it. It took me a little time for it to occur to me that she was demonstrating something. I sat up slowly and made to copy her, moving my hands as she did. She shook her head fiercely and pointed to my head.

Inside, she seemed to be saying. *Push away the pain inside.* This was easier said than done.

Trying to engage my brain when it was so sore seemed a sadistic thing to do but, then again, this was clearly a girl who knew something about how the mind worked. As soon as I concentrated, it was like touching a copper wire to an electric current: the pain started to flow around my head rather than throb and shoot. Still, I closed my eyes and pressed against the pain, leaning into it and absorbing its full strength.

Not being able to bear any more, I gave in and sank down onto the sofa again, laying my head on the soft, cool cushions. Now that the pain had arrived, I knew my speech would have returned, though it wasn't perfect yet.

'Leeavv me,' I said out loud. The glow of the lights crept under my closed eyelids. I opened one eye again; she frantically tried to attract my attention. I left the eye open, which I felt was about the most I could offer her.

'*Up, up,*' she mouthed.

I sighed. Couldn't she see I didn't want a lesson right now? I moved up on to my elbows and tried again to push against the wall of pain. I could only withstand a few seconds of it then collapsed weakly before retching. This time I turned away from her and put one of the cushions over my eyes, hoping she'd take the not-very-subtle hint.

My dad must have been standing outside his office, which was the room next to the library. He was shouting in Italian. Between the glowing girl and my dad, I might have been better braving the stairs to get some peace.

'Have the blood results come through yet?' Annoyance was in every word. I could just about hear Lorin's soft voice, though it was not distinct enough to catch what was being said.

Then my dad shouted, 'Nothing? I don't believe that.

Take more blood, run more tests. I thought they were scientists, they have enough PhDs between them. Tell them they are missing something significant. I will cut their grants if they don't get me a result, and soon.'

I looked at Abigail whose lights were breaking up and disappearing. Surely he wasn't talking about her? I sat up on the sofa and put my hands over my head, hearing footsteps moving across the marble hall and the door opening.

'Don't turn the lights on!' I shouted, too late. On came nine glittering chandeliers, each one threaded with hundreds of reflective teardrops of glass. The pain was orchestral in its range.

'*Giraffa?* What are you doing in here?' my dad said, his voice full of concern. He left the door open, but closed off the lights immediately and moved over to my sofa. He knelt down in front of me, taking my hand and squeezing it in sympathy. 'Shall I take you upstairs?'

I nodded a little. He picked me up using the kind of careful hands with which you lift a newborn baby, taking care not to jolt me in any way, and held me to him for a second, resting his head on my own.

'I miss you being small. You used to fall asleep in all sorts of odd places in this house, and I would find you and carry you to bed like this,' he said before moving off.

My head was teaming with questions for my dad. He was so contradictory. He'd been so busy the last few days and I'd become so caught up in whatever was going on that I'd forgotten he was always kind. Though talking when I felt this grim was the thing I least wanted to do, the need to have some answers took precedence even over the migraine.

He started to move up the stairs.

'Dad, I heard you saying something about taking blood and tests. Who were you talking about? Was it your friend's daughter, the one who was screaming the other night?'

We were half way up the stairs by now. He was breathing quite hard and stopped and leaned against the polished wooden handrail for a second to catch his breath.

'No, *Giraffa,* what has given you that idea?' he said before heaving me up a little and continuing on upward. 'Do you remember Diana, she was my assistant in Florence?' I did vaguely. 'Well, it is very sad; she has cancer, and at present she has an infection. Her temperature is dangerously high, but they can't pinpoint the infection. Broad spectrum antibiotics aren't working. I have my own specialists working on her blood, but they are not coming up with anything.'

Dad pushed the door open with his shoulder and took me over to the bed where he laid me down gently before sliding my shoes off. He busied himself around the room, closing the shutters and bringing down the blinds, altering the air conditioning slightly. I felt pathetically grateful as he pottered around. Then he came and lay down next to me on the other side of the bed, taking my hand in his own and holding it to his chest.

'Don't worry. I won't really pull their funding. I just want them to do the best they can for her. She is a nice lady.'

My brain was burning, but being in the total dark and not having to look him in the eyes, I admitted my petty crime. It seemed like the perfect opportunity to bring it up.

'Dad, I need to tell you something and you are going to be mad with me. The other day, just after the statue arrived, I was in the ballroom looking out of the window when you came in with a girl. I don't know why I didn't come out – I know I should have done. I saw you ... taser her, I think. Did I see that?'

I expected him to shout and throw my hand away for spying on him. I'm not sure why I thought this would be his reaction as he'd never so much as raised his voice to me as far as I could remember. Perhaps it was just what I felt my low behaviour deserved. Instead, he shocked me by sounding perfectly calm, although he spoke with a slight tremble in his voice.

'That must have seemed odd to you.'

'It did, and I've been worrying about it ever since.'

'Sweet, you mustn't.' He rolled on to his side so that his body was facing me. His voice was full of concern. 'That's probably why you are suffering today with the migraine. You should have come to me and asked right away.' He brought my hand to his lips and pecked it. 'It's a difficult story to tell you because it began with noble enough intentions, but now I regret having become mixed up in it all.' His voice was soft and sad like a low note played on a cello. 'I've told you about Marco's friend, Abigail, who you heard screaming on your first night here. What I haven't told you is that at the end of last summer...'

He paused and swallowed.

'At the end of last summer, something really terrible occurred.' His voice cracked a little. 'I told you about the disappearance of Pierro, my business partner and great friend, but I didn't tell you that I know what happened to him. He was murdered ... by Abigail.'

'What? No, that's impossible. The girl I saw was smaller than me. You have to be wrong.'

'I assure you, it is entirely the truth,' he said in a voice heavy with fatigue.

'Why isn't she in gaol then?'

'She's sick. I told you that. I don't know all the details of what happened, but Pierro was trying to help her. He insisted that we use her on Sergio's exhibition last year. After the exhibition, I know that she went to stay in his summer house and when he was there on a visit, she murdered him.'

'What about the police?'

Dad shook his head. 'The decision was taken out of my hands. It was complicated, Francesca. Do you remember Roberto, my assistant, who worked for me for many years?'

I nodded.

'Roberto was Pierro's brother. He found the body. I'm not clear on all of the details, but he feared that the circumstances were such that his brother's reputation might have been damaged if the murder had gone public and he took it upon himself to prevent that happening.'

'What? That's insane! Are you saying he covered it up?' I said, unable to believe what I was hearing.

My dad sighed. 'I'm sure you can sympathise about the pain he must have been in at that moment. I believe his questionable actions came from a place of deep love for his brother. Myself, I was particularly concerned for the safety of the girl. Roberto said she was nowhere to be found, but he was raving that he would kill her himself if he found her. Marco was staying with me when I received the call and being in shock at the news, I let the whole affair spill out to him. He pleaded with me to intervene and help her. He argued that she could be treated properly in a psychiatric unit and kept safe until Roberto was more himself. If you see her hands, you will see how ill she really is. It's very, very sad. In honesty, I couldn't see how committing a sick young girl, not much older than you, to a life sentence in prison, would help the situation anyway.'

His voice pleaded with me to understand.

'That wasn't for you to decide,' I said, pressing my fingertips into my tender temples.

He gave a hollow laugh. 'Your mother, the detective, would agree with you.'

'And so Abigail is here to be protected?' I asked.

'I did tell you as much of the truth as I could. With a little help, we located her and had her sectioned, but after several months, Marco was concerned that the doctors were drugging her too much and she would never have a chance to get better and so I agreed to let them treat her here until a way forward could be found.

'I thought Sergio's statue would be a good distraction for her; it would give her days a focus. She was outstanding at her work. The other day when I showed her the sculpture, she tried to pull something from her bag. My security adviser had insisted I carry a taser when dealing with her, just in case. Her movement was so strange and I misinterpreted it. I assumed she intended to attack me as she had Pierro. The taser was on its lowest setting, I promise you. I had no idea she would faint.' His voice faltered. 'As you can see, my *Giraffa*, I'm in an almighty mess all built with good intentions. I lie awake at night worrying about it. If I could go back to last year, I would have called the police immediately. It's actually a huge relief to be able to tell someone.'

I felt tears rise up in my eyes. My poor dad had been carrying around this burden. I could relate to the strain of keeping a secret for months on end, but the seriousness of this one must have taken its toll. We held hands in the darkness and I nestled closer to him. We were quiet for a while as I tried to take it all in. A mess was right. I ran my mind over all he'd told me; I should have talked to my dad sooner as Blake had told me to do.

After a while, he stood up. 'You should get some rest now.'

I felt very close to him. 'Thank you for telling me the truth.' We held hands for a minute and he moved off towards the door.

Less than two hours after Dad left, when I'd fully reached a blissful place where there was no more pain in my head, someone switched the light on.

Blake knelt down at the side of my bed, eyes level with my own. I let out a breath.

'What can possibly be this urgent?'

The ice in his blue eyes glinted. 'Come on, get up. You are not going to believe what I just found out.'

Chapter 9

'I need to show you something.' Blake tugged at my arm which was totally uncooperative and fell limply down the side of the bed.

'Why do we need to go now? I just want to be left alone,' I bleated.

I opened my eyes. His expression had a hint of sulk making me feel guilty like I was faking or something. The small amount of sleep had made a big difference and the pain had lessened. The awesome drugs worked this time and numbed my brain. I was now squarely in the land of headache rather than migraine.

'Alright, alright, help me up and I need my…'

Blake handed me my sunglasses. I sat up and took his arm to lean on as I felt so out of sync.

'This had better be good, Blake.'

'It is,' he reassured.

Blake called an Uber. 'Marchione Street, Porta

Nuova,' he confirmed with the driver. I laid my head back against the headrest, feeling weak.

'Sergio had better have told you something *very* interesting to be worth forcing my zombie-self up and out, 'I said.

'He didn't say much, only that he knew Abigail and he'd met the artist you mentioned, Terry Gerrard, at his exhibition last summer in Florence.'

'Did he tell you anything more about Abigail?'

'He said she's an incredible craftswoman who works colouring statues. Pierro connected them last year. You know how indiscreet Sergio is. Well he was tight-lipped throughout the whole discussion, but I did get a few juicy details which I'll tell you about when we arrive. There was a caveat: he made me swear that anything he told me would not get back to Dad.'

'Weird,' I said and Blake nodded. 'How did you coerce him?'

Blake looked smug. 'I'm good at that kind of thing, and Sergio fancies me. He's propositioned me a couple of times.' I felt an acid sting of jealousy at the base of my throat. Though I didn't speak, I wasn't quick enough to barrier off the anger in my eyes and Blake chuckled. 'Don't be annoyed with me.' He smiled, enjoying the torment he was causing.

'Oh, don't rub it in,' I said, closing my eyes to block out the unfairness of life.

The cab dropped us off outside a contemporary skyscraper. There were two slender free-standing signs outside the entrance declaring the address: 76 Marchione. Standing on its doorstep, I felt dizzy looking up. It had the profile of a windsurfer's sail and the reflective titanium skin of the Guggenheim Museum in Bilbao which seemed to ripple as it rose. Fortunately for me, the day was overcast and so the reflections were a soft blue-grey which was just tolerable to my delicate eyes.

Blake hardly even glanced at it. He led me into the reception and dealt with the receptionist, but my eyes were captured by an amazing Antony Gormley sculpture made of fine wire, twisted around so that the lines looked like a three-dimensional scribble, apart from a distinct body in the centre. It was exactly like seeing a sculpture of Abigail's manifestation.

Blake walked across with two passes and barcoded cards. 'How did you get us passes to come in here?' I queried as he fastened my pass on for me.

He looked confused by my question. 'My mum arranged them.'

I followed him through the electronic turnstiles. My head hurt more when I looked anywhere other than straight ahead, but it was hard not to. The public space of this building was vast: designed around a huge atrium, it was planted to give the feel of an indoor garden. Water was running over stone surfaces that twisted around the space. There were shops, a café, three restaurants, a gym, hairdressers, all for the staff, and first class contemporary sculpture everywhere I looked.

Blake was focusing on where he was going, or perhaps had been here many times before, because he headed straight for the lifts without a glance left or right. He had lucked out taking me here when my appetite for art was at its weakest. On any normal day, I would never have been able to pass such amazing sculptures without suitable reverent pauses at each one.

Travelling up in the lift, I was struggling with myself over whether I should tell Blake about Dad's confession. It was something that could get Dad in a great deal of trouble and he hadn't said I could share it. On the other hand, Blake was playing fair with me. My brain couldn't cope with ethical dilemmas right now; it was too much like pummelling a bruise.

We arrived on the eighteenth floor, and from the lifts we walked into an almond-shaped lobby. The lighting was atmospheric and only a few notches up from dim. The white marble floor had a dark strip inlaid which looped, crossed and turned in upon itself like a hand-drawn doodle. On the wall facing the lifts, a long elliptical mirror was mounted in the centre dividing two solid wooden doors. Both doors had electronic access pads. Blake stepped forward and took a card from his pocket which he swiped across the device, letting us inside.

'Did they give you that at reception?'

'Nope, I swiped it from my mum's purse. I'll put it back later – she'll never know.'

'Devious – I like it.' I smiled at him and could see he enjoyed the approval.

We entered into an open-plan museum the size of a football pitch. There were dozens of rows of display cases in lines from one end of the room to the other. He flicked a switch and all the lights in the cases came on.

'Wow, I wasn't expecting that!' I stepped forward and gazed into a glass case. It contained a brooch designed as a salamander. It was exquisite: solid gold except for some emeralds inlaid along either side of its spine. There was a date and a name printed on a small card. The case next to it held a bell, in gold, which looked rough and rugged like a ship's bell and the material seemed far too grand for its form. The next had a small leather-bound book with tiny handwritten notes inside. I couldn't really read the italic scrawl, but there seemed to be mention of chemicals and some drawings of materials.

'What is this place?' I asked Blake. He was looking into another case a few rows up.

'This is the collection I told you about that my mother curates, along with most of the other artwork in the building. Dad seems to be *the* official custodian of it. I always understood that it was just a collection of precious and beautiful things, but it's owned by the Alchemy Society.'

I walked from one case to another, looking at a wide gold bracelet beautifully engraved, a ring, a coin.

I lifted my head. 'A lot of it is jewellery?'

He walked over to me and pointed at the ring. 'Gold – nearly everything is made of gold, and not just any gold, but alchemist's gold. Sergio says that this guild protects the real history of alchemy.' I must have looked particularly stupid because he said, 'You know, alchemy … turning lead into gold. You did go to school, right?'

'In my school, we did chemistry rather than alchemy, and I'm fairly sure that it's not physically possible, so don't sass me when you are the one not making sense. Alchemy is a myth.'

'Well, this is the bit that completely blew my mind. According to Sergio, there have always been people who have the gift, but apparently this secret Society has been making sure no-one knows that. They've been combing the world for hundreds of years, looking for special people and enslaving them. The objects here are a cache of evidence proving that alchemy is possible.' He lifted his arm and waved it over the display cases. 'They have airbrushed history of these objects so that there is no physical evidence of the truth.'

I took a deep breath and looked around at all the treasures in cases. 'You are saying they made the real history of alchemy vanish?' I shook my head.

He nodded. 'Cool – ha? And though Sergio wouldn't confirm it, my hunch is that Abigail is one of these people.' He wafted his hands over the case below him. 'And that's the real reason she's in Dad's care.'

'What does Sergio really know about anything?'

'He did say he thought there was something *special*

about her.'

'How do you get from there to her being an alchemist?'

Something caught my eye, a slight movement. I looked along the many rows stretching ahead of me and saw my dad standing at the far end of the room with Lorin just behind him. My eyes locked on to Dad's and I felt a deep blush rise to the surface of my skin. Seeing my expression, Blake jolted upright and spun round.

'Hey, Papa.' Blake raised his arm in a wave. He looked completely relaxed. 'You've never shown me this collection, it's so cool. I just popped in to see Mum and I wanted to show Frankie the art. By the way, she loves the Antony Gormley in reception – might be a good tip if you're thinking about Christmas.' He said this in a light-hearted voice and actually followed up with a laugh, which would have been impossible for me with facial muscles that seemed to be frozen.

The room was long, and as he was at the other end of it, I couldn't see Dad's features well, but his stance was rigid like he was holding on to his control for dear life.

'Glad to see you've made such an excellent recovery, Francesca.' He didn't sound glad. 'How did you get in here? It's a restricted area.'

'I asked the cleaner to let us in. He wasn't about to deny the boss's son.'

I couldn't help but admire how casually Blake was managing to behave. He even drifted to another display case and peered in. I felt like my lungs were full of treacle, they were so slow to breathe out. I hoped against hope Dad hadn't overheard our conversation. Blake had said Sergio would get in serious trouble.

'Lorin and I are driving back to the house. Have you seen enough?' Dad said in a voice that you might use if you caught a thief rifling through your cupboards – *have you taken enough*?

93

I fumbled for words, nodded and moved mutely towards him.

By the time we were standing in front of the lifts again, I had started to regain some oxygen to my brain.

'Why are you here?' I asked.

Blake, Lorin and my father looked at me like I had just asked what planet we were on.

'This is Papa's company, I thought you knew that,' Blake answered.

If Blake had said our father was the Italian president, I couldn't have been more shocked. This was far beyond what I'd ever imagined my father's business to be. The building was like Google headquarters. It couldn't be one man's private company.

As my unsaid *oh* outlined on my lips, the doors of the lift opened, but only my father and Lorin stepped forward as it was almost full.

'We'll see you outside,' my dad said, getting in the lift. Several people inside greeted him before the doors closed.

I immediately turned on Blake, who was pressing the buttons to call another lift. 'This is Dad's company? And, by the way, you're a good liar!'

'Not really, you are just terrible, and what were you looking so guilty for?'

'He probably overheard us and we weren't supposed to be in there. I couldn't help looking guilty.'

Blake shrugged. 'You'd better ditch the guilt if you're going to help that girl.'

***

In the car, Dad only spoke a few words. He told me he had plans to attend a political gathering that night which I had no desire to do. The journey home was tense; even Blake's unrepentant brazenness had wilted with Dad's alabaster anger. He got out part of the way back home, mumbling excuses about having plans. *Thanks, Blake!*

It did give me an idea for a surrealist sketch of Dad, though: a portrait in profile drawn in the style of a classical marble bust, serious, art without emotion. From the neck down, the body was transparent and inside was a swirling pit of red-hot lava bottled by a cork in his throat. It wasn't even just a fancy; this was exactly what I sensed sitting next to Dad.

I beat a hasty retreat to my room to let him calm down. I needed to talk to a friend about normal stuff and Skyped Kristin, asking her if she might come over for a few days. She didn't think she could as her parents had arranged to take her and her sisters away as soon as she got back from Barcelona. I didn't tell her what was going on where I was, though I really wanted to. She was bubbling over with holiday news and gossip, and what I had to tell seemed weird in comparison. She filled me in on the current drama: Pete, a boy from our old class, had kissed Tilly and now Tilly's boyfriend, Patrick, had decided to fly home. From absolutely nowhere I felt a wave of tears prickle my eyes and emotion welled up in my throat which I tried to choke back down. I wanted to be there having that kind of holiday – not on my own.

I slumped into my grey armchair with my legs draped over the arm rest, dropping my neck back over the other so that I was staring at the elegant patterned plasterwork on the ceiling. What Blake had told me couldn't be true. It was an insane explanation for a collection of museum objects. I knew that nuclear science had enabled the atomic structure of elements to be changed, but the idea that it could be done some other way – a mystical way – was too much for me. Blake was getting his information from Sergio, who could not be considered a reliable source.

I'd ask him outright and see his reaction. Knowing Sergio, he'd probably crack up and we'd laugh at Blake's gullibility together. I was feeling supremely lonely anyway, so seeing Sergio was perfect.

I texted to see if he fancied going out. *Always,* was his reply.

After a shower, I put on tight jeans, boots and a sparkly vest-top. As I straightened my hair, I thought I'd better go and apologise to Dad and make it up with him before going out. Not seeing either of my parents very much meant that I didn't like being on bad terms with them. When I'd been at school, some of my friends used to tell me about the rows they'd had with their parents at the weekends. My mum and I both tended to smooth over arguments, keenly aware of how precious our time together was. I reflected that this was probably the first time I'd ever really angered my dad.

While I applied my make-up, I thought about Abigail and what she'd been trying to show me. The idea that I might be able to control my migraines was a novel one: I knew exactly who had the whip and it wasn't me. I hadn't contacted Terry yet; I felt a bit guilty. My plan was to talk to Sergio that night and see if I could get any more out of him than Blake had. I turned on the slick new laptop that Dad had provided in this year's room makeover and tapped Terry's name into Google.

He had a website. An East End boy turned artist who lived in Venice and had exhibited widely throughout Europe. He was famous for painting two types of work: melancholic scenes of city life and portraits of his beautiful wife, Thérèse, who had been a fashion model. There was a photograph of them together; his wife was African-American with the darkest, glossiest skin imaginable, substantially above six-foot tall, delicate and exceptionally beautiful. Oddly, she looked vaguely familiar, but I couldn't think why. There was another photo of her on the catwalk in Milan in an Egyptian style headdress and make-up.

There was a picture of him too. He was thick-set – *rugged* was probably the most flattering description you could give him. He could not be described as handsome. He had fair hair, light eyes and the kind of blue-white skin that reddened but never tanned. It would have been hard to find two more contrasting characters to make a pair.

I looked at his gallery. Instantly, I realised why she looked familiar. Dad owned one of Terry's paintings with her as the subject and it hung on the staircase wall. She sat with her back to the artist. Her hair was up and she was naked from the waist up. He'd caught her as she looked over her shoulder at the viewer and gave the most seductive, welcoming smile. I clicked through the other pages revealing hundreds of portraits of her from every angle.

There was an email address. My finger hovered above it. He didn't look particularly sinister. He was a fellow artist after all. I looked at various blog posts about what Terry added to the art scene, how much Sotheby's had sold a painting for in New York, articles analysing his style and comparing him to all sorts of other artists. Then I came across a blog by his wife, Thérèse.

Thérèse was an aspiring playwright. She wrote a blog about performance, writing and choreography. The odd thing was that she had stopped posting on the blog last year, though before that she had evidently updated it several times a week since 2010. Her last posts didn't suggest that she was considering terminating it. In fact, her last post had been the first instalment of a three-part series about a Victorian playwright who had written about the slave trade. The last two parts had never been uploaded.

I clicked through to her Twitter link and saw that her

last tweet had been August last year too. This did seem odd. I left Terry and Googled her. Newspaper articles about her being a missing person filled the first page. There was some suggestion that it might be to do with the dirtier side of high-profile modelling and it seemed that an investigation was ongoing.

I went back to Terry's email address and clicked on it, sending a brief message saying that Abigail was with us in Milan and that she'd asked me to contact him, adding the address. Shutting down the computer, I felt the same way as I had about spying on Dad. It was underhand and I was meddling in his business. I would have preferred to tell him, but I wouldn't be able to explain how Abigail had asked me to contact Terry without telling the truth, and Blake had warned me not to do that. It did sound crazy. I didn't want to be made to see a psychiatrist.

I felt compelled to look at Thérèse's portrait, which I usually walked past dozens of times a day. I sauntered downstairs and stopped on the landing where it hung. She did have a rare beauty: her African heritage had given her glossy skin a few shades darker than her eyes, which were the colour of warm cocoa. Her hair was piled up revealing a long slender neck that met her shapely shoulders. Though her pose was entirely modest, there was something in the tilt of her head and the way the light hit her eyes that made it seem suggestive.

My dad's office door was open and the lights were on. I popped my head around the door, but he wasn't there. It did look like he'd soon be back. The desk was clearly in use with note pads and papers out, and a cup of coffee which was still lightly steaming suggested I'd missed him by moments, so I slipped in to wait for his return.

It wasn't a large room considering the size of the house and Dad's constant use of it. I wondered why he hadn't chosen something more significant. There was no guest chair as this wasn't somewhere he invited guests, so I went around his desk to sit in the swivel chair and wait. I spun for no reason and saw the rows of hardback economics and business books fly past me on the hand crafted shelves. The computer was on, and without giving it too much thought, I jiggled the mouse and saw the desktop appear. One of the files was marked Argent. The name seemed familiar. I couldn't help myself – I sat forward and double clicked on it before I'd even thought whether I should or not.

Inside were three files. The first was labelled blood and there were dozens of scans of results. There were unfamiliar medical words written at the bottom of the page. My conscience nudged me – if I'd attended some medical lectures I might have known what they meant. The second file was labelled Genome and within it was one file named Map, the other Sequence. Nervously, I looked up, but though my view of the hall was partly obstructed by the door, I couldn't hear anyone returning. The final folder said Drugs. I clicked inside this one and found a spreadsheet. At the top, the name said Abigail Argent. There was a long list of names with numerical scores in rows next to them.

These must be her medical records, though I couldn't imagine why my dad needed to be privy to such detail.

An email notification popped up at the bottom of the screen.

Dear Domenico,
We are delighted to accept your invitation to see the latest acquisition. I doubt there will be any at the Society who will not attend what promises to be the event of our age. We look forward to seeing you.
Leslie Grayheim

I could hear footsteps echoing across the hallway. I shut down all of the files as quickly as I could, spun in the chair and dived towards a door which I assumed was a bathroom. As my eyes swept the small room, my heart sank as I took in shelving with ring-bound files, some stationery and even a few coats hanging on a rack.

I closed the door and stood inside, in the dark, trying to slow my breathing. *Oh no!* I was in a cupboard, not a bathroom. Blake had been right – I did not react well under pressure. Adrenalin must inhibit my strategy centre. Why had I behaved like a frightened rabbit? I should have stayed in Dad's seat and acted like I'd been waiting for him. Sloping out of a closet would seem much more suspicious, and if he found me in there, my hiding would seem like a pattern rather than the pure stupidity it was.

I was berating myself so thoroughly that I didn't listen to whatever was going on in the office and was completely unprepared when Lorin opened the door and tried to enter. Not expecting to find a stowaway, he jumped backwards while I gasped and staggered. Some boxes stacked up against the wall hit me behind the knees at the sweet-spot which made my legs fold up under me. Of course, the mouth of one of the boxes swallowed me.

'*Merda*,' he exclaimed, bashing the light with his hand and putting my undignified position completely in the spotlight. He dived forward to pull me up. 'Frankie, what are you doing?'

I wish I knew, I thought as I got to my feet. I put my hands up to shield my eyes, but really to shield my face which displayed a perfect blend of embarrassment and guilt.

'I thought I might have another migraine coming on; they come in clusters. I ran in here, but it isn't a bathroom. The lights make it worse.' I leaned across him.

'Can I turn them ... off?'

The room was tiny, and as I reached across him, my awareness of our proximity came into sharp focus. I slowed and felt a thrum of attraction thrill through my body. Colour rose in my cheeks; our mouths were inches from each other and I couldn't help but stare. It was as if his lips had hypnotised me, particularly his generous lower lip and its shapely line. His were only a little higher than my own. That's when I flicked the switch. Apart from a tiny sliver of light where the door hadn't closed fully, we were in complete darkness. I could feel his warm breath on my face, and knowing precisely where his lips would be, I lifted my chin, hoping they would touch.

Having fantasised so much about doing just this and more with Sergio, I had no real expectation that the dream would come true, but Lorin was not Sergio. He brushed a fleshy thumb across my bottom lip. The sensation was so exquisite and unexpected that my legs nearly folded up again. Putting one hand on my neck so that the fleshy thumb lay across the collar bone, he pulled my head towards his and kissed me fully and without hurry, deeply, involving every millimetre of my mouth in a way I'd never been kissed before. Time warped; I wasn't sure how long we kissed, but several hours would not have been enough for me.

When he did break away, he was out of the room in less than a beat. I remained inside for a few more minutes, keeping my eyes closed to prolong the stolen sensation.

Chapter 10

Sergio peeked into my room at nearly 9pm and looked me over.

'Ready?' he said, but his expression said, *you can't be.* 'You do know where we are going tonight? The hub of highbrow chic – 10 Corso Como.'

I glanced down at my clothes, which I'd thought looked perfect a couple of minutes ago. He pushed past me and marched into my walk-in wardrobe, letting out a sigh as if he had to do everything in life himself. I leaned on the door frame, watching him work the wardrobe in a professional way, unlike me who tended to settle on the first item that came to hand. As he tugged out little dresses and held them up before discarding them onto the floor, I told him about what I'd been doing since I'd last been in Milan.

'If you must talk, then at least undress at the same time,' he said, snapping his fingers at me. He was never interested in other people's lives unless they related directly to him. I slipped off my T-shirt and gave him the next instalment about revealing all to Dad.

Sergio was looking for shoes. He was kneeling to examine a low shelf.

'Do you think he'll help me, Sergio? Do you think I'm good enough?'

Peeling off the jeans, I stood in a turquoise bra and G-string. The closet lights lit my body and Sergio sucked in some air and raised his eyebrows.

'*Bella*! I'd like to sculpt you. What a heavenly body you have.'

The colour rose in my cheeks. I looked up at him from under my lashes and flicked some stray hair away from my eye line. Pouting, I put on my best mock-temptress voice.

'Shame you only want to sculpt it. Maybe you could upgrade that thought to bedding it.' As I said this, there was a light knock on the door and Lorin came in without waiting. I spun and opened my mouth. The words I'd just uttered seemed to hang in the air and I felt like he was reading them.

Lorin didn't look away, but stared past me at Sergio, who was on his knees less than a metre from me.

'Your father asked me to let you know he's booked a private viewing for you both to see the Robert Crumb exhibition on Thursday at Hangar Bicocca, 1pm.'

He said this without taking his eyes from Sergio. The news was so thrilling that momentarily I forgot the situation was awkward.

'That's amazing! I tried to get tickets for it, but couldn't.'

Lorin turned, his face expressionless. Message delivered.

My blush came late, but it was as vivid as any could be. What must he be thinking of me? An hour ago I was kissing him in a cupboard, now I was semi-naked with another man in a wardrobe.

As the door closed, Sergio said, 'People don't smoulder enough in modern life, but he knows how to work that anger. It surprises me that he seems immune to my advances.' Standing up, he handed over the chosen outfit: a silk slightly transparent fitted shirt, which was a shimmery midnight shade and was as light as cobwebs, and a short black skirt with Jimmy Choo heels.

'He's straight, that's all.'

'Usually the straighter, the better,' he said, winking at me evilly as he buttoned up the shirt. '*Bella*,' and he ran his fingertips along the collar and down the v of my shirt. Taking my hand, he led me down the never-ending staircase. Dad came out of the library as I tottered past the door. Sergio turned and puckered his lips, sending Dad a little kiss, and breezed out into the courtyard towards the side door, dragging me with him.

He climbed into a cab, the engine of which was running. It must have been waiting for him the whole time.

'You must have the hide of a camel, Sergio, to stay standing after the Medusa-stare my dad just gave you.'

'I can assure you my hide is a soft satin, not that you'll ever have a chance to find out. You are too sensitive.' He put his arm around me and I laid my head on his shoulder. 'Your dad needs a little disobedience. Think how dull his life would be if everyone scurried around pleasing him all of the time.'

Number 10 Corso Como was an unpretentious looking building from the outside with its speckled stone walls, iron railed balconies and plants with cascades of foliage falling downward like wayward hair, but it wasn't quite the same within. It was a unique space allowing you to combine the pleasures of cocktails, food, fine art, books and high-end retail. We started on the top floor, the rooftop bar where the plants were highlighted with delicate fairy lights. We sat beneath its sculptural pergola and Sergio ordered cocktails, insisting on tinkering with all of the recipes. Then we moved on to the shopping space where we spent over an hour giggling over some of the more ridiculous items and their overinflated prices. By now, it was quite late, and though the gallery was closed, Sergio flexed his celebrity muscles just because he could. Within ten minutes, the doors were open to us.

He ordered our custodian to fetch more cocktails. Though the gentleman was clearly too senior to be sent on errands, he obliged Sergio as so many people did.

Sergio had no interest in what was on display and draped himself over a rectangular leather seat, face down. I moved around the plinths where some ugly contemporary ceramics were on display.

'How can you be so disinterested? Something might inspire you.'

He snorted. 'Not here.' He ran his fingertips back and forward along the blonde wood on the floor. 'This wood has more to offer.'

'Where do you get your inspiration from?'

'Euch, you sound like one of those deathly boring magazines that Jack - my new agent, who I *hate* by the way – makes me talk to *all the time*.'

'Wasn't the last magazine you were in Italian *Vogue*?'

'I see you haven't given up your stalking habit altogether.' Half his face looked pleased, but the remainder was squashed into the buttoned leather surface of the seat.

'I keep my hand in.'

'That means something quite different in Italy.' His hair flopped over his eyes and I had to inhibit my inclination to stroke it away.

He turned on to his back, staring at the ceiling, and I

could see the marks left by the chair on his cheek.

'You don't need to find inspiration in other people's work, Francesca. It's like you are looking for scraps in other people's bins. Trust yourself: you are good enough. So good that I would bet all my money and my beauty that your father will help you. I think you have more talent than anyone I have seen in the art world for a very long time – apart from *moi*, of course.' He pouted his lips, batting his eyelashes and giving me a smile brimming with superiority. 'A little warning, *carina*, which I'm quite sure you'll ignore: everything comes at a price with respect to your father. He has been very good to me, *very good*, but he's a man who deals in favours. That's a unique kind of currency, and payment is often much harder than parting with cash.'

I looked at his serious face. 'Is Abigail an alchemist?' I asked.

He stood up and walked across to me, taking my hand. 'Darling, I haven't a clue, and frankly, I don't care. None of it has anything to do with *moi*. Where are those cocktails?' he said, turning and dragging me out of the gallery to find them.

***

When I woke the next morning, I was determined to continue the having-fun theme that I'd enjoyed the night before. I would go to the swimming pool today in the centre of town. It was a social space to sunbathe and I'd push myself to make some friends.

I got ready in light clothes and packed a bag for the day. Making my way downstairs and into the hall, I noticed a flicker of movement in the ballroom and realised the tall decorative doors were uncharacteristically closed. I went to peep through the slim panes of glass which were set into them.

Abigail was there. For once, she was not in lights, but there in the flesh, and she was working on Sergio's sculpture. I tried the door handle, but it was locked. She heard the rattle of the handle and walked over to the glass, looking left and right of me to see if anyone else was there. We stood inches away from each other.

'Are you okay?' I said.

She put her hand to her ear and I raised my voice and tried again. She shook her head. I wasn't sure if she meant she couldn't hear me or she wasn't okay. With wood and glass between us, a real conversation wasn't looking likely.

Seeing her at such close range shattered all my confidence in my father's story. I didn't imagine all murderers to be stereotypic bad guys, but she was just too fragile. To kill another human must require some steel in the character, and this girl looked gentle, kind even. She tucked some stray hair, which was otherwise fastened in a ponytail, behind her ear and turned back to her work.

On the floor was an array of tools, a large Calor gas container and blowtorch, and on several dustsheets were containers with liquids and pastes inside, green pads and steel wool. Four of the windows were ajar by a few inches and held by stays, making them too narrow to squeeze through. I could hear the radio playing faintly through the door.

The statue's surface looked even brighter than it had been when it first arrived; she must have done something to it already. Picking up a brush, she gave the statue a pat with one hand like you might do to an unsettled horse. She fired up the blowtorch making it burn fiercely and began to heat the surface back and forth. This continued until the surface must have been very warm before she flicked one of her brushes laden with chemical across a rag and then pressed it to the hot surface. I saw the steam rise from the touch of the damp brush.

The area she had done turned a burned black.

I wondered what she was doing. She continued onward in what became a meditative flowing motion, heat, flick, touch, steam, heat, flick, touch, steam, and occasionally she would pause to re-dip her brush in the fluid.

Soon the surface of the angel looked like some terrifying hell creature. The colour was almost the opposite of the satiny pink surface that it had originally been. Then she stopped and turned off her blowtorch for a minute or two. She picked up a green pad, which looked like the type you clean pans with, and moved to the back of the statue which she had just worked upon. I could see as she moved the pad across the coal colour that the shade shifted; it became more silvery. She worked the pad in a circular motion across the broadest areas of the body.

When satisfied, she selected another chemical and a larger brush, fired up the gas again and played it over the area, but more gently this time. When she plunged the brush into the chemical, flicked away the excess and touched it to the surface, the result was a deep russet brown, which as she continued to work deepened into the most glorious, robust red. She moved quickly over the angel's back until the majority was covered.

By this stage, I could tell she had lost me. I had faded away for her and she was totally entranced by her work, as I was when I was drawing. I envied her that place she was in; I knew it well. She changed chemicals again, this time without switching off the blowtorch, though now she only used it infrequently to tickle the surface and ripen its heat. The bronze moved from red to a fresh green and from green to a crisp white, and finally the richest royalist blue I'd ever seen.

I felt a surge of excitement. The colour was so vivid and so unexpected. I'd been sure Dad and Sergio would have kept the angel light and golden in shade. The blue was beautiful, but strange all the same. It didn't look like paint because it had a depth and richness that paint couldn't imitate.

The doorbell echoed through the house. I felt irritated; I didn't want to be disturbed. Anyone using the main door would be coming to see my father and I wouldn't be able to stay in the hallway. I waited for someone to come up and open the door. After a delay, the bell rang again. It struck me as odd that no-one seemed to be rushing to answer it.

The bell sounded a third time.

At my mum's house, I wouldn't think twice about answering the door, but here simple things were more complicated. My dad probably had a designated door attendant who would be sacked on the spot if he was found to be absent from his post, plus I was sure there would be a code required to open the door. Lorin always did it for me if I went out that way.

It sounded for a fourth time. I walked tentatively across the black and white marble tiles, picking up my phone and pushing Lorin's number. I felt really stupid; I couldn't believe that I was actually going to ask permission to answer a door. The call went to voicemail, so I slipped the phone into my back pocket and went over to the door. It had two handles, one which was an old-fashioned push-down type and the other which was higher up and was a pull-to-open. I waited a second before pulling and pushing down simultaneously.

To my surprise, it swung towards me, light as silk. Only the most sophisticated engineering could make such a brute behave that impeccably. It was so unexpected that I didn't pull my head out of the way quickly enough and the door bashed me in the temple. I squealed in pain and rubbed my head very fast.

Distracted, I didn't notice immediately that the man on the doorstep was holding up a gun. He lifted it directly to my head and took a step forward, pushing me back inside.

I've had moments of fear in my life, but those were fleeting. This was something different: the painful spark of fear didn't go out, but took hold and began to rage. My breath lodged in my throat and I seemed to choke on it.

'I'm Terry Gerrard,' he said. 'Take me to Abigail, *now*.'

It was a second that took an hour to pass as I stared at the end of that gun, hypnotised. As he walked forward, I stepped back like we were in some kind of scripted dance. My perspective only widened when his name penetrated my addled brain.

'I was the one who emailed you,' I stammered as if this might make him put his gun away and apologise for his bad manners. I took my first good look at him. I wasn't immediately sure how old he was because his hair and his face told different tales. His face had very few lines, but his hair was white. I looked to his eyes for confirmation only to find an intensity that did not reassure me that his trigger finger was well guarded. He had the type of physique that looked like he could walk through solid concrete.

He didn't close the door fully, but left it slightly ajar.

'I know who you are, I just want Abigail,' he said in a gruff voice without breaking eye contact. Fear was making my eyes and the back of my throat sting.

I nodded. 'She's in there.' I pointed to the ballroom, screaming in my head, *'Where the hell is everyone?'* He flicked his gun, indicating I should lead the way.

I didn't like the idea of turning my back on a man with a gun, but I couldn't continue to walk backwards and potentially fall down the few steps to the ballroom space so I spun. He had his arm around my neck before I'd even hit 180 degrees, and I realised he had no real need of the gun now because he could snap my neck like a twig.

Just in case I was a little slow on the uptake, he pecked me with his gun on my already bruised temple and growled, 'Hurry up!'

I shot forward even faster than he'd expected, resulting in me partially strangling myself. As we reached the ballroom door, I mumbled, 'I don't have a key. It's locked.'

Without waiting a heartbeat or getting me to move aside, he lifted his gun and shot the lock in the elegant oak doors several times. Bullets rebounded, sparks flew, and I tried to turn and curl up to protect myself, but he held me fast before barging us both forward, using me as his battering ram.

As I met the door, I lifted my arms up to guard my face from the impact, but fully expected to be knocked unconscious by the blow. Fortunately, it had been built more for beauty than security, and in its wounded state, it seemed to swoon and give way. We were through in seconds. I staggered over one of Abigail's pots, kicking it hard so that it spun almost to the windows, its contents being flicked all over the floor.

Terry hauled me up roughly. In frustration he yelled, 'Up!' which I had no choice about anyway as he was man-handling me the way you might a soft toy.

There was no tender embrace in this reunion. Abigail didn't delay a second. My feet barely encountered the floor as I was rushed back past the annihilated door into the hall.

Less than a dozen steps from freedom, their winning streak waned. Though the hall remained empty, the front door banged shut as if closed by an invisible butler. It locked electronically. Terry spun, searching out the possibility of another exit. The immense staircase, corridors and landings, which minutes before had been unoccupied, now featured a small army of men, all with guns trained upon the three of us. Prior to now, I'd always assumed the staircase to be a decorative feature, but now I saw its tactical merits. They had the advantage of height and had their prey in a space with nowhere to hide.

Rather than feeling safer, I felt my fear crank up. This was going to be a stand-off. Terry pushed Abigail back behind him. He put pressure on my neck, making me gulp for breath and pull at his trunk-like arms uselessly. I saw him take a glance over his shoulder towards the ballroom. While he was assessing his options, my father exited his study with Lorin, whose eyes immediately sought my own.

Dad didn't look at me. Terry relaxed his arm very slightly, and just the way that water trickles and then flows when a hose has a kink released, so my tears came. Not for years had I felt such a childish desire to run into my dad's arms for safety. My love for him swelled and burst and I felt a gush of pain at the thought of never feeling his arms around me again. Then another, slightly sourer, thought occurred to me: had they been in his office the whole time? It was probably the trauma of the situation mixing a cocktail with my emotions, but suddenly I was raging with anger. Had I been set up? The door was unlocked and there had been no-one to answer it and yet they'd been in the office, and where had all these men sprung from?

A dozen strides from Terry, my dad reached inside his navy suit and pulled out his own gun without breaking step. He lifted it and pointed it at Terry, who stood firm.

'Domenico,' Terry spat out the words like he was tasting rotten cabbage.

My dad looked like the heavyweight champion of control. He adopted the most superior expression he had in his arsenal and said, 'I think you should take your hands off my daughter.'

'I wonder if you care about *her* a tenth as much as I cared about Thérèse. You crushed us.' Terry's voice was strangled with emotion. 'And for what? Some deluded myth; a Midas complex!'

I jumped as he shouted the last phrase directly into my right ear, so scared that I shut my eyes, just wanting to block the entire situation out. I was definitely missing something: Terry's voice had the vibe of right being on his side. He sounded wronged.

'You are referring to Thérèse Gerrard, I think. She went missing last year. I read about it in the papers.'

'Don't play games with me,' Terry shouted. I was so close to his body that I could feel his unhinged anger spilling into me. Lorin moved even closer to my dad; I wondered whether he would take a bullet for him. Chauffeur, assistant, errand boy, was he a bodyguard too?

I tried to will my dad to hear me. *Please, if you are playing games with him at this moment, please don't.* His radar didn't seem to be on because he smirked a little at having riled Terry up.

'I always admired her. I even bought a portrait.' My dad inclined his hand towards the staircase which we were slightly in front of. Terry swivelled and I with him. The armed men hadn't changed positions by even a whisker so it seemed. This time our eyes moved past them to the first landing where the colossal staircase split and the giant oil painting of Thérèse hung.

'No.' One quiet word like a dramatic chord at the end of a symphony. He snarled, 'You must have no shame. How can you look at her every day when she no longer breathes because of you?'

I held my breath. I had an awful sinking feeling like I was going down into deep water; the sense of dropping further into something that it was likely I would not come out of. I had thought this situation was all about Abigail, but clearly it was much more than that. There was Pierro's murder, and now Terry was laying another, but at my dad's feet: Thérèse.

My father's voice cut through my thoughts. 'You are out of options, clearly outnumbered and there is nowhere back there to get out.' He sounded so reasonable, as if he were giving a tourist directions. I couldn't hear the slightest hint of anxiety. He actually tutted when he saw the mess Terry had made of the door as he looked past the shattered barrier into the ballroom. 'The windows in there only open slightly, and if you decided to throw yourselves through them, which I don't advise, you would find the land drops away on one side of the property on to a road.' His stance was that of ringmaster, legs astride. His energy was supremely confident; he was sure the lion would bow.

I, on the other hand, was feeling like I was a hair's breadth from my heart exploding out of my chest or using up its lifetime quota of beats just in this scenario. It didn't seem possible that it could continue to beat so hard and fast much longer. *Young people could have heart attacks*, I thought vaguely.

Terry must have been thinking over his options because he didn't respond to my dad's enquiries straightaway. My instinct was that he was going to do something desperate. Trapped as my body was, my brain was careering about like an out-of-control train: I was going to die and my life hadn't even started. I wanted to be an artist. If I died now, I would never have had sex! This hadn't seemed that urgent before, but now it seemed of the utmost importance. I looked at Lorin.

He was already looking at me, but we were not thinking the same thing. I held his eye and he bent his right arm, clasped his hand, and slowly moved it backwards.

Then he looked down. I followed his glance; he lifted his foot slightly and, in slow motion, made a stamping movement, stopping before it hit the floor. I shook my head subtly. He repeated the movements, thinking I didn't understand.

I knew exactly what he was suggesting. He wanted me to hit Terry in the ribs with my elbow and stomp on his foot, but I had no belief that I could injure a man built like a rhinoceros. I doubted he'd even feel my elbow make contact.

Terry's voice boomed above me. 'I won't leave Abigail here with you murderers. She's better off dead than running from your cult for the rest of her life.'

'And Francesca? Will you kill her too?'

My dad's tutorial style of speaking was beginning to annoy me. The hallway seemed to be humming with expectation. I could feel tears slipping from my eyes again. I looked to Lorin. He pursed his lips; I read them as saying, 'Hold on.'

'Do you want to see Terry dead, Abigail? Being a patron of the arts, I wouldn't want to see such a talent wasted, but I'm sure the police will find in my favour, even if he is shot through with a dozen bullets, seeing as he has broken and entered my house and kidnapped my daughter.'

Suddenly the power shifted from Terry to Abigail and this was an intelligent move. I couldn't see her, but I felt like my life was better off in her hands than in Terry's. Everyone seemed to be holding their breath. I couldn't help a sob escaping, which echoed in the hallway.

Abigail moved past Terry. Now she was shielding him, and she spoke with a voice which I realised I'd never heard before. It was raspy, perhaps from lack of use or maybe because it was blunt with bitterness. She approached my father and spat the words into his face.

115

'Not another drop of blood will be sacrificed by my friends for you.'

'What about my friends?' Dad opened his arms and circled her so that he was alongside her when he spoke the next sentence. 'I don't remember you extending much mercy to Pierro.'

She was wearing fingerless gloves as she had been every time I had seen her in the lights. She pulled them off and shook the palms of her hands at him, revealing a landscape of monstrous scars across her skin, and then turned to Terry.

'Let her go. It's not fair to involve her. It makes you the same as him.'

'They've dragged us into their world, Abi. We didn't want to be here. We can't play fair if they play dirty.' Terry's voice softened when he spoke to her. 'They won't shoot us if I have her.'

Abigail turned and looked at my dad and back at me. She looked like she was struggling to inhibit something. Her body quivered and was tense at the same time, like vibrato played on a string. Her eyes suddenly looked very strange; different to how they had only seconds before. There was something unnatural about their colour as if someone had added a dab of sienna, but not mixed it well.

'You of all people should know them better than that,' she said to Terry, and in a commanding voice she repeated her demand. 'Let her go.'

Terry may care about her infinitely, but he disagreed with her and he tensed his arm. I gasped and fought his strength, thrashing like I was drowning. Lorin took two steps towards Terry, who pulled me backwards. My father directed his words towards Abigail once again.

'We could always do a trade.'

Terry relaxed his arm slightly, enough for me not to pass out.

'If you do what I've asked of you, he can go free.'

My heart was clattering about uncontrollably. I couldn't have heard correctly. My dad had just offered a trade, but not for me?

She shook her head. 'I can't, and if I agreed, how would I trust you'd keep your word?' Anger lashed the tail of this sentence. She tried to sound strong as she negotiated, but I suspected she was losing the battle to remain inside her own body, perhaps due to the stress of the situation. She was definitely fighting to stay in control of something.

'There're at least ten witnesses here. Do you think I could get away with cold-bloodedly murdering a man if there was no cause to? It's a little different if he's holding my daughter hostage. There's really no need for the guns if we all behave in a civilised way.'

Terry made a noise somewhere between a snort and a laugh. 'I think our definitions of civilised are a little different. I'll hang on to mine a little longer, thank you.'

My dad shrugged like it didn't matter to him either way.

'Do we have a deal, Abigail?'

She nodded.

Terry couldn't reach out to Abigail, what with me in one arm and the gun in his other hand, but I knew he wanted to.

'You don't have to do this,' he said in the voice he used just for her which betrayed the other side of his character: the man he used to be.

'Yes, I do,' she said in a deadened voice.

Without delaying for a beat, my dad seized upon the affirmation and led the way into the ballroom. My eyes were never far from Lorin's and I thought I saw a micro-expression of annoyance pass across his face before he followed my father. Abigail moved in a contrived way like she had to concentrate on each step of this basic function. Terry followed her, bundling me like I was little more than a bag of washing. Then the armed men marched down the stairs in formation, following behind us like a firing squad.

Chapter 11

As Abigail came through the door, she darted off to the left hand side of the room and pulled one of the small historic weapons from the wall that Dad kept on display there: it was a dagger. The gunmen trained their sights on her.

Dad shook his head and gestured to them to lower their weapons. 'Let's all calm down a little, shall we?' The armed men inched further into the room creating an outer circle of muscle around the main players with Sergio's statue at the centre, whose deep blue patina made it look more daemonic than angelic.

'You have chosen my favourite blade of the collection, Abigail. It's a Roman *pugio*, which was an extra weapon carried by a Roman soldier. Isn't it a beauty? And so unusual because it's made in bronze, not iron,' my dad said in his most charming voice. Everyone was staring at the leaf-shaped blade with its delicate grooved lines running from hilt to tip.

'I imagine you would appreciate it more than the others, Abigail,' he added with a genuine touch of deference in his voice.

My head gave a throb. I was so confused. *What did Dad want her to do? What were we doing back in the ballroom?* Abigail was holding a knife and he seemed to be giving a history lesson. I stared at her, trying to interpret the body language. She looked at my dad like he was a cockroach she'd found in her sandwich. I thought there was a good chance she would take a run at him and attempt to stab him.

Abigail looked down at the blade; perhaps her respect for craftsmanship prevented her from ignoring its finery. Terry was fidgeting. He had his head turned towards the windows and I felt like he was re-evaluating them, which made me want to pull in the opposite direction like a dog on a leash.

I sought the devastated skin on her palms. The scars were clearly intentional, so angular were they in their shape. The surface was mountainous and in various shades, from angry red to the palest of pink, but as far as I could see there was no unblemished skin and the lines did not fall below her wrists. They didn't seem like the work of suicide attempts.

I felt Terry flinch as Abigail took hold of the dagger and cut herself across one palm, then gripping the dagger in her bleeding hand, she cut across the other. She dropped the dagger to the floor and laid both her damaged hands upon the statue's surface.

A light tremor went through the room, enough to make the glass tears of the chandeliers chime against each other like five hundred toasts about to be announced.

'Please don't do it,' Terry whispered, and only I and Abigail heard. She glanced at him and in her eyes was that swirling daub of sienna and an apology, and then she closed them in concentration.

Everyone else in the room stood stock still and hardly dared to breathe. Terry was holding so tightly around my neck that I tried to shift my body in order to gain a slightly more comfortable position. I happened to glance at Lorin. Despite the situation, I nearly laughed out loud.

His hair was standing nearly on end, and so was the hair of the four men nearest to him. All of them were unaware, and they looked completely ridiculous.

I shuffled again to see more. 'Stop squirming,' Terry chastised and gave me a tug.

Now my dad's hair was rising up too. There must be some kind of static charge building up in the air. I turned back to Abigail and could see something else. Every so often, she flickered. I saw a momentary glimpse of her outside her body surrounded by lights, but then rather than stay there, she moved back inside herself. It was as if she was being shaken in and out of her own body.

She was pushing so hard against the sculpture that I was expecting to see her blood pouring down the surface, but the blood seemed to be defying gravity and holding its location. I could see shimmering lights growing around her perimeter. They were building in density and energy. The air felt thick with so much static and the lights were beginning to engulf her. I could hardly bear to continue looking at her when she turned her head towards me, caught my eye for just a second and, as she turned back, screamed.

'NOW!'

I thought a bomb had exploded. Every person in the room was thrown backwards off their feet several metres as something physical hit us all. I had seen her propel the lights outwards across the room before they consumed her.

Both Terry and I were on the floor, but having the

slightest bit of notice that something was about to occur, I had the advantage. His arm had cushioned what would have been a concussing blow to the back of my head as we both hit the floor and slid along the perfectly sealed satin wood. He did hit his head, and apart from the shock, was winded too. I slipped his arm and rolled away a fraction before he could clamp down upon me once again.

As I gained my feet, the room swam with strange energy. The floor no longer seemed to be horizontal – one minute falling away and another pitching upright. Terry swung his foot in my direction and made contact, managing to make me stagger, but not fully trip. I threw myself forward, hitting the ground inelegantly between two of the armed guards who had fallen nearest us.

I moved far enough from Terry that I felt safe, before looking at Abigail. She was still the nucleus of the lights, though I could see they were changing. They went from flickering shards that only I could see to a blinding density that affected everyone in the room. It was just like an enormous headlight had been turned on and directed into all of our eyes, but after a moment my eyes began to adjust. Some of the men were shouting. It seemed no-one could bear to hold their eyes open, and as a consequence no-one could see except me.

I had only one desire: not to be reclaimed by Terry. I began by crawling and then made it up on to my feet and towards the door. I glanced to see if Terry was follow-ing, but the dense, sharp light was protecting me by searing everyone else's eyes, keeping them down on the ground. My desire for safety was countered by my curiosity at what Abigail was attempting. I stood by the shattered door.

The light was consuming. I felt like it was inside me and out. Even with my sight, I was disorientated and felt the tug to leave the room in case I passed out. It was only when the men's voices cried out that I realised I was becoming dizzy because the room was heating up, fast. It wasn't long before it was feeling unbearable. I sank onto the step and pressed my face against the cold stone and whispered promises into its surface.

'If I ever get out of this, I won't stay in this house.'

When the heat peaked, it felt as if my skin was about to melt and drip onto the floor. It was like being in the centre of the sun in a dream. Only then did the oven turn off and the light fade away. For a while, this change was as excruciating in its own way.

One of the men closest to me was curled up and crying. Terry was down on the floor like he had been knocked out, his gun still in his hand. Our group was a complete wreck: bodies were scattered all over and had obviously tried to escape the situation as they had migrated from where they'd fallen after the first blast. Nearly all of the armed men had dropped their weapons; some looked as if they might be concussed; one was still unconscious. There was the sense that we'd been in a bombing.

My dad, who was furthest away from the statue, was on his feet first. I staggered back up to mine and moved towards him. I'd never seen his hair anything but perfect; now, one side was plastered against his face while the other stood straight upright, but it was his expression of fury that was most remarkable. On the floor at the foot of the statue, unconscious, was Abigail. Everyone's eyes were on the statue and mine joined them, but apart from two dark handprints in dried blood and a slight smear below them, it looked exactly the same as it had before: it was still patinated a peacock blue.

Terry made a move towards Abigail, but a couple of the men, who were on their feet and had reclaimed their weapons, rounded on him. My dad walked around the sculpture as if looking for some trace of change; I could see him swallowing down his disappointment.

'Lorin, do you think you could possibly take Francesca to her room and make sure that she has everything she needs after her distressing ordeal?' my dad said in a forced voice.

I left the ballroom with Lorin at my side. I wanted to get out of this room, away from the sculpture; away from Terry and Abigail and her lights; away from my father and his lies. Lorin shut what remained of the double doors as we left the room.

I put my hand on the banister of the staircase and looked at it shaking like it wasn't my own. Lorin placed his hand over mine, sliding his fingers between my knuckles and squeezing.

'Hey, it's alright. It's over. Come on, let's keep moving.'

I looked at him. His dark hair, which was usually swept off his face, had fallen across his eyes; it made him look younger. He put his arm around my waist and half held me up as we walked up the stairs. I leaned into him and felt warm tears slip from my eyes again.

'Shh,' he soothed.

We were on the landing a few steps from my room when I heard a single gunshot echo through the vast hall. Lorin anticipated me. He jumped backwards, raising his hands out in front of him to steady me like I was a spooked horse.

'What are you doing?' I tried to push past his solid trunk.

'Frankie, please listen to me. It doesn't concern you. Leave them to sort things out.' His voice was low and he spoke slowly in calming tones.

'Like hell it doesn't!' I yelled at him, feeling anger flash in my eyes. 'Someone might have been killed.'

'Frankie,' Lorin's face was pleading, 'trust me, there

are enough people downstairs to take care of it.'

'It could be Dad.'

'Very unlikely.'

'Terry? Would my dad kill Terry?'

'No. There would be no need. Terry was completely outnumbered.'

The fight drained out of me. He reached out a hand that wasn't entirely steady. I dodged it like it held a razor blade. *How dare he stop me moving freely in my own house?* I turned and climbed the last few steps to my room.

Safe inside, my back against the door and my head slung back, I was forcing my tight chest to expand and take in a deep, calming breath when I was propelled forward several paces by the door being shoved inwards. Lorin's body collapsed into my room like a tree that had been felled, face pressed into the carpet. I stared at his body. My brain could not compute. Had he been shot? No blood. Heart attack? I dropped to the floor, my hands shaking so violently I couldn't control them enough to touch him.

'Are you alright?' I panted. *Stupid question!* 'Lorin, please, what's wrong?' Holding my breath, I began to shake him.

A twitch went through him. He rose up like he was lifting himself into a cobra pose, pushing his torso off the ground, and stared at me with glazed eyes. My breathing rolled out again in relief. Then he made a grab at me, grinding the flesh of my arms between hands that felt like they could crush steel. I was so surprised that my reaction was an incoherent sound: part scream, part sob. His expression contorted as I tried to wrench his hands off me. We grappled on the floor – a tug of war with no rope.

'Lorin, stop it, stop it!'

He stilled, seeming short of breath. He ran his eyes

around the room, searching for familiarity. I said his name, softly this time, and his focus turned to me. His expression was so lost that it pushed away the immediacy of my own trauma.

'It's okay,' I whispered. His pupils widened and I leaned forward, placing my arms around him as gently as I could, resting my head on his shoulder. His breathing remained stilted, but it slowed. He buried his head in my shoulder and I felt tears touch my skin as he clasped me like a drowning man clinging to driftwood.

When his breathing slowed, he whispered, 'I'm sorry. That hasn't happened...'

A knock on the door and my father's voice made him pull away and regain his feet. He put out a hand to steady himself, but the wall was several feet away and he staggered. He rubbed his face as my dad entered the room.

Chapter 12

Dad didn't seem to notice Lorin's odd stance.

'Thank you for your kindness, Lorin. Please arrange for some sweetened tea and brandy to be sent up immediately,' he said. Lorin left the room on autopilot. I stared after him, not at all clear what had just happened.

'How are you?' Dad said, examining me with eyes that were gentle, not those of a killer.

The fear was beginning to die down, but I wasn't feeling much of anything else other than a pervading numbness. I had a sense that I'd been betrayed somehow. My mum was always picking me up for exaggerating. We could witness the same event and yet I would interpret it differently, adding whole new layers of implied meaning that drove her detective's brain wild.

I sat down on the bed. He followed me, putting an arm around my shoulder, squeezing me tight and kissing the top of my head.

'Thank God you are alright; you were so brave and smart. I couldn't be more proud of you. I don't tell you that often enough. You saw your opportunity and went for it. Not everyone would have been able to think like that in the middle of a crisis. I'll send her away, I promise. She can go to another hospital. I am wiping my hands of the whole situation. I had no idea she would bring such danger into our lives. Terry Gerrard ruined her life and nearly yours too.'

'What do you mean?'

'Terry Gerrard is poison. He seduced Abigail while she was staying with him and working in Venice. Then when she realised he had no intention of leaving his beautiful wife for her, she lost all reason and ability to function normally.'

'Terry implied that you'd killed his wife.'

'Ridiculous. The man was discovered to be having an affair with Abigail, who was a friend of his wife's and at least fifteen years her junior. Naturally, she left him. He blamed Pierro for that because it was him who had told her. Pierro had been in love with Thérèse for many years. In fact, he'd known her since she was a child, and when he saw what was going on, he seized his opportunity. Not a gallant thing to do, but the act of a man deeply in love. When Thérèse told Terry she was leaving him, Abigail assumed that this was a good thing, but Terry spurned her. Abigail blamed Pierro, which was why she murdered him.'

There was a knock at the door and one of the staff brought in a tray. He set it down on the coffee table. My father got up and poured a cup of tea for me. He passed it over with a hand that shook enough for some of the tea to slop into the saucer, then took a brandy glass and lowered himself onto my grey armchair.

'You asked her to do something. What were you talking about?'

'Her therapy, what else could it possibly be? She won't cooperate with anything the doctors are trying to do with her. I'd asked her to undergo DBS: deep brain stimulation therapy. It's a type of electric therapy treatment. It's very well documented for treating Parkinson's disease, but new research is showing that it is benefitting those with severe depression and other psychiatric disorders. Several doctors have advised me that it's her best hope. The studies are very positive, but she wouldn't agree. I understand why, it's invasive and unpleasant, but with the right support, she stands a much better chance of beginning a normal life again.'

'There's something you're not telling me. What about your alchemy collection?'

Dad looked confused. 'What does that have to do with this? It is not *my* collection. I am president of a society which is interested in the history of alchemy, and with that role comes the custodianship of the collection, but I am also president of the Milliardo Foundation, CEO of my own company and several smaller charitable foundations. Are they relevant too?'

'So you aren't keeping her because you think she could be an alchemist?'

It was like a bomb had gone off. 'What?' he roared, jumping to his feet. Some of the brandy splashed on the arm of my chair. He was more furious with this comment than he'd been at Terry holding a gun to my head. His eyes flashed and the colour in his skin rose. 'I am protecting her, Francesca, not keeping her! She would be in gaol if it weren't for me.' His voice thundered. 'All I've ever wanted to do is help her.'

I sat quietly, trying to sift the story for truth. 'But why did we go back in the ballroom? Why did she take down that knife?'

'Oh ... I see why you are coming to these conclusions, but you have the situation back to front. It's not I

129

who wants her to be an alchemist, it is entirely her own delusion. It was one of the reasons she was so heavily medicated in the hospital because she was obsessed with the idea. We took her and Terry into the ballroom because strategically it was a better location to disarm Terry. The hallway was not to our advantage. When she grabbed that knife from the wall, we all thought the same thing: that she intended to hurt herself, but when she turned around, did you see her eyes? Did you see them changing and swirling and turning yellow? It was very strange – mesmerising, in fact, and I'm only human. In that instant, I did think maybe I was wrong. Pierro told me he thought there was something highly unusual about her. After what we witnessed, I realise I should have taken his comments more seriously. She has an incredible psychic strength; it is obviously why she is so unbalanced.'

My shoulders slumped. 'Oh, Dad, I don't know what to think now. Did someone kill Terry?'

His whole face stretched in astonishment at my question. 'Of course not. What would give you such an idea as that?'

'I heard a gunshot.'

'He took a shot at one of the guards. Fortunately, they were wearing a vest. *He's* fine, though you're a credit to your mother, worrying about him after what he did to you.'

'Where is he now?'

'The guards have taken him to the police with the CCTV footage of his entry.'

'He'll tell them about Abigail.'

'He knows he has to be careful not to get her implicated in Pierro's murder, plus I doubt they will take much notice of him with the evidence against him. I was so frightened he would hurt you. It really is sad. He was such a talented artist, but he's as unhinged as she is.'

'And where did all the men come from?'

'That was Lorin's doing, and I will never argue with him again about the money I pay for security. This year, he doubled my wage bill by adding a heavy stipend for more security, and whenever I quibbled about it, he said it was essential. When you answered the door, our security guard had it on CCTV and immediately pressed our emergency support button. Those men were here in less than five minutes and it was as if Lorin had done that drill with them a hundred times. They just fell into position.'

Not being quite as delighted with Lorin as usual, I layered sarcasm into my voice. 'Before we give anyone a medal, I think when an armed man trots up to the front door without anyone noticing, *probably,* there are still a few hitches in the security arrangements.'

Dad nodded.

My brain was in a tangle. I was starting to feel guilty. Could I have misread the whole situation? If I had then, no doubt, I needed several years of therapy to work out why. Completely different thoughts to those I'd had five minutes ago fluttered across my brain. Dad was a private man, but that didn't make him a guilty one. I should have more faith in him, but the scenario was so strange and so complicated.

Finishing his brandy, he walked around to where I sat on the bed. He leaned in and kissed the top of my head.

'I need to ring your mother and explain what has happened. She'll want to speak to you, of course. I don't think now is the time to tell her about the difficulties at university, do you?' I shook my head. 'We'll leave that for another day.'

Dad returned to check in on me every couple of hours that day. It was the only way I knew time was passing. At each visit, he tutted at the quantity of drawings around me as the floor became carpeted with them.

Terry had invaded that calm place in my head where my art came from and was reaping havoc. Details poured out of me like pus: Terry's rough hands upon me; his mouth close to my ear; his stance; the look in his eye that said, *'I don't care if I kill you'*. The only way to get him out was to draw him out. And then there was Lorin, my Lorin, fighting with me on the floor.

By early evening, my eyes were dry with exhaustion. At nearly ten o'clock, Dad insisted I break away from my desk. As he kissed me goodnight, he added, 'Well, *Giraffa*, this trauma may be the making of your art career, though I'm not sure I'll be able to part with a single one of your drawings at any cost.'

Each visit, he had gathered great armfuls of my work up like my mother would laundry.

I found the sanctuary of sleep impossible to locate. My thoughts about Terry and Lorin tangled. I had wanted to draw every frame of Lorin's face while we fought and after to give me answers to what had happened, but I wasn't that stupid. My father might have seen the sketch. My brain buzzed like a live wire. Binge-watching TV yielded a path into a fitful dream around 4.25am.

***

My phone buzzed at about 8am. It was Blake, and I didn't even get to say hello.

'You total bitch!' he shouted down the phone. 'I run off and help you. Go investigating for you, get my mum to let us into her work to see things we shouldn't even know about, and you don't even call me and tell me about some major event, relevant to what we were looking into, that happened in our own father's house!' His voice was so loud I had to move the phone away from my ear by inches. I woke to the fact that he was completely right. I should have called him, but I was damned if I was going to apologise when he was braying like a donkey, so I felt the most eloquent and annoying thing I could do would be to hang up.

Dropping my head back on the pillow, I shuffled down into my divinely soft bed and pulled up the duvet to my ears. Three colossal strikes and Blake careered into the room, plumes of furiousness rolling off him.

'You are something else!' he yelled. I sat up in bed and all the tiredness and repressed aggression from yesterday surfaced in a heartbeat.

'I'm sorry that you weren't the first person I called after having a gun held to my head, but strangely enough, you're not that important to me!'

His face was blank, but the volume of his voice dropped a little. 'What happened to the ballroom door? It looks as if it's been driven through by a tank.'

'Actually, it was me who was driven through it, not a tank.'

Blake threw himself down in the armchair, annoyance written all over him. 'I don't get you. Two days ago, you were begging me for help.'

'That's not fair. Something shocking and scary and dangerous happened here yesterday. Not calling you was the least of several stupid things that I've done over the last couple of days. Abigail asked me to contact Terry Gerrard, and he turned out to be a psycho who nearly murdered me.'

I gave him a summary of yesterday's events and told him about Dad's explanations. This time, I held nothing back. Blake sat silently and whistled when I came to the end.

'I wonder how much of what he says we can really believe. It sounds to me like there could be more to this Terry story than Dad's version suggests.'

Now it was my turn to shout. 'Why do you have to

133

say things like that? I feel like you've punctured my relationship with Dad. You are forever making cryptic innuendos and now I am doubting Dad the whole time and it isn't fair.'

Blaming Blake for my betrayal of Dad certainly felt better than accepting the blame myself.

He raised his eyebrows at me. 'Excuse me for having an opinion.'

I felt anger loosen my tongue. 'Where do you get this whole "I'm-so-badly-done-to" thing anyway? Dad is going to take you into the business. You just hadn't made him see how much it means to you. If you want someone to take you seriously, you have to stop with all the silent kicks and speak up for yourself.'

'Like you did? From what I heard, it was my mother who did the talking.' Blake stood up, looking sourly at the wall of novels. 'Perhaps the promise of your dreams coming true is what is making you so eager to ignore some of the subtleties of yesterday's events. I imagine you're ready to forget all about Abigail and the Society now that you're going to become an artist.'

His voice was taunting.

'And what if I am? Yesterday was awful and I don't want to know anything else about any of it. I just want to have a nice summer and draw. In fact, yesterday's events have given me a little perspective and put my priorities in order. The extent of my ambition is to have a summer romance and spend my days hanging out at the pool, losing my anaemic blueness instead of being haunted by a possible alchemist.'

'Bet you're proud of those sturdy principles.'

'Why is it all my responsibility? What the hell do you want me to do? I can't help Abigail. I tried and look what happened. Why don't you get out!' I shouted, standing up on my bed and pointing at the door.

'You can dole it out, sister, but you can't take it?' he

sneered at me as he sauntered towards the door. 'I'll go and get some breakfast and leave you to calm down. Obviously, you're not a morning person.' He slammed the door as he left and I joined his childish act by sticking out my tongue.

Blake's words rankled. He hadn't been there yesterday. He didn't know how terrifying it was to be caught up in something like that. Surely, I was entitled to prioritise my own life, and he was behaving like I was walking away from Abigail, leaving her hanging by her fingernails from some precipice. I knew why his opinion made me so angry: it was because I suspected he was right. I wondered how she was today; I imagined she would be recuperating, and her hands must be a mess.

I showered and dressed and considered calling up Kristin. She would give me a good dollop of common sense, but could I tell her all this on Skype? We wouldn't be able to dissect it in the kind of detail I craved. I knew I owed Blake an apology. I'd said things I shouldn't have, but he shouldn't have come in guns blazing – no-one would be anything but defensive under that kind of fire.

I dragged my heels downstairs. Glancing towards Dad's office, I wanted to see Lorin and I didn't. I'd flipped what had happened with Lorin back and forth in my head during my wakeful night, and I still couldn't account for his behaviour. I suspected he was avoiding me. He could have come to my room last night if he had wanted to explain.

I walked across the hall to the breakfast room, not relishing the possibility of eating breakfast with a cranky Blake, but Dad was with him, finishing a coffee. Their heads were close and they were talking in an animated way. Blake looked flushed and glanced with irritation at the disturbance.

Dad rose and kissed me on the head. 'Blake, we can

discuss this a little more in the car. I'll see you later, Francesca. I'll collect you from here at 12.30 for the exhibition. Are you feeling up to it?' He caught my chin and held my head, looking at me as if I were a child who might be coming down with measles.

I smiled. 'Yes, not even yesterday's life-threatening drama could stop me wanting to see Robert Crumb's exhibition.'

Dad smiled and stood. 'Coming?' He looked at Blake who nodded and stood, gulping down the last of his coffee.

As Dad left the room, I stopped Blake. 'What were you two whispering about so secretively?'

'Just taking your advice and making Papa see me.'

I grabbed some rhubarb jam and piled it up on my croissant.

'Good for you. I'm sorry. It was an awful day yesterday.'

'I might not have forgiven you so easily, but Papa has asked me to come to the office with him this morning – first time ever.'

Happiness shone from Blake's face, the complete opposite of twenty minutes ago. It stuck in my throat that his barbed words had been all about me ignoring aspects of Dad's story for my own gain, but he wasn't about to refuse the hand offered to him. I swallowed the lump down with my croissant.

Chapter 13

Dad was picking me up at lunchtime so I went back to my room to read and ended up falling into a deep sleep for a while. I woke with a start over two hours later and staggered up in search of Paolo to blend me something substantial enough to keep my eyes from closing again.

'This is the Kalashnikov of coffees. It will annihilate your fatigue.' He passed me a tall glass held in a silver frame and held his breath as I took my first sip: more fiery than whisky, more bitter than quinine and with an aftertaste that made a scorpion chilli taste mild. I wondered whether this concoction was legal.

I felt the perverse pull of wanting to return to the scene of the crime and took my coffee into the ballroom. The room was the antithesis of yesterday: serene and empty. The sculpture had gone, along with all of Abigail's tools and materials. Guilt cut into my conscience: if the statue had been moved, she might have gone too.

I sat down in one of the window bays and looked out over the view, which was so hazy it looked as if tracing paper had been laid over it. I rubbed my forehead as the fog of sleep was blasted away by Paolo's coffee, and in the space it created, yesterday's events were re-enacted. New thoughts and questions were surfacing. Could I live my life as normal when she was locked up somewhere? Was Terry alive or dead? Did I believe my father's explanation? Could he lie that convincingly? Being locked up because she was suicidal or had murdered someone was one thing, but the ugliness of being locked up because of some mythical gift would make made Dad a psychotic monster.

When Lorin laid his hand on my shoulder, I jumped three feet in the air.

'You're like an Aborigine with your silent motion.'

I swallowed down the shock with a mouthful of scalding coffee. He moved me along the window seat so he could join me. I stiffened and slid further than necessary.

'Good coffee?' he enquired. Small talk was an interesting choice, but as an expert in denial, I couldn't be a hypocrite. I gave a tight smile.

'I think Paolo has mixed in amphetamine instead of sugar.'

'You're dressed very brightly today.'

I looked down at my lemon skirt and vivid orange T-shirt. 'I planned on having a rich bronze tan when I wore these, but I don't seem to have had much time for sunbathing so far.'

'You look lovely.'

'I was just thinking about Abigail. Did they move her?'

Lorin hesitated. 'You need to ask your father. He wouldn't be happy if he knew I'd told you anything.'

'I doubt he'd be *happy* if he knew you'd kissed me,

but you did.'

He dialled down the volume of his voice so that it was barely a whisper and moved closer.

'I shouldn't have.'

That was a thousand paper cuts dipped in vinegar. I couldn't keep the sting out of my voice.

'It can't matter whether I know or not, surely? Not being able to figure out where she's kept is driving me mad. I've toured the rooms, but none of them are locked.'

'She's still here, but she goes tomorrow,' he mumbled.

'How are you ... after yesterday?' I blurted out and heard the clang of irony, but the question broke the tense atmosphere between us. Some hair fell across my face and I tucked it behind my ear as I waited for a response. With a slow hand, he gave the tendril its freedom again.

Turning his back to the door, he lowered his eyes to my lap.

'I told you that I left the army because I'd had enough. That wasn't true. It was on my second tour, I began to experience ... episodes. They gave me counselling, and named the behaviour panic attacks, but instead of going away, they became more acute to the point where I'd lose awareness of the present and become disorientated. After a while, I was given a general discharge on medical grounds, which is not the end of a career that any soldier wants.'

'Did something particular happen to start them?'

'No, it wasn't one event that caused it, but we did see a lifetime's worth of violence and cruelty during our first tour. One day, the anxiety just invaded my life when previously it hadn't been there. Yesterday's was my first in seven months. I was alright until the moment I felt you were safe and that's when it started. All I could see was that look in Terry's eyes. Desperate people have a certain look. You were so close to…'

He broke off as he felt my hand slip over his. Yester-day's fear clawed at my throat and I felt an overwhelm-ing need to be held and protected from the spectre of danger that hung between us. His eyes met mine and I moved towards him, wanting to lay my head on his shoulder, but he jerked away. His eyes darted up to the far corner of the room. My eyes were tugged along by his and I saw a security camera which I'd never noticed before.

He stood up. 'She's in the annexe,' he said in a voice barely louder than the rustle of the cushion as he gained his feet. Before I had a chance to respond to his explana-tion, he was half way to the door. I considered following, but what was there to say? *I'm sorry for you*. The indignity of pity was a humiliation I'd suffered often enough. I would rather seem cold than insult him with that. He needed time to trust me and remember that I had more experience than most in the area of mind-hijacking.

The annexe was such an obvious place. How had I not thought of it? I got up and walked upstairs to the second floor where, instead of bedrooms, several rooms had been knocked into one large space to house my dad's personal art collection. The room was kept in darkness when not in use to protect the paintings, which included works by Rembrandt, Titian, Caravaggio, El Greco, and even a drawing by Leonardo da Vinci. Dad was *persona non grata* at some of the most famous art galleries in the world as he'd outbid many of them for key pieces which they felt should have gone into the public domain. Dad had no such scruples and a seem-ingly unlimited art budget.

Today I wasn't interested in the art. Moving the heavy blackout curtains aside, I looked out over the courtyard and beyond that to the more utilitarian space behind the kitchens enclosed by a high wall. At the furthest end, there was a building that had once been a garage and had been extended above. We called it the annexe, and when I had been young enough to need a nanny, that's where they had lived each summer.

The gallery was significantly higher than the annexe but, to my surprise, I saw Abigail sitting on the floor alongside the window – a ball of misery. Her legs were drawn up so that she could rest her head on her knees. I tried to wave, but she didn't notice me. The lower level rooms only looked over the courtyard and were not high enough to see the annexe. I wondered if I could open the window, but that proved fruitless as it was drilled shut.

Leaning against the glass, I felt defeated. There wasn't much point in getting her attention anyway: I couldn't be any material help, but I thought, *If it was me locked up, any contact would be welcome.* I looked down at my bright T-shirt and a thought was born.

I whipped off my top. I wasn't wearing a bra so I covered my breasts with one arm and waved my T-shirt frantically back and forth. She didn't see me immediately so I waved harder. Perhaps it was only luck, but something made her look up.

We were a distance apart, but her expression of desperation hit my heart like an arrow meeting its bullseye. Clasping my T-shirt across myself, I pressed my face against the glass and we stared at each other. I just wanted her to know that I hadn't forgotten her. It was a very basic human exchange and lasted less than ten seconds before I was pulled backwards away from the window by two strong arms.

I lost my balance and thought I was going to fall, but was hauled up on to my feet. I started to struggle against whoever it was and spun until I realised it was Lorin.

'What the hell are you doing?' I said, regaining my feet and facing him in fury.

He stood still, looking daggers at me. I tried to cover

myself up with both arms.

'Keeping you out of more trouble! There are several guards out there. Do you want them to see you like that?'

'And if they do?' I said in the full knowledge that people showed more wearing a bikini.

'You're his daughter. It's not a good idea to put yourself on display like that.'

He nodded his head at my partially covered upper body. A small amount of shame spiked with anger made me defensive.

'I wasn't showing anything,' I yelled.

'Keep your voice down. That's not how it'll be told around the house.'

I gave him my most patronising stare and slowly dropped my arms to my waist, revealing my top half fully. I slipped my T-shirt over my wrists in an unhurried way and lifted my arms up high over my head. For a second, the orange T-shirt stayed like a flag waving on high, and then it fell over my head and I tugged it down into position.

'Well, if I'm already going to be talked about, you may as well tell them something worth listening to,' I said as I set off past him.

A step away from the door, he caught my wrist and spun me round, pushing me back against the door. His mouth was on mine, and this time it was a completely different kiss from the last one. It was as forceful as the last one was gentle. Though I was only a few inches smaller than him, he lifted me up and pushed me against the door. I circled his hips with my legs. He pressed his whole body against mine and held me securely, our mouths perfectly level, then slid his hands along the underside of my thighs. My skirt had ridden up and his long fingers rested at the crescent of my behind. I was glad I wasn't relying on my legs to hold me; they would never have managed it. For someone so passive in his daily life, he kissed with no reserves, pouring out everything he was feeling.

'Francesca.' It was my dad, ready to take me to the exhibition. Lorin and I stopped, our bodies tensing in sync. We opened our eyes, but he did not pull away instantly.

Dad called again and this time Lorin released me. I regained my feet and he stepped away, looking confused for a moment. I opened the door very slightly to peer out over the balcony and see where Dad was. Lorin stood slightly behind me and laid a hand on my waist.

Dad was wearing his glasses and seemed to be reading a printout. Lorin pulled out his phone and pressed a number on his favourites list. I heard the phone in Dad's office ring and saw Dad disappear in there.

'Go,' said Lorin, giving me a small push. I bolted from the room and along to my own. Safely inside, I leaned against the door. That kiss had a lot of potential. If Dad hadn't come back, that could have escalated. I took a deep breath and tried to calm my heart, which was racing. I felt like a bottle of champagne when the cork has been popped; excitement effervesced out of me. I would have to calm down otherwise my dad would be suspicious.

The wall phone buzzed loudly right next to my ear and made me jump sideways.

'I'm ready,' my dad said pleasantly down the receiver.

I had to stop myself yelling, 'I know!'

***

We sat in the busy gallery café at Hangar Bicocca, a contemporary art space that was more multiple aircraft hangars than gallery in the former Pirelli factory. I was wondering whether I might be able to get Dad to lean on whichever contact he had here and arrange a further visit for me. I loved Robert Crumb: dubbed an underground cartoonist, he had made the leap into big time art with his iconic style, as I hoped I might do one day, but I hadn't been able to concentrate. I could think of nothing other than Terry. My brain was congested with yesterday's scenes which made me blind to the masterpieces on the wall.

Maybe I needed a change of scene. I could visit Kristin in Barcelona for a few days, gain a little perspective and hopefully dry out from the fear that seemed to have soaked through to my bones.

Dad put his hand on my wrist. '*Giraffa,* you are not listening to me. I was telling you about my thoughts on your future. I wish you had not hidden this secret from me for so long. I could have helped you sooner. It troubles me that you do not feel that I would have understood.

'I think you should stay in Milano after the summer. I will hire two or three of the best art tutors I can find and they will help you develop. Also, you might go and spend some time with more established artists abroad so they can mentor you a little. We will hire a beautiful studio space, and once you are settled in, I will bring some of my friends to view your work. You will have to work as hard at encouraging them to buy as you will creating the work. Being an artist is only ten per cent about creativity, the rest is about becoming someone they want to know and buy. By the time you have your first exhibition, I think we can ensure that your popularity will be established.'

Excitement overtook me. This was beyond my wildest dreams. I'd never considered the idea of staying in Milan. My mum would hate it and I wondered if she'd even agree, but I thought it likely that now Dad had decided he wanted this, he wouldn't allow it to be derailed easily. It would be a world heavyweight battle between two titans. Staying in Milan had some appeal, Lorin for one, though the big downside was that I had no friends here.

As if he needed to convince me, Dad added more to his case.

'It would be wonderful for you to be here and for us to get to know each other better, and I am not entirely unselfish. Abigail weighs on my mind very heavily and I can confide in you about her.'

He kept his eyes low when he said this as if embarrassed to admit it. I was touched that he seemed so excited about the plan. I leaned across the table and threw my arms around him.

'Thank you, Dad, that does sound completely incredible. It's far better than I'd ever hoped, but wouldn't it upset your life too much having me around? What about all your *liaisons*?'

I teased him, using my best French accent. He clasped his hands together, prayer-like, and raised his eyes to heaven.

'What liaisons? I am as celibate as a monk,' he said and grinned, his face becoming all nose. 'You don't worry about that. If you're behaving badly, I'll send Lorin up to deal with you.'

I couldn't control my smile from breaking out with that comment. *Better and better,* I thought.

***

Well after midnight, I lay in bed, unable to sleep again. My eyelids were tender and I couldn't stop rubbing them as my eyes felt dry. I wondered if Paolo's Kalashnikov coffee was still percolating through my veins. My mind was stormy and worries pitched and rolled like waves:

Lorin and the nuclear level mess that would inevitably ensue if my dad ever found out; Terry's arm around my throat, driving me through the ballroom door; Abigail and her possible gift; the offer my dad had made to me at the exhibition today.

I got out of bed and decided to go down to the kitchen. It was very unlikely that any of the staff would be there now, so I might make myself a late-night snack. I padded down the dark carpeted staircase and noticed a flicker of light from underneath the office door. My first thought was to dash back up to my room to put on something a bit sexier than pyjamas. Then I noted that the light didn't look regular somehow; it seemed to pulse, and I realised that, even for Lorin, this would be working very late.

I moved down the remainder of the stairs and across the black and white tiled floor of the hallway. Could it be my dad? I wasn't sure if he was in or not. I held my breath as I pushed the handle down and swung open the door in a single movement. It was Abigail's signature glow.

I felt an urge to hug her, which was ridiculous as she wasn't really there, and why was her light in here anyway?

She smiled at me. I came in and shut the door. I didn't even need to turn a light on, she was so bright. She mimed at me, tapping her head and then opening her hands and raising her shoulders. *'How's the head?'*

I twisted my hand back and forth: *'So-so.'*

She finger spelled in the air, h-a-v-e – y-o-u-? then lifted her hands to her temple and gestured as she'd shown me in the library, pushing her hands away from her head. I shook my head, feeling a bit guilty, but really life had been extraordinarily mad recently and I didn't understand why she thought this would help.

She beckoned to me. As I stepped into her haze, she

reached out and tried to pull my arm forward, but like a ghost she couldn't make contact. I came even closer.

We stood almost toe to toe, so close it felt like the air was denser. I was aware of it the way people are aware they're in water. She was smaller than me. I felt static running along my skin like my body was conducting current. She couldn't physically touch me, but her aura surrounded me; every hair on my body seemed to be primed and standing to attention. She made the familiar gesture of pushing away from her temple and then closed her eyes, and I followed her lead.

This time I was not in raging pain, so letting my mind push outwards wasn't punished by a cerebral beating. I just relaxed and tried not to think about the fact I had a body encaging my thoughts. I tried to free them, but as contrary as cats, they refused to be directed. I opened one eye; Abigail was staring at me.

She mimed pushing against something heavy like she was trying to move a rock. I closed my eyes and tried again. This time, I didn't think of myself outside of my body, but of expanding my body's boundary. This took more effort. She was right: it did feel like pushing something that didn't want to move.

Those lights of hers were so familiar: they were the same stuff as my migraine markers. My migraines always began in my temples, the same place I often saw the images that became my drawings. I pushed there, outwards from my temples. I could have kicked myself – that's what she'd been telling me. This place was so much more flexible. This place felt like the walls were made of elastic.

My periphery was already wider than usual, and then, like a snowflake falling, I saw my first dazzling light. It hovered and another joined it; I watched them grow. Now there were clusters; I held my breath. The pain would not be far behind, the thunder after the lightening.

The lights grew and grew until they were hard to see, and then I opened my eyes and saw Abigail clapping her hands together. It felt like I'd gone deaf. Even though we hadn't been speaking, I knew my ears had been working, detecting little background sounds. Now there was nothing; it was a silence deeper than I had ever encountered. I looked at her, uncertain.

The office door swung open. I turned in fright, expecting whoever it was to shout. Lorin entered the room. He didn't turn the light on and seemed completely oblivious to me or Abigail. I watched him walk a couple of paces towards his desk, looking as if he were about to put the desk lamp on, but then he stumbled and fell onto his knees. I looked down in horror as I realised he'd fallen over my body which was lying as if asleep on the floor.

My eyes felt like they were burning. The lights around me were very bright. Lorin staggered up and switched on the desk lamp before trying to shake me awake. As I watched, panic gripped my core. How could I get back in my body? She hadn't shown me how to get back in my body!

I looked at Abigail in utter terror. She was indicating to me to calm down, which seemed the most ridiculous thing to say to someone in my position. Lorin was now checking my pulse; I could see he was saying something to me.

Returning to my body began with a feeling of being pulled from very far off – the way it can feel when you are being woken from a deep sleep. I had the sense I was travelling, and when I opened my eyes again, I wasn't standing but lying on the floor, looking up into Lorin's concerned face. My hearing returned and, though he wasn't speaking, I was aware of sound again.

I felt incredibly nauseous. I sat up and bent my head between my knees. Panting, I felt the saliva gather in my mouth. I swallowed it down, closing my eyes and trying to breathe deeply.

By the time I felt better, Abigail had gone and Lorin was bombarding me with questions which I couldn't seem to process. His mouth was moving, but what was coming out didn't come together into anything familiar. It felt like my thoughts had been crushed like a car sent for scrap. There was something familiar about this state: it felt like my condition post-migraine.

I felt deeply tired, and the one thought that did get through my slow brain was *bed*. I didn't attempt to speak; I was fairly sure that my fluency in gibberish would have him insisting I see a neurologist in the morning. I walked towards the door of the office, across the dark hallway and up the moonlit staircase. Lorin didn't follow. I turned on the stairs to see where he was. He stood in the office doorway, silhouetted by the light blazing behind him, just watching me ascend.

Chapter 14

Sleep had eventually come, but there'd been an under-current of a headache constantly present. It was hard to reach that place where sleep was restorative because just as I did, the ache would yank me further away again.

Next morning, the first thing I did was reach for my phone. I had to tell Sergio about Dad's offer. I gave my head a prod to see how it was feeling: almost normal. Excitement fizzled. Last night, I hadn't been able to appreciate it, but I had experienced something awesome: a way out of my evil migraines, if only for a while. Then a doubt crept in. It occurred to me that I might not be able to repeat it without Abigail's presence; somehow coming into her lights had helped me.

I wondered if she'd been moved already. What if I never saw her again? Without really knowing her at all, I realised a kinship had been growing between us, and after last night, we seemed to be even more tied.

I had a quick shower and slipped into some white cotton shorts, flip-flops and snug yellow T-shirt which outlined all my curves. Adding a brush of mascara, I got my sketchbook and pencils ready and went downstairs. I didn't fancy breakfast alone, but thought I would grab a coffee-to-go from the breakfast room and maybe walk to Castello Sforzesco.

Paolo was a sight to behold. Most days he did single cups as and when they were required, but this morning, he must have a big order because the machine was fully cranked up and billowing out great gasps of steam. He worked the large chrome thug of a coffee machine with all the skill of a seasoned engineer. Given a chance, he would have taken me on a personalised tour of every spout, lever and knob. My fingers twitched at the sketching opportunity and I pulled out my pencils as I waited, sitting on the bar stool. Paolo didn't even see me, so intent was he on his order. He was tall and bald, and I drew him as an octopus with arms flailing wildly, some with coffee cups in them, others with tiny steel jugs. The steam was making him sweat, and I paid particular attention to the expression of concentration he wore and the perfect roundness of his shiny head.

'You are too cruel.' Lorin's words dropped over my shoulder, making me jump. 'I forbid you ever to draw me.'

'Well, I'm not agreeing to that,' I said, adding a few more steam clouds to the sketch. Lorin took possession of the bar stool next to me. Paolo caught sight of him and the harassed vibe dialled up a notch.

'Can I add a cappuccino to go, please?'

He looked like I'd asked him to give me his kidney.

'Why's Paolo so busy?' I asked Lorin.

'Your father has a meeting with builders, engineers, surveyors, architects. He wants to add a basement to the house. They are looking at plans and I'm getting coffee.

I needed to see you.'

'Did you?' There was too much hope in my voice. I cringed and kept my head down, concentrating on my page. I hoped he couldn't see my colour rise.

His voice was apologetic. 'Your father would like you to visit him at Marchione Street at 10.30 this morning. He says to wait and you can go there together.'

'Tell him I'll make my own way. I feel like walking this morning.'

Lorin reached forward, paused my hand, which hadn't quite finished the sketch, and pulled the paper from my pad. 'Can I have this?'

'I don't know why you'd want to. It's very silly,' I said, lifting my eyes up and being hit by how sexy he looked this morning. His eyes were bright and his hair was wayward, some falling about his face while other curls arched upwards. I had to exert substantial will power not to reach up and touch him.

'I need more *silly* in my life, Francesca.' There was a pause where my mind shot back to the panic attack he'd had in my room. 'What happened last night? Was it a migraine or did you sleepwalk?'

I wasn't keen to admit to either one. The last thing I wanted was to be pitied by him or thought of as an oddity who drifted through the house like a ghost in the night, but I was saved from further explanation by Paolo having the coffees ready.

'*Andiamo!* Let's go,' Paolo yelled, thrusting my cappuccino at me and shouting, 'Ya! Ya!' at Lorin like he was a horse who needed to spring to the gallop to bring the stagecoach in on time.

***

Blake was in reception at Marchione Street when I arrived.

'Hey, what are you doing here?' I said in surprise.

152

'I'm renewing my pass for archives. I can't even slack off up there as there's no mobile phone reception – the rooms are fire proof, theft proof and probably nuclear bomb proof. Someone's got to put last year's files in storage.' He laughed, but without humour. 'Not quite what I was hoping I'd be doing. I'll get you a pass too.'

I stood and looked at the sculpture which had reminded me so much of Abigail the first time I'd seen it and now represented me as well: incredible. Blake handed over my pass in a plastic wallet. He had a hard plastic pass which looked more permanent.

'Dad has asked to see me. Will you take me up there?'

'Nothing better to do,' he said, leading me towards the lifts.

We rode up in the lift to the thirty-third floor.

'You are going to be wowed by Papa's office,' Blake said with enthusiasm. We came into a lobby of the same shape as the one that had led into the alchemy collection, but this one was decorated entirely differently. It was white with a pale polished limestone floor. There was a contemporary tapestry behind a walnut reception desk. Blake smiled at the receptionist and she waved him through.

Dad was speaking on his phone and stood, nodding to us. It was the largest office I'd ever seen, laid out like an apartment with defined zones: work area, lounge area, meeting room area, rest area and small art gallery. I walked the floor, taking it all in. His work area had a computer with three screens and the desk was roughly the size of a double bed. The meeting room space had a long black boardroom table with around twenty chairs and a couple of bronze sculptures upon it. The rest area had an inviting grey chaise longue in one corner, at the furthest point from the computer. Alongside it was a small table with a couple of books on it. The view from every angle of the office was breathtaking, looking over the whole of Milan.

'*Ciao*, Francesca. *Ciao*, Blake.' Dad hugged and kissed us both. 'Do you like the office?' The more I gushed, the more pleased he seemed.

He picked up his phone and pressed a button. 'The *Inglese et un espresso*,' he said before replacing the receiver. I glanced at Blake – only two drinks?

'Come and sit over here.' He indicated to the seating area which had a selection of chairs, none of which looked as if they'd been designed for sitting on. I chose one which was suspended from the ceiling and was more like half of a Christmas bauble than a chair. He sat on a pair of red lips.

'Blake, in the morning you can report to Stacey on the thirteenth floor. I've arranged for you to assist her. Back to work.'

Dad dismissed him with a wave of his hand. Blake nodded.

'Of course.'

He glanced back at me swinging in the bauble as Dad's secretary brought in a silver teapot, coffee pot and biscuits and laid them out on a coffee table.

'Thank you, Micala.' Dad smiled at her and then turned to me. 'Shall we get it over with?'

I looked at him blankly.

'Shall we call your mother about *our* plans?'

I took a deep breath, bit my lip, and nodded my head.

'Yes, let's do it.'

'I know Blake wanted to stay, but I think this will be like a visit to the dentist without anaesthetic for both of us, so let's not have an audience to see us sweat.'

I nodded and my bauble swayed. I must remember to tell Blake why he wasn't invited to stay.

Dad went over to his desk and brought across a portable phone. I pushed my hands between my legs and squashed them, shuffling from side to side.

'Nancy, darling, so nice to hear your voice,' Dad purred. 'A marvellous opportunity for Francesca has come up.' I could hear Mum objecting before she'd even heard what it was that he had to say. Dad was smooth and coaxing: a man with a talent for negotiation. 'An international artist wishes to mentor her. He thinks she could be *very* successful. We were thinking she could defer university for a year and explore this opportunity.'

At this white lie, he winked at me. The decibel level that my mum's voice reached caused my dad to lift the phone away from his ear and pull a face while she vented.

'I would advise you strongly to consider the offer. It has been clear since Francesca arrived that she is unhappy at university, and if you insist she continues, I would not be surprised if she did drop out entirely. Yes, of course she's here.'

Mum blasted my eardrums off. She rattled off her objections so fast, I couldn't even follow all of what she was saying. Phrases like, 'Ridiculous plan', 'Whose idea was it?', 'Not going to happen' walloped my eardrums. There was nothing to do other than let her blow herself out. Occasionally, I looked at Dad for direction. When her pace slackened, I chipped in, making an effort to speak in a firm tone.

'Mum, I don't want to fight with you, but deferring for a year is a good compromise.' This set her off again. She spoke so fast, I only heard snippets: 'You'll never go back', 'I'm not stupid', 'Ruining your life'.

'Mum, I hear your objections, but I'm an adult and I won't be bullied. You knew I didn't want to do medicine. I've given it a try and I'm not happy. Please take some time to think it over and we'll speak again tomorrow.' I looked at Dad, who motioned *cut the call* by

155

drawing his hand across his neck in a slicing motion. 'Goodbye, Mum,' I said, ending the call with her still half way through a sentence.

Dad and I looked at each other and laughter overtook us.

'That went well, I think,' he said and I sat back in my bauble chair, laughing with relief.

'Poor Mum, she'll be even more furious that I cut her off.'

Dad poured us both our drinks and I came and sat next to him. There was companionable silence for a moment or two before Dad spoke again.

'Francesca, I want to ask you a favour. Would you be prepared to help me with Abigail?'

My stomach tensed. I had not expected this. I felt guilt pinch because my instant reaction wasn't more gushing. Helping her would bring us together, and I knew that the more involved I became, the less likely it was I would ever rest easily.

I swallowed that mouthful of selfishness down. 'Of course, I'll help.'

'She will be staying here in Marchione Street from now on. I'm so pleased you care enough to help,' he said, stirring some sugar into his coffee. 'Is it true that she can move outside of her body and you can see her?'

I felt my face flush and fumbled my tea so that it spilled slightly on my leg.

'Ouch!' I hopped up, spilling more tea on the floor, and grabbed a handful of tissues which sprouted from a leather-clad box on the coffee table. My mind was whirring as I dabbed my legs and then the spill on the floor. Things were starting to make sense. Blake whispering to Dad over breakfast and telling me he was making Dad see him; the sudden change in his status. He'd shopped me and told Dad what I'd told him in confidence. Worm!

I took a deep breath and sat back down. I didn't think there was much point in lying; I was so horrible at it.

'Yes, sometimes.'

'This fits in with the event we witnessed in the ballroom when Terry took you hostage. It's more evidence that she has incredible psychic power. It is so important that we understand it fully. I am sure that it is the root of her mental health problems.' He was conveniently sidestepping my ability to see her amazing psychic power. Anxiety was flickering inside me.

'Who is it so important for exactly?'

'For her, of course, but we cannot ignore the fact that her ability could give us insights into the human brain, mental illness, brain damage. Psychic power is anecdotal, but we have the means to study it and move ourselves towards answers to questions scientists are desperate to solve.'

'That doesn't sound much fun for her.'

'I am giving her an opportunity to help humanity. It will be a means for her to make amends for what she did to Pierro. It must be better than being in a prison for the rest of her life.' He leaned forward and touched my hand. 'My sweet girl, don't you remember that her power threw more than a dozen men to the floor? It would be wrong to pretend it didn't happen. I will ask very little of you, only to be a part of a minor exercise.'

'You won't hurt her?' I said, looking into his ice-blue eyes.

He looked hurt. '*Giraffa,* what an awful thing to say. Of course I would not hurt her. What kind of man do you take me for? You can think of it as a way of thanking me for all that I plan to do for your career over the next few years.'

That hadn't taken long. Sergio had warned me that there would be a price. I wondered what my father had had him do in order to further his own career. Every cell in my body wanted to scream at him and tell him he shouldn't put me in such a position, but then a little part of me heckled, '*You know you don't deserve this ticket to all your dreams, so if you've got any sense, you'll grow up and pay the piper.*'

Chapter 15

'If I'm going to be working here, I want a permanent
pass for your building.' This was a tiny request, but it
meant more to me than he realised. I wanted an opportunity to snoop around his alchemy collection a little more.

My Dad laughed. He sipped his coffee; he knew the
deal was done. 'An hour's work doesn't constitute
working here. Why would you want a pass?'

'You've got the best contemporary art collection I've
ever seen and you never told me about it. I'd like to draw
some of the sculptures so I'll need to keep coming in and
out.' I felt the strength of the lie and this made me
bolder. Blake would have been proud of me.

'Done,' he agreed.

'Is there a day that you would like to get the ... exercise done?' The word exercise stuck in my throat. Who
were we both kidding?

'You can get it over with straight away if you'd like.

I don't see the need to leave it and let you worry over it. Let me speak to Micala.' He stood up and walked towards his desk, picked up the telephone and pressed a button, speaking in Italian. 'Hello, please can you tell Lorin that we will be ready to visit the lab straight away. Tell him to make the arrangements.' He caught my eye. 'And can you inform reception that I would like a pass organised for my daughter. She'll collect it later.' He paused, listening. 'First name is Francesca and for twelve months.'

The glass bauble chair was so deep that I could lie back against the cushions so that my torso was almost flat with my legs dangling out. It swung slightly. I did not like the sound of *the lab,* and, even worse, Lorin was going to witness my lack of morality. What would he think of me when he watched as I took part in tests on another person? It couldn't be a turn on. I comforted myself with the thought that his presence made him complicit, which turned out to be not much comfort at all.

Lost in my own head, I hadn't realised that Dad was waiting at the door, ready to go. He cleared his throat. I sat up and hopped off the bauble. The strong moral core which my mother had spent all my life fortifying was weighing heavily on my conscience.

We went down a very long way in the lift, and when the doors opened, I wanted to step backwards instead of forwards. There was nothing inviting about this space. It was an industrial looking area with breeze block walls a few metres from the lift entrance. The floor was mud-coloured concrete, the walls were unevenly whitewashed and the ceiling was low. I wasn't always great with artificial lights; some could bring on a migraine, and these were the worst of the lot: yellow and overly bright. There were no windows so I imagined we were below ground.

As we stepped out of the lift, the air felt tepid. Though I couldn't see a single person, I could hear a hum of blended chatter coming from somewhere behind us. Dad led me around the back of the lift, and when I saw the rest of the room I really wanted to bolt.

The space in front of me was vast, but there was no reference to the styling of the other floors with their welcoming lobbies, artwork and fashionable staff. It had the feeling of an underground car park, but without a single car. In the centre of the huge space, like an island, were two open-plan laboratories alongside one another.

The floor of the working zone was distinguished from the rest of the space by a bright yellow square painted on it. The square was divided up by the laboratories located either side of a central aisle which had been painted white to match the units and work surfaces. People dressed casually, compared to upstairs, moved between the different lab spaces, undertook tasks at the bench or worked at computers. There must have been seventy-five scientists.

Beyond the laboratory was a further zone. It was in line with the yellow square, but set apart by a rectangular white zone. There were two large boxes, each made of glass, adjacent to one another with one shared glass wall between them. They were around two metres high, and were like two contemporary sculptures of ice cubes.

'Are we in the right place?' I queried.

'Shh,' my dad soothed, slipping his hand into my own. We walked along the white aisle between the labs. Some of the scientists looked up and nodded to my father as we passed; they all looked busy. My eyes found Lorin, who was sitting between two men at a bank of computer desks. On the desks were several monitors.

I slowed as we approached the cubes. 'I'm not sure I want to do this, Dad.' I could feel the hairs on the back of my neck standing up.

161

'Darling, this is a very simple exercise. Don't let the props upset you.' He squeezed my hand.

Lorin got up when he saw my dad approach. I tried to catch his eye. 'Everything is ready,' he said without looking at me.

Dad stopped to talk to the men at the monitors, leaning over their shoulders. I stared at Lorin; he didn't acknowledge me. I knew that he couldn't be too friendly, but surely ignoring me would seem weird too? Still I had more to worry about than Lorin's behaviour. I looked at the cubes set on small plinths; they were scary!

'It is time to hand you over to the professionals, Francesca. Lorin will stay to supervise, and Daniel will be running the exercise.'

I wanted to shout at him, 'This is not an exercise. It's an experiment!'

'You're not staying?' I said, my voice forced up to an unnaturally high pitch by a feeling of growing panic. I'd assumed that he would be with me for moral support.

'I have to take a phone call and there is nothing I can do here. You have the best of the best on the team and I can't imagine you'll be more than half an hour.'

I looked at Lorin, desperate for a little reassurance, but he only had eyes for a computer monitor. *Not helpful!*

Dad gave me a squeeze. '*Ciao, Giraffa,* and thank you,' he said, touching my cheek, then he turned away and strolled towards the lift. Daniel took over. He was blond, tall and had tiny eyes; my fingers tingled to draw him as a ferret. I stored his image mentally for later. He looked even more ferrety by sticking his neck forward while intently attaching a circular disc below my collarbone with body tape and clipping a microphone on to my collar. Then he took me over to view the monitors on the desktop, showing me lots of graphs and columns of numbers, none of which I was interested in. He introduced me to Leon, a solid man who looked about as animate as an oak tree.

'When you are in there, they will be taking readings from your monitor and Abigail's. We also have some equipment in the viewing spaces which will be able to give us more data. We are just trying to build up a picture of her capabilities.' Daniel sounded at ease. 'You will have to remove your shoes and socks, I'm afraid. You shouldn't be cold. It's just because some of the sensors are in the floor. Are you ready?'

I took a deep breath and nodded. 'I suppose so.' I sent over one more glance at Lorin, but got nothing. I was plotting a sturdy kick in his shin as I walked past him.

'Let the other staff know that we are about to start,' Daniel instructed Lorin.

Lorin walked over to a man and passed along the message to all of the people working there. Within a few minutes, they were grabbing their bags and making their way to the lift.

'Let's move across, Francesca.' Daniel indicated towards the cubes. As we walked, he spoke. 'Let me explain what we'd like you to do. We want to try and view Abigail in her psychic state. We will be unlikely to actually see her, but our equipment should be able to pick up a great deal and form a picture of what is going on. We are going to put you both in different boxes and ask her to move across to you. When you can see her in your box, I'd like you to tell us.'

'Is that it?'

'Yes, that's it. Are you ready?'

'As much as I'll ever be.' I tried to smile, but my facial muscles seemed to rebel at the request. I removed my shoes and socks. 'If it feels like betrayal, it probably is betrayal,' I mumbled to myself as I hovered around the cube's base. I knew what I should do: I should tell my dad that I didn't want a career in art at this price, but even thinking it was hollow. I knew I'd do just about anything for it, but he never should have asked me, particularly so close to the Terry-trauma.

When the room was empty apart from Daniel, Leon and Lorin, the lights dropped low in the lab space and came on in the cubes. Lorin came towards me and escorted me up a couple of steps to a glass door on one face of the cube. He held it open for me.

'How sweet,' I said, rolling my eyes. 'I wish it looked more like a restaurant rather than a gas chamber.'

This was so messed up.

Once I was inside, he closed the door and returned to his place.

'You aren't claustrophobic, are you?' Daniel's voice came over a speaker, and as I couldn't see him very well with the outside being darkened, it seemed like he was an invisible presence.

'If I said yes, would you forget the whole thing?'

Daniel didn't answer which I took as a *no*.

A door was opened on the other side of the lab briefly, and with the light behind it, I could see Abigail in silhouette, sandwiched between two largish men in white hospital scrubs. As they walked through the door, Abigail saw the cubes and her body quivered like she was about to bolt. One of the orderlies expertly took hold of her wrist and gave it a tug as you might a naughty toddler who didn't care to cross a road. He bent and whispered something in her ear; she stiffened, but then moved forward more meekly. I couldn't make out if his words had been soothing or threatening.

My breathing became shallower as I waited for them to arrive. Anxiety hurried my heartbeat along and I wondered how I would be able to look her in the face without shame being written all over mine.

Her entrance into the cube was inelegant. She ground

her feet into the floor, but was jostled in by her attendants – one of whom remained inside with her. After giving him the kind of look usually reserved for dog mess on a favourite shoe, she turned her attention to me and walked over to the glass wall that we shared. I was glad to see that she looked well. Her hair was clean and was tied at the nape of her neck in a tiny ponytail. She wore jeans and a tight-fitting shirt which looked new.

She laid her gloved hands on the glass and pressed her face up against it.

'I'm sorry,' she mouthed.

I couldn't hear her properly. What? Why was she sorry? I didn't understand. That should have been my line. I looked at her in confusion.

Daniel must have started talking to her because I could see she was listening to something, and in that moment I realised. It hadn't been Blake who had told Dad I could see her projection – it had been Abigail. That's why she was sorry. Why had I trusted her over Blake? Why had I assumed that she would keep my secret? In fact, it was a ridiculous assumption that she would ever have been on my side.

The next thought was even less welcome. Maybe we weren't here to find out about Abigail's ability, which with all that had taken place in the ballroom with Terry was already pretty well drawn. It must be about testing me.

'I want to get out!' I shouted. 'I don't want to do this!' I flew towards the door and pushed at it with every ounce of my strength, but, of course, it didn't give. 'Let me out!' I yelled.

Daniel's calm voice dropped in again. 'Francesca, this will be done with soon. Please don't be frightened, there really is no need.'

I was now hammering on the door and kicking at its base. I was absolutely certain that if I didn't get out then something very bad would happen. Fear is like fire: once it catches, it spreads and doesn't take much to become out of control.

'Francesca, calm yourself,' said Daniel. He didn't realise that calmness and logic were never going to extinguish this possibly illogical terror. I felt tears spring to my eyes.

'Let me out! Let me out!' I sobbed, banging the door with my fist. Why wouldn't he let me out? The words out, out, out, circled my head like birds in a flock.

Lorin came to the door. There was no impassive expression now. When his eyes met mine they locked and I read misery in them. As he opened the door, I tried to barge forward. He blocked my way and pushed me gently back while entering the cube himself. He had the upper hand when it came to scrimmages. All I could do was hammer on his chest and feel my feet slide backwards along the metallic floor as he moved through the door. As soon as he was in and the door was shut, he put his arms around me and spoke softly into my hair.

'Frankie, it's alright.' I slowed my fighting. 'I'll stay with you. It's okay, really. You don't need to be scared.'

I looked up into his face, unable to stop the tears falling down mine. He held my head between his hands and slid them down my hair, settling them at the nape of my neck, then leaned down and whispered into my ear. I felt the touch of his lips on my lobes and closed my eyes, wishing we were anywhere else.

'Frankie, listen to me.' I was completely still now, holding on to his strong arms. 'This will be over quickly if you cooperate.'

I leaned my head against his chest and felt the tears fall onto him.

'Are we ready?' Daniel said. I turned my head to where he was sitting and nodded.

Lorin stepped away and stood like a bodyguard in the

corner of the cube. I turned to look at Abigail who closed her eyes. The only other time I'd seen her leave her body was when she was catapulted out of it by the taser. This time, it was different. She began to glow very slightly, and the glow built until it was all around her, then she stepped out and her body fell to the ground like a dropped coat.

I wondered if I'd ever master such control over this ability. It looked so easy for her.

Daniel's voice came over the speaker. 'Can you see anything, Francesca?'

I nodded. 'Yes, I can see her ... aura,' I confirmed. 'That's all you needed, isn't it? Confirmation? Let's end this now.'

'A little longer, Francesca. We'd like to try and get as much data as possible so that we don't have to repeat the exercise. Let's just see what happens, shall we?'

'No!' I shouted. 'Let's not.'

'Frankie, you've been wonderful already, but try to be a little more patient. It really won't be much longer,' said Daniel.

Abigail moved towards the glass wall that we shared, and within a moment, she was inside my cube. She came towards me and her lights swirled around us. I felt a static sensation raise every hair on my skin. She pointed outside the cube and opened her hands questioningly.

'*Wanna go?*' she mouthed.

I'd never wanted anything more, but now I didn't trust her. If I went then Daniel would know for certain that I could project too. Certainly the sensible thing to do was not to show my cards or do anything unusual. Then, it was only her word against mine. She moved outside my box and beckoned for me to come. I shook my head.

I was so focused on her that when I felt a slight buzz and a tingle against my feet, I hardly registered it.

Abigail's projection was hovering at the periphery of

my cube. She was staring at the floor.

The second time I felt the buzz because it was much more uncomfortable and rose up my legs. I jumped. Abigail waved her arms back and forward frantically at me. I glanced at her, but turned to Lorin.

'What are they doing?' I asked him.

'Just monitoring.'

Lorin was wearing shoes with rubber soles so he hadn't felt what I had.

'Feel the floor. It feels like they're sending electricity through it.'

He bent down and touched it. 'I can't feel anything,' he said, looking at me with honest eyes.

When the first real pulse hit me, I couldn't think or breathe or react. It was like being burned alive, but only for a moment. Abigail was shouting at me, and this time, I listened.

Closing my eyes, I sent my consciousness up into my temples and pushed outwards. Abigail wasn't next to me this time and my focus scattered like marbles dropped on a shiny floor. Then Daniel and Leon gave me a real bolt. Electricity surged up my body, and my brain felt like it was being squashed against my skull. There was enormous pressure for a moment and then, like a river bursting its banks, my consciousness flooded out of my head and I found myself in Abigail's silent world.

My body lay on the floor and Lorin was at my side. He stroked my blonde hair, which had fallen over my face, and turned his head, seeming to be talking to the men at the desk outside. I looked for Abigail who held her hand out to me, and without thinking whether I could or not, I walked right through the glass. It was like walking on someone's shadow. I felt like I should be aware I was doing it, like it should have substance, but there was none.

She stepped forward to me and lifted her hand as if

she were going to hold mine, but of course, there was nothing to hold. Seeing her lights overlap mine was so odd, like a memory of feeling rather than a reality.

I turned and ran down the white strip between the laboratories. It wasn't like running normally where you can feel your feet and the floor; it was more like running on a trampoline where you can take longer steps as the floor gives. As I moved further away from my body, I felt anxious for it. What tests might Daniel do to it if I left it behind?

As we approached one desk, Abigail came alongside me and pointed. On the bench was a tooth, a molar. She turned around and pointed at her mouth. I shuddered. *What was my dad doing here?*

I ran towards the lifts. Abigail didn't seem to like that idea and directed me towards a stairwell. Just as we moved through some doors, I felt the tug at the back of my head that I had felt last night when I was returning to my body. This time the sensation was amplified by a thousand. Nausea overtook me as light and consciousness were blurring and spinning. I hoped I might black out, but I didn't.

At the exact moment that all the sensations rolled into an unbearable torture, the world stilled, which was a new form of disorientation.

'Frankie, Frankie.' I could hear Lorin's voice. I tried to open my eyes, but it felt like the elephant-on-my-head phase of a migraine.

'I'm going to be sick,' I blurted out. Lorin was in the way. I couldn't turn on to my front and had to lean across him and retch three times. *Why was Lorin always around when I did this?*

I lay back, panting. I wasn't in the cube, at least. Lorin's face looked anxious and pleased at the same time. That journey back into my body had been much worse than the previous one. Perhaps it was worse when you were further away from your body.

'Oh God, Lorin, I feel like I've been run over.' He handed me a small bottle of water to sip. I raised myself slightly on to my elbows and drank before handing it back and collapsing down again.

'Do you remember what happened?' Without knowing it, he'd given me a storyline which would avoid the need for too many questions. With my brain so fried, I'd never have thought of it.

'There was a man who put a disc with wires on my chest. He looked like a ferret.' Lorin covered his mouth so I didn't even get to enjoy his rare smile. 'I remember getting upset, you came in. They hit me with electricity and then I passed out. Do you have some Ibuprofen?'

'You got very upset. I need to ring your dad and tell him you are okay.' He rubbed his forehead in the way people do when they are trying to erase stress from within. 'I'll get you some pills. Are you sure you don't want your migraine medication?'

I shook my head. As he moved away from me, slipping his phone from his pocket, I felt anger replace his presence. Had he known they were going to shock me? He must have known. He was supervising the whole thing.

I couldn't think straight.

Lorin returned without my pills. He slipped his arms under me and stood up.

'I'm to take you to the hospital wing for observation. They will give you pills. As a precaution, your dad insists you stay the night.'

Chapter 16

Dad's voice arrived before he did. I'd only been in the room for about five minutes. The door opened and he rushed in, looking flustered.

'What happened? I was taking my call when Lorin messaged me to say you had collapsed. Did you hit your head? We are having a CT scan just in case.'

He sat down on the edge of my bed and I looked at him.

'They used electricity on me.'

'No, Francesca, you have hit your head. They would never do that.'

'I assure you they did. They hit me with electricity. It came through the floor, which was when I blacked out.'

'No.' He was shaking his head, but the protestation grew less assured as I stood my ground. His eyes grew wide and his eyebrows disappeared towards his hairline. I studied his face for any trace that he'd known what they'd done, but found nothing.

He stood up very slowly without speaking. Though control was in every movement, he gave off the vibe of a volcano about to blow. I felt the rage below the surface. He walked towards the door.

'Dad?'

He turned and looked at me as if he'd forgotten I was there.

'Back soon, *Giraffa,*' he said in a low voice that sounded scarier than when he let his temper rip.

Half an hour passed, and a nurse came to take me for a scan. I wondered if nurses were also doing this to Abigail, and if they would be holding both our brains up to light boxes and comparing them. Dad was waiting for me when I returned. The nurse made a show of helping me into bed which I didn't need.

'The scans are clear: excellent news. It was probably just a panic attack, but I'd like you to stay here tonight, just in case,' Dad said. 'I have asked Lorin to stay so you have a familiar face, and he can bring you home in the morning. I brought some magazines from the shops in the reception area, and some chocolate. Lorin will bring a bag from home with clothes. I rang your mother to tell her what happened.'

'What did happen, Dad?'

Walking over to the bed, he dropped a kiss on the top of my head and tried to draw me to him, but I pulled away. I wanted an explanation.

He sighed and perched on the bed next to me. 'I have let Daniel and Leon go. They were senior members of my team and I trusted them. I don't know why they took it upon themselves to go beyond my instructions. Perhaps, when dealing with groundbreaking science, there is always that temptation to cross a line. It is why ethics is such a fundamental part of the study of science.'

He gazed at me sadly.

'You don't blame Lorin?' I said.

'No.' His surprise was a relief. 'Lorin had nothing to do with it. He was there only to support you. I am sorry, *Giraffa*. I let you down today.'

He swallowed and looked down. I studied him. His eyes walked the cotton weave of the sheets covering me. Did I believe him? I wanted to, but it felt like a reach. My hunch was that people didn't defy my father unless there was a very good reason – I couldn't imagine the likes of Leon and Daniel doing that.

'So you weren't testing me?'

He looked up. 'Why would I need to do that? I've always known you were outside the ordinary spectrum. How else could you draw like you do?' He smiled and slipped his hand across to mine, not holding my hand but allowing our fingertips to touch.

'I'm trying to help her, Frankie. Please don't imagine it's any more than that. I want to make her better than she ever was.'

We sat in silence for a few minutes. 'I'll see you in the morning,' he said, getting to his feet. As he crossed to the door, my emotions trampled my logic. I had to be wrong. My dad would never do anything to hurt me – he was my *dad*.

'I ... bet Mum was pleased to hear from you twice in one day,' I said.

'My ear is still stinging. I'll ask the nurse for some drops,' he said, cupping his ear and flicking his eyebrows comically.

***

A nurse brought my bag in and I was reunited with my phone. It was almost 5.30pm, but I didn't see Lorin until nearly 10pm. He knocked at the door and opened it only enough to allow his head and shoulders through.

'I'm next door if you need me,' he said. He looked at me, his expression unsure. His hair was very messy as if he'd run his hands through it a thousand times.

'Come in for a minute.'

He glanced down the corridor and looked at his watch, then came in. He turned off the over-head light and the room darkened. I shuffled up and he lay down next to me, but on top of the covers, and put his arm around me. I turned my body slightly towards him.

'Weird day,' he said, to himself as much as to me.

'Yup,' I agreed, my lips in the crescent of his neck.

'I could do with a drink, though a hospital is probably not the best place to find one. Why did you agree to take part in these tests? I was so angry with you when you arrived.'

Ah, that was it.

'Did you know they would shock me?'

I felt his body tense. Then, in a sudden movement, he rolled over so that he was on top of me, looking down, pinning me beneath his body. Supporting his weight on his elbows, he trailed his fingers from my temple to my cheek and below my collar bone to the centre of my breastbone. His face was very close to mine, his lips were parted slightly.

'Where did you go?'

When I didn't answer immediately, he kissed me gently and ran his tongue along my lower lip before kissing it alone.

'The monitors were beeping and the screens were going mad with data, and then suddenly there was nothing except them shouting that you'd gone. Your father has been so angry.'

I turned my lips down in a mock frown. 'Poor Papa.'

His proximity was making my body sing. My hormones had dropped any grudge against his underperformance as a knight-in-shining-armour. A surge of adrenaline blew through my body.

'How much do you want to know?'

His eyes held mine in the darkness. He kissed me, and this time it wasn't gentle. He let me feel the weight of his body, the strength it contained, the potential it had.

'Very ... very ... much,' he replied slowly.

He pushed himself up, forcing my euphoric high to plummet, cupping my jaw. My blonde hair grazed his hand.

'But even for you, I don't want to get sacked, and in about seven and a half minutes, there will be a nurse along to check on you and tuck you in for the night. I imagine that she wouldn't turn a blind eye to me sharing your bed, and you should be pleased to know that I'm not interested in a six and a half minute sprint.' He stood up. 'A little later, we'll take a walk around. This building has plenty of rooms where we won't be disturbed.'

***

As soon as my heart returned to a normal pace and my desire began to dissipate, doubts crept in. During a whole academic year in a university town with not much to do, I'd had encounters where I could have begun my sexual education, but I'd stood back from taking the final step in each instance. Though it was hard to admit to anyone but myself, I recognised that avoiding any emotions that took me to extreme places had become an ingrained habit. It was my Kryptonite. I'd learned as a child that getting crazy with excitement, anger or stress made me vulnerable to being grabbed and abused by a migraine. I was only safe in that calm inner world in my head where all my drawings were born, and so I kept within my safe zone as much as possible.

I felt like ringing Kristin, but she'd probably be out at a bar and no doubt would be several cocktails south of

175

sober. I had such mixed feelings about Lorin, I wanted someone else to make sense of them for me. I knew I wasn't in love with him – yet. Did that matter in this modern age? Certainly not to most of my friends. But the attraction between us was strong, and I knew I was teetering on the edge. It was doubt that kept holding me back – doubt about the potential fallout when my father found out and Lorin's unbalanced behaviour after the Terry incident.

Lorin knocked softly on my door. I slipped on the canvas shoes I'd been wearing that morning, feeling the lack of appropriate clothes. Normal people got to have dates and flirt in their best outfits. I was wearing an aquamarine vest top and mismatched pyjama bottoms, and I felt anything but sexy.

Lorin took my hand, but he walked in front of me as we moved along the corridor. There was a nurses' station which was unattended and a seating area which Lorin and I slipped past. The hospital wing ended at a set of double doors and we moved back into the main building which was instantly identifiable by its sloping walls and atrium.

Lorin paused at a small bank of lifts and then walked past them to a door where we found the stairs.

'Much safer,' he murmured to me.

They may be much safer, but I would arrive wherever we were going out of breath, and probably sweaty, to add to my ridiculous attire. We only walked up seven floors, but as each floor had two sets of stairs with a landing between them, my libido was certainly not in the same place it had been about half an hour ago.

We came out of the stairwell into a long corridor with glass offices running along one side of it. Each had a small meeting room table, several chairs and artwork on one wall, smart boards on another. We padded along the carpeted corridor until we reached a door that wasn't glass, but wood.

Lorin opened it with an electronic card and we slipped in. As the door closed, Lorin passed his card over an electronic panel. There was a loud click and the light on the panel went from green to red. My heart gave a little flutter.

The room was large and open plan and looked like a grown-ups' common room. There was an array of Chesterfield-style chairs and sofas in some madly bright colours and textured fabrics gathered in groups throughout it. Lorin turned on task lights on laptop workstations close to a well-stocked book shelf.

'Would you like something to drink?' He indicated a bank of coffee machines which were set into one wall. I nodded.

'Can you make cappuccino?' I came to sit down at a long glass table which ran the length of the coffee machines.

'Of course. It's a skill all Italians have, though I cannot boast that I am as proficient as Paolo.' He didn't exactly smile, but there was humour in his eyes.

I actually needed the coffee. I was usually an owl, happy to stay up all night drawing, but I was feeling a lot more tired than usual. The events of the day must have taken their toll.

Within ten minutes, Lorin was at the glass table next to me and we were both sipping cappuccinos. Despite my stupid clothes, it would have been a perfect moment if it wasn't for the fact my mind kept darting back to Lorin's unseeing gaze as he fought with me on the floor during his panic attack. Not that I felt inclined to bring up the issue of panic attacks. He looked very handsome in the low light and the little that came in from the city lights outside. I lifted up one leg and rested it on his chair. He dropped his arm and cupped my calf.

'Are you here to get back at my dad for shouting at

you all day?'

Damn, Frankie, close mouth when thinking. He leaned forward so that our eyes were level. I saw a spark of anger and thought he was going to tell me to go to hell.

He said, 'Partly. Aren't you?'

'He hasn't shouted at me all day.'

'No, but he did electrocute you.'

'That was Daniel,' but I felt my confidence in that statement sway.

Putting down his coffee cup, he leaned forward and placed both his hands on my thighs, running them down to just above the knees and then back up in reverse. He kissed me then: desire with a dash of cappuccino. As he felt me respond, he slipped his hands below my thighs and pulled me out of the chair and on to his so that I sat astride and slightly above him. His hands cascaded over my body and his stare became intense, those eyes drinking me in, as if he couldn't get enough of the sight of me.

My fingertips were dragging through his dark hair, and his had found the skin beneath my vest top and were gripping on to my waist. I understood the phrase 'consuming passion' – I felt like he wanted to consume me. Feeling the pressure of his kisses increasing, I pushed him away gently to gain a little control. His face looked almost drugged with what he was feeling. I began to unbutton his shirt, unhurriedly. He tried to drag my hands aside, the delay an irritation, but I insisted, sliding his shirt over the curves of his shoulders. Light and shadow played on his contours. I felt the twitch of temptation to set aside what we were doing and find a pencil and paper to draw him.

Once I'd let him kiss me again, he stood up and turned 180 degrees without any suggestion that the weight of my body made any difference at all. So slowly

I was hardly aware he was doing it, he bent at the waist. With one arm splayed across my shoulder and the other on the small of my back, he lowered me to the table's surface where he slid his fingers downward to my waist, gripped the base of my camisole top and lifted it above my head.

When the top snagged my hands, keeping them out of his way, he brushed my nipples with his thumb, sending a thunder of feeling through them. Whatever his motivation, I figured this was probably worth a migraine and not a bad way to lose my virginity.

I had my eyes closed while he was doing something delicious to my midriff. When they fluttered open for a second, I thought security had discovered us as someone had turned on all of the lights. As my eyes burned and struggled to adjust, I let out a yelping scream and pulled at Lorin's shoulders frantically.

Chapter 17

Lorin pulled away. I leaped off the table and made a grab for my top, which was on the floor, and covered my breasts.

It took a second to register the shards of light, the hazy glow. Abigail stood in the room and didn't look the slightest bit embarrassed by her discovery of us.

'What?' he said.

I couldn't do much more than stare at Abigail, who was standing right next to Lorin and looking amused. She was shaking her head. This irritated me. For a minute, I couldn't think what Lorin knew. Should I tell him she was there? Probably not, but he was one step ahead of me.

'She's here, isn't she?' I looked from Lorin, who was doing his shirt up and tucking it back in, to Abigail. She went towards the door and beckoned me to follow. I followed her with my eyes.

Lorin looked almost wild. He grabbed my wrist.

'Listen to me, you don't want to get too mixed up with her. I know a lot more about what is going on here than you do, and the more you associate with her, the more connections people will draw between you. That can only be bad for you.'

'What people? What do you mean?'

'Being able to see her and even move out of your own body is one thing, but vanishing with her implies you are colluding.'

'Who cares even if I was?'

'The Society.'

'Dad's Alchemy Society? He told me that had nothing to do with Abigail.'

Lorin didn't answer.

'Am I in danger?'

'Possibly.' He moved closer to me and whispered into my ear. 'Standing with your father is a strong, strategic position, but being seen as her ally puts you more at risk.'

At this point, Abigail disappeared through the door. I felt a strong urge to follow her and Lorin read my thoughts.

'Please don't,' he said in barely a whisper.

'I need answers!' My head was spinning. 'I need to know whether my dad is a philanthropic businessman with an interest in alchemy, trying to do his best with a psychotic girl, or a murderous, kidnapping megalomaniac who doesn't care who he hurts to achieve his fanatical ends. She might be able to give me those answers.'

'She hasn't steered you too well so far. You nearly got murdered the last time you tried to help her, and don't forget too quickly about Pierro who, so I'm told, died a death no man would want to experience.'

I shook my head. 'It doesn't add up. She's not much

older than me.'

'That doesn't mean anything.'

'I can't give you any evidence. I just know that I don't feel like I'm being told the whole truth; it's all corners and blind alleys. Abigail and I have something in common. She's taught me something about myself. These migraines have blighted my life, but now there is some meaning to them.'

'You're giving them meaning they don't have. She's taught you a...' he floundered for the words, '...parlour trick.'

'It's not a trick, it's a solution – one that finally works. You wouldn't refer to an asthma drug as a parlour trick!' I yelled at him.

He shook his head. 'It's not the same.'

'It's better than suffering!'

He took a deep breath. 'Play this right and your father could make you the Leonardo of our generation. Otherwise, you'll end up being someone who was good at drawing once.'

This was a slap. 'You're telling me not to dig too deep and leave Abigail alone.'

'Because I care about you.'

'Would you do it?'

'I've done a lot worse for a lot less,' he said, turning away.

'What does that mean?' I said, catching his hand.

'I'll tell you another time. My own mistakes,' he replied, not meeting my eyes.

'Just tell me – should I trust my dad?'

He nodded. 'Where you are concerned, you should.'

'And, will he do the right thing by her?' I wanted a positive answer. I searched his eyes for one.

'Don't ask me that.'

'Because he's the devil? Or because you're *his* man and not mine?'

'No.' He paused and his eyes softened. 'Because I don't know myself.'

***

I was tucked up in bed that night by Lorin's alter ego, Dad's fastidious assistant, instead of by my brooding boyfriend. It was anyone's guess whether it was the late night coffee, the adrenaline spike from our argument, the itch of anxiety that seemed to be constantly with me since Terry's invasion or pitching back and forth over what the real reason was that Abigail was being detained, but the outcome was the same. I seemed to have lost the road to sleep and I ended up listening to music until the dawn dropped through my window.

Sometime during the night, I made a plan for the following day: I needed to take another look around the alchemy collection. The first time had been only a glimpse, and although I wasn't quite sure what I was looking for, I felt it was a source of information I hadn't properly explored. When Lorin came to escort me home, I tried to dissuade him.

'I'd like to do some drawing here today. There's no point in going to the palazzo only to have to come back again.'

Lorin shook his head. 'Your father wants you home.' His eyebrows said *and that's that*. We were a little wary of each other on the journey. My mind flitted about like a caged bird. Last night's conversation had me doubting the wisdom of staying in Milan. I curled my hands into fists, feeling the nails bite my palms at the idea of walking away from becoming an artist, but I knew I would risk an awful lot for a chance to live that dream. Home meant getting a job, any job, and life wouldn't be filled with art or Lorin.

A text from Blake was a welcome distraction.

Heard you hit your head – if I have to do more filing I might consider doing the same.

'I feel a bit sorry for Blake. He was so excited to work with Dad, but so far he's been doing mindless tasks.'

I realised I'd spoken this aloud when Lorin's shoulders relaxed a little.

'I thought your father might have taken him under his wing a little more, but perhaps he wants to give Blake an opportunity to rise through the ranks on his own merit.'

'Not a lot of point in being the boss's son if you don't get any advantage.'

As Lorin turned into our street, I saw Dad come out of the house. The night I'd spent thinking had turned him into the ultimate cartoon baddie, so when I saw him lift his hand in a wave as we pulled closer it brought me up short.

Dad opened my door and enfolded me in his arms. With his arm around my waist, we walked inside.

'Feeling better?' he enquired, studying my face.

I tried not to let all that was going on in my head tamper with my smile.

'Absolutely!'

'Sergio is here and he is waiting for you. If you are sure you are okay, I might permit visitors.'

'I'm fine. I've been desperate to do some drawing with Sergio.'

His phone rang. He looked at it and scowled. 'I must take this.' He answered and asked the caller to hold. 'I have to go to the office today, but tonight there's a private party at the Teatro alla Scalla. You like opera, don't you? I thought a group of us could go together – Blake, Sergio and a few others, if you are feeling well enough?' He pushed the phone into his chest. 'Go out to the courtyard, I'll come.' His hand signalled for me to go with a twitch of the fingers.

Sergio was stretched out beneath the pergola, looking like the male model he would have been if he hadn't had the ability to sculpt. I dropped into the recliner next to him and he poured me a glass of iced tea from a jug at his side. He lifted his sunglasses and cast an eye up and down.

'You look awful! I suppose you finally got lead poisoning from sucking on all those pencils. Your dad said you were in hospital last night.'

'I got electrocuted when Dad was experimenting on Abigail.' I turned my face up to the sun.

'Yeah, right,' he scoffed.

I tapped him so that he moved over and lay with him on the sleigh-style sunlounger. He slipped his arm around me and I nestled down so that my head lay on his shoulder. He squeezed me close.

'It's true, though it is the short version,' I said.

'The long version sounds worth hearing. That Abigail is a curse. I wish she'd never touched my statues.'

'I thought she turned you into a megastar?'

'I'm sure the world would have realised my genius eventually even without her. Since I met her, I've lost an incredible agent. She'd better not cost me one of my only friends too.'

I turned my body into his a little more and pushed up on my arms so that I was looking down on him, our faces very close. He lifted my hair away from my face and raked it between his fingers. I looked at him through my lashes and something passed between us – he knew how Pierro had died.

'You mean you don't want to lose one of your devoted slaves,' I said. Our bodies laughed in sync.

A yawn took me by surprise and I burrowed into his body again like he was a downy duvet, feeling myself relax the way I'd yearned to do last night.

'I seem to have lost the ability to sleep at appropriate

times,' I mumbled into his chest.

'Electrocution does that to a person,' Sergio said, stroking my arm with his long sculptor's fingers. 'Why don't you come with me to stay in my villa in Nervi, Liguria? It is a place with gilded beaches and pretty restaurants, very quiet. You can sleep all day and draw all night if you wish. I have to stay here for just a few more days to attend the event that my angel statue was commissioned for, but after we could go.'

'Yes!' He knew what I needed better than I did: the possibility of gaining some distance, and perspective, but I had no more time to ruminate on the divine idea because my father's voice smashed our peaceful moment.

'There are enough seats out here for everyone!' His bark made us turn to where he was standing across the courtyard. I wondered how long he'd been observing. His stance was rigid and his eyes bored into Sergio like I was sharing the lounger with a black mamba.

'Just enjoying your daughter, Domenico, she's so delicious,' Sergio said, giving my body a stroke as I sat up. He was squinting at my dad, who was standing with the sun behind him.

'That was Jack on the telephone. He says you have missed four deadlines for your upcoming show.'

Sergio huffed and stood up, wanting to get a little further away from the waves of anger rolling off my dad. He moved across to a small table where there was a jug of lemonade sitting in a container of ice.

'He says you are impossible to work with; he's threatening to quit the team.'

Sergio tilted his head back and made a noise of frustration in his throat. Though he wore sunglasses, I could tell that he was rolling his eyes.

'Let him! He's such a big baby, always bawling his eyes out to someone.'

'He's one of the best in the business. It took me several months to get him to join us. I will not be pleased if you lose him.' The fierceness in my dad's voice made me want to disappear and his anger wasn't even directed at me.

'Spending time with Francesca always inspires me. I was thinking about doing a nude of her next.'

I saw the nuclear bomb go off in Dad's eyes. The Golden Boy had just been annihilated. I anticipated what was about to happen and let out an incoherent noise to warn Sergio, but I was too late. Dad threw a punch which hit him on the chin with all the impact of a wrecking ball. Sergio crumpled like he was made of paper. He looked up from the floor at my dad, his eyes wide with surprise – a childish look of vulnerability on his face like a naughty toddler who doesn't understand why he's been slapped. His hand quaked as it rose to his chin as if he was unsure whether he'd find it there at all. I scrambled over to help him. My dad glared with such force, I felt his gaze push me back. Not having had much sleep can be the only excuse I had for realising so slowly that this rage wasn't entirely to do with Jack.

'Get on to the phone and beg Jack's forgiveness! Lorin will take you to Jack's office where he will sit in on the meeting that you seem incapable of turning up to!' Dad's face was puce and his brows were drawn down like they were readying themselves to pounce. I willed Sergio not to say another word. Silence spun around us, and when Dad was satisfied that there would be no further challenge, he turned away and left the courtyard.

Sergio rubbed his chin. 'Good left hook.' He lifted up his sunglasses so I could see his slanting aquamarine eyes. 'That really hurt.'

I nodded sympathetically, stroked his hair away from his beautiful face and pulled him to his feet before he slumped into the nearest chair. I grabbed ice out of the almost empty drinks container and wrapped it up in a serviette. Kneeling at his feet, I pressed it to his jaw and he put his hand over mine.

I heard footsteps echoing across the courtyard. Lorin stopped behind me and passed a phone to Sergio over my head.

'Jack on the phone for you,' he said.

I stood up. Shaking his head slightly, Lorin rolled his eyes at Sergio's behaviour. My loyalty was divided, so as the conversation between Jack and Sergio began at a halting pace, I mimed *going to get a shower* and both Lorin and Sergio nodded.

I'd hoped the shower would blast away the weariness that was beginning to weigh me down. It did, but it left exhaustion in its stead. My white sheets whispered to me seductively as I moved past the bed to get fresh clothes. Checking my phone, I found a text from Sergio saying he'd be in touch later. Though I didn't envy him the next few hours, I couldn't have been more thankful for an excuse to collapse onto the bed.

***

I didn't get back to Marchione Street until nearly 3pm. Sergio had texted me while I slept saying he'd be there if I wanted to meet. I texted him on the way and got myself a cappuccino when I arrived as I hadn't felt safe asking Paolo for another of his special brews. The silk kites in the atrium caught my eye and I decided to take a few minutes to draw them as they were hanging directly above the café. The artist had displayed the enormous brightly coloured kites as if they were in their most animated state. Some swooped and others tugged on their strings; one soared high while its counterpart was caught as it plummeted. I didn't draw them as they actually were, instead making them abstract with dashes of colour, but I stole the artist's flair for momentum which couldn't be improved upon.

'I like that.' Blake's voice broke through to the peaceful drawing place I'd been in. He sat down at the table with an espresso. 'I'm on a break. I'm working in Mum's department today, shadowing her.'

I kissed him. 'I'm glad I've seen you. Been meaning to ask you, now that you are a seasoned employee, if you'd be able to reveal what Dad does for a living. I've been trying to get a straight answer out of him for years.'

I added a few strokes to the sketch before laying it down.

'I don't think you can call me an expert yet, but I'm beginning to think we have been a bit hard on him. I think the reason he's so general about what goes on here isn't only about him being secretive, but because it's so diverse. It's not like it is one business dealing with one product. It's more like two businesses per floor. He has my mother's division which is rare objects, then there's a proper art department, which buys for investment and sells plus organises lots of loans to other galleries all over the world. There's also a whole floor dedicated to conserving, storing and packaging those art works. There's a division that deals with concrete manufacture globally, another that deals with international bauxite trading, another that deals in gemstones and mining, several that are doing something with software, then there are some dealing in patents and a particularly large one dealing in the manufacture of pharmaceuticals. I'm on shipping tomorrow which involves import/export of a whole range of items. I haven't even scratched the surface either. I'd like to work in the mail department or IT, then I'd get an idea of all that there is here.'

'So you haven't come across anything sinister? I was beginning to think he must be dealing in something really awful like arms to Syria or harvesting body parts.'

Blake shook his head. 'Are you here to see Dad?'

I scanned the ground floor area. I'd had enough of waiting around for Sergio. 'I'm going to go up to the eighteenth floor to do a bit of poking around.'

'How are you going to get in there?' As soon as Blake said this, I realised there was a fundamental flaw in my plan. I didn't have the specific pass to get into the collection. I looked at Blake with dog eyes, clasped my hands together, put as much desperation into my expression as I could.

'You are a nightmare,' he said, shaking his head as he stood up. 'I've got a lot more to lose if I get caught these days.' I kept up the pressure. 'Oh, come on then...'

I jumped up and bounced along behind him to the lifts. 'I really appreciate it, super-brother.'

'Yeah, yeah,' he said, his mouth twitching with annoyance.

As we waited for the lifts, he stroked his lips with a finger and I felt him scrutinise me.

'How are you doing after the Terry Gerrard invasion the other day?'

'Grown a conscience, have you? I don't seem to remember you asking how I was when you were blasting me for being a bitch.'

The lift arrived and the doors opened, allowing four girls to exit.

'Hi, Blake,' chorused the girls, one adding a flash of her eyes, a squeeze of plump lips and a flick of long lashes.

Blake pressed a button on the lift pad and inclined his head to the girls, giving them a half smile. As the doors closed, I couldn't help teasing him.

'Hi, Blake,' I mimicked, pouting and squeezing my cleavage together.

'They all know who I am. They are only thinking ch-

ching.' He shrugged. 'I owe you an apology. Lorin told me how terrifying the whole thing was. He said you'd been lucky and that it could have gone either way. I thought you were exaggerating when you told me what had happened. You should see someone about it – talk it over. You look ... tired.' His keen eyes hovered around mine, which must have been underscored with shadows.

'The only person I want to talk to is someone who knows what happened to Terry after I got out of his way. Dad said he had him taken to the police, but I'd like to know that for certain.'

'Why? Do you think he might come after you again?'

The doors opened revealing another almond-shaped lobby. We stepped out. I felt tenseness in my temples and lifted my hand, stretching across my forehead to squeeze them between fingers and thumb.

'I don't know – there's just been a lot going on.' I realised I'd better not say more as I hadn't told Blake about Dad's experiment and he was likely to blast me all over again if he found out I'd been keeping something else involving Dad from him. I wasn't in the mood for another showdown and I really needed the access card.

I glanced around the lobby. This one was furnished differently to the other floors I'd been on. Blake entered his mum's department, leaving me to enjoy the deep velvety-pile carpet and console tables with bright sculptural flowers on display. I slipped my shoes off and passed my time by stroking the divine softness of the carpet with my feet.

Blake came out after about ten minutes. Slipping the card to me as he might tip a valet, he glanced at the corner of the room. I followed his eye and saw the camera.

As if we were both onstage, he said in a performance voice, 'I would be interested to know if you locate anything.'

I played my part too. 'Of course – I thank you sincerely for your assistance.'

I smiled to myself as I rode down in the lift to the eighteenth floor. Blake wasn't funny in a jokey or slapstick way, but he had a sense of the ridiculous in life which made me feel closer to him.

I slipped into the room the collection was housed in and looked at the cases nearest the door. I moved along, looking for snippets of information. The first row I came to had a series of cases with items labelled Subject Johns 1648, Subject Cairn 1827, Subject Gillrow 1902. The term *subject* made me shiver. It seemed a strange one, like the labels were referencing lab rats rather than people. The lab we'd done the experiment in yesterday sprang to mind. Dad was so insistent that the reason Abigail was being detained had nothing to do with the Society's interests, but my certainty was fracturing.

A few cases further along there was a small book, hand bound and brittle with age, that had its first page open. The paper was stained and the surface was speckled with marks like liver spots. It had become so dry it had the crispy quality of a desiccated leaf.

The first page read:

Book 1
The Alchemist Society, 1447
"We seek and protect the truth"

So the Society was established in the late middle ages. Not a period known for its human rights.

I passed on to another box which held a map of the world, hand drawn, dated 1673. On the map were little symbols of a sun in nearly every country in the world. Inside the suns were numbers. Some countries had several suns. I looked at the key. The suns represented subjects. In 1673, the numbers involved were high.

Moving on, I found a circular pendant made of gold engraved with a snake eating its own tail. A card in the case read:

Prior to 1907, this pendant was given to all members of the Alchemist Society who had located and secured an alchemist. The symbolism of the snake is a link to the Society's origins in the Brotherhood of the Snake.

I was just thinking how much this reminded me of witch-hunting when I heard several voices speaking in Italian in the lobby. One voice was louder than the rest, and I recognised it immediately as Blake's. He was trying to warn me they were coming in. I looked around frantically for somewhere to hide; I didn't want to be caught in here, particularly if Dad was with them. He had been so annoyed with me last time. There was nowhere obvious to go. All I could do was clamber along to the end of a row and sit against the cases. They wouldn't see me if they passed my aisles. Sitting on the floor, I hugged my knees and heard the door open and conversation drift in.

A troop of people walked past the opposite end of my row and up to the far end of the room. They must be having a meeting in here; there was a conference table at the far end. I reached into my bag and turned my phone on to silent then texted Sergio.

Me: Help! Am hiding in room on 18th floor, there's a meeting in here.

Him: Stay hidden. When done meet me in café.

I heard a woman's voice open the meeting. I recognised it immediately as Vero's.

'This is my son, Blake, who will be sitting in on the meeting. Let's get started. Our annual event will be taking place in three days' time. Are all the arrangements in place?

'There has been an unprecedented one hundred per cent acceptance rate for the event.' There was a murmur around the table. 'The statue is in the building and will be moved into position the day prior. Julio, how about the cage?'

Cage? That didn't sound good. Was Dad's event going to be a lot more raunchy than I'd imagined? Maybe that was why there were so many acceptances. I couldn't think of any other reason why a cage might be ordered.

'It will be ready by the end of tomorrow. They have never let us down yet, but we must acknowledge that to make such a bespoke item in such a short time has been a challenge.'

Julio went on to talk about the difficulties the manufacturers had had, then Vero asked individuals about catering, drinks, audio-visuals and security. After receiving their feedback, she rounded everything up.

'Thank you, everyone. Please keep me informed of any changes by email.'

The group filed out, all except two men who continued to talk.

'Daniel, tell me about Abigail.'

My ears pricked up. Was this ferrety Daniel whom Dad had said he'd fired?

'She's well.' It sounded like him.

'Feedback on yesterday's experiment?'

Ha! The man had said experiment, not exercise, and then I thought, *That's not good!*

Daniel cleared his throat before starting, his voice wavering slightly.

'Some surprising results, actually. The experiment confirmed that Abigail is capable of moving psychically, and Francesca can as well. The CT scans showed that there are regions in both their brains which are very similar and atypical in comparison to other specimens.'

I stiffened. I didn't like that.

194

'Judging from the length of time that we lost their energy yesterday, both subjects have the psychic strength to move a significant distance from their bodies. We have already put measures in place to prevent Abigail projecting, though revisions of the procedures are occurring all the time.'

The other man asked, 'Would you say that Francesca has the characteristics of a person of interest to the Society?'

My breathing did an emergency stop. Daniel didn't answer immediately.

'I would say further tests would be needed to establish that for certain. Francesca reported that the situation had caused a panic attack, and she had passed out. We need to look at this again. It complicates the results. What we do know is that first we had an energy reading in Francesca's cube and similar in Abigail's. Then the energy level in Abigail's cube dropped and her body fell, suggesting she had left the cube. At that moment, there was almost double the energy in Francesca's cube. Then, there was virtually no energy reading in either cube, and our portable equipment could not locate either of their energy signatures until the point we woke them.'

The other man's voice became quieter, and to hear him, I had to crawl forward so that I was at the bank of display cases closest to the conference table.

'Daniel, this puts us in a very difficult position. We cannot treat Francesca as we would any other potential subject, but with her markers, I am intrigued. Unlike any of the Society's previous subjects, Francesca's medical records and family history are known in detail which would be incredibly helpful. We would potentially be able to challenge the historical assumption that this ability is a gift and consider whether it is in fact a region of the brain that is able to be developed like a dancer's ability to control dizziness.'

'I agree,' said Daniel.

I wanted to stand up and shout at them, '*No, no, no!*'

'Psychic ability has always been the most common marker for selecting a potential subject. With the results we took yesterday, if this was any other subject, there would be no question of taking the next step.'

Though it was the height of summer, I felt goose-pimples form along my arms. I did not like where this was going.

'Just think, Daniel, if Abigail lived up to our expectations and we had someone else with the same potential gift at a different stage of its maturity, how revealing that would be.'

The excitement in his voice was horrifying. I'd thought psychic meant seeing the future, having visions, seeing ghosts. I couldn't do anything like that. A metallic taste crept into my mouth. I could feel the first tears break their bank and escape my eyes. My mouth must have been open as the tears mixed with saliva and ran to the back of my throat, making me swallow a couple of times. I battled with myself not to make a sound.

As I sat there listening to them indulge in their fantasies, I cried with incredible control in total silence. The hot tears ran in continuous lines down my cheeks. It was a self-fulfilling prophecy: I had chosen to dig until I revealed something ugly, and that was exactly what I'd done. It didn't sound like my dad knew anything about this plan, yet. Of course, he wouldn't allow it.

There was only a fraction of me that had any doubt.

Chapter 18

When I finally got out of the room, my thoughts were
sprinting like a greyhound after a rabbit. I wasn't safe. I
could ask Sergio if I could stay with him, but would I be
any safer there? I knew Lorin's opinion: stay close to
Dad. I thought about calling Blake, but I wasn't certain
where his allegiance lay now. I felt like my life was
imploding. The best bet was my mum, but telling her the
truth without sounding like I was a basket case was a
whole new dilemma.

I came out of the lifts on the ground floor and went in
the opposite direction from the one that led to reception
and the café. I walked along to the atrium outside the
hospital wing and sat down on one of the seats that
looked out to a small grassed area where there was a
contemporary sculpture by Allen Jones of a gymnast
doing a backbend. I put down my bag and tried calling
my mum. As expected, the call went to answer phone.

She was based in Canary Wharf in London and her building had the worst reception. She'd call me back fairly soon.

Sergio was sitting in the café tapping his phone when I got there. Looking up, he immediately rose with a concerned expression on his face. He kissed me twice.

'If I can smile today, then you should be able to too. Let me get your coffee.' I shook my head, but he ignored me and went to the bar to queue.

'Could Ms Francesca Milliardo please come to reception? Thank you,' boomed a receptionist's voice over the public speaker.

I suddenly felt like I couldn't exhale. The air became a rock that had got lodged in my throat. I could hear people behind us exiting the lifts. I glanced to my right as two security guards rounded the corner of the café, walking towards me. The guard behind and to the left locked eyes with me. I wrenched mine away and noticed the guard on the security barriers talking into his radio device, staring at me as he did so. My body quivered with fear: they were coming for me.

I sucked in the tiniest shallow breath and looked wildly at Sergio, who put an arm out to calm me. Slipping it, I bolted like a racehorse shooting forward when the whip is raised. I dipped my neck so my security pass scanned through the barrier without me breaking step and then rose on to the balls of my feet and raced right past the reception desk. Just before I moved through the entrance doors, I threw a glance inside to see who was following, but only noticed Sergio standing a couple of metres from the café, looking at the air I'd filled moments before.

I turned right down Marchione Street and zig-zagged between the pedestrians. About three streets away, my phone rang in my pocket and I craned my neck to look behind me before slowing for a pace to glance at the screen. Seeing a McDonald's, I darted inside. It was heaving with people and I pushed myself into the nucleus of the crowd before answering my phone.

'Err, what just happened?' Sergio said.

'Did you see anyone come after me?' My eyes darted about the restaurant. *I should have kept going.*

'No,' he said in a slow, amused tone. 'Even I haven't come after you, but I do have your bag.'

'What?' I hadn't even noticed I didn't have it.

'Er, that's why reception was calling you. Someone handed it in.'

I was losing my mind. Humiliation ran through my veins, making me squirm. I told Sergio where I was and he walked to meet me with the most leisurely gait, shaking his head.

'I do love you,' he said, holding his hands up and then giving me two smacking kisses, one on each cheek. 'You're such good value. I can never predict what you're going to do next. I thought you were going to vault those barriers like a champion hurdler. I wish I could draw like you. It would have made the most marvellous sketch.'

'It's not funny,' I said, seeing the humour in my head, but definitely not wanting to admit it.

'It was funny,' he said through pursed lips, nodding his head.

'Come on. I want to get home as soon as possible. I'll tell you all on the way.' I made him power walk across Milan and filled him in on the previous day's experiment and what I'd overheard in the meeting.

'Is this why we have to walk so fast? I don't know what you're concerned about – your dad will protect you.' Sergio puffed like an octogenarian.

'That's what Lorin says.'

'Since when do we confide in Lorin?'

I ignored his question, uncertain that Sergio could be

trusted.

We arrived at the palazzo's steps. He gave me a hug.

'Try not to worry too much. I'll be at the party in Marchione Street. The angel statue was commissioned for the event. I can report back to you any juicy details about the cage.'

I kissed him goodbye. 'I'm not certain I'll stay in Milan. I'm going to talk to my mum and see what she thinks. Why are you laughing?' I added in an annoyed voice.

'Just thinking of you hurdling the security gates. It's going to amuse me for quite some time.'

***

I needed my passport. I went to my chest of drawers where I kept it in with my T-shirts. Rifling through the drawer, I felt a twinge of panic. My travel documents seemed to be missing and I was sure they had been in there. I yanked the drawer so that its mouth was fully exposed and pulled out every item without regard to the fact they had been pressed and placed so perfectly by one of the staff. There was no passport.

Though I was sure I hadn't put it anywhere else, I pulled at the drawers below frantically, even tugging them off their runners. The panic was rising which inhibited my thinking so that I looked in more and more unlikely places. I dropped down and looked under my bed, through the books on my bookshelf, the cupboards under my bathroom sink. I dragged the rug up in front of the fireplace and threw it on its back so that its binding was on view. I ran to my cupboard and pulled out the suitcase I'd emptied; there was nothing in the pockets or inside the lining.

I went through the pockets of my coat, the jeans I'd worn on the journey here. I went to my shelf and looked to see if I'd laid it on top of my books. Just as I started running my hands along the base of the mattress, even though I knew I'd definitely not hidden it there, the phone rang.

'Mum!' I steeled myself for a storm of anger.

'Frankie, I'm about to go into court. I've been awake all night worrying about all this. I've booked a flight to Milan in two weeks so that we can discuss everything face-to-face.'

My words came out wrapped up in a sob. 'Mum, I'm scared...'

She cut me off. 'I'm scared too. I'm begging you, please don't throw your life away. This is the most important decision you'll ever make. Deciding it's a mistake in a year or two will be too late. You can always carry on the drawing in your spare time – you don't have to lose that part of you.'

Her voice was so desperate, it had knocked out the veneer of her London twang and her Scottish brogue was loose.

'Dad involved me in an experiment...'

She sliced into my words. 'Your father is a ringmaster. If you put your career in his hands, you won't ever feel like you're deserving of any success you achieve.'

She had lost her grip on the reins of her own fears and they were galloping away from her.

'Mum, please, you need to listen to me!'

'Not everyone is clever enough to study medicine. You are one of the lucky ones. You shouldn't walk away from this opportunity to save people's lives. With your dexterity and creativity, you'd make the most magnificent surgeon. Frankie, I'm being called. I have to go. Just don't make any final decisions until I come out to Milan, okay? Text me later. I love you, angel.'

Feeling disconnected from her in every way, I slumped down on the floor with my back against the bed and let my neck flop backwards. Then I started to cry.

***

Sergio would not answer his phone. I felt too freaked to stay on my own in the house so I raced around to the flat he was using. Blake wouldn't be out of work until at least 6pm, or maybe much later if he was trying to impress Dad, so it was no good calling him.

Sergio was staying in a flat on the corner of Scuole Palatine which was walking distance from the Duomo, but had the inconvenience of trams in constant motion outside his window and the fact he had to dive between shoals of tourists just to progress down the pavement. The communal door downstairs was propped open so I walked up.

As I arrived on his landing, I saw his keys were still in the door. Although he ribbed me about my eccentricities, he was as absent-minded as I was. I'd been locked out so often at home that Mum no longer allowed me to take house keys out with me, but instead left them with an elderly neighbour who was nearly always in.

A chink of doubt opened up in my head: maybe I was creating my own drama. With my track record, it was possible that I had lost the passport. I opened the door and let myself into the small, shadowy hallway.

'Sergio, you left your keys in the door,' I called through the flat, but it felt still. Was it possible to go out and leave your keys in the door? I hadn't managed that before, but it sounded like something I would do in the fullness of time. I popped them on the hall stand.

Just to be sure there hadn't been an accident, I checked over the rooms. They all opened off from a small hallway. The flat was not large, but it was furnished with style. A galley kitchen was tidy – I doubted he'd ever cooked a thing in it. The sitting room had a leather sofa, an Eames chair and a sinuous Arco lamp. One wall housed the neatest bookshelves I'd ever seen, with items that had been selected to complement the colours of the books' spines and so carefully placed that a ruler had certainly been used to ensure perfection. On a coffee table was a solitary cup. The bedroom had a very tall window throwing light on the bed, which was unmade. There were clothes in a pile by the door.

I wandered into the kitchen and found some Rooibos tea in a cupboard. Not Sergio's usual choice, but as he was subletting, it was probably the owner's. Making myself a cup, I suddenly had an idea. I would take a snap of myself doing something silly in one of the rooms and then text it to him. It should make him laugh and hurry back.

I stood on the coffee table with the bookcase behind me so he recognised where I was, pouted my lips and tried to do a 1920s flapper kick. It was hard to take a selfie like that without falling over and the shot was so-so. I jumped down and looked for a better location: his bed.

Scooting over there, I put my tea down on the side table and tugged off my shoes. I dived under the duvet, inhaling his smell on the covers. Above the bed was an original artwork by an artist I didn't know, but it was striking and couldn't be mistaken. I wriggled around until I got my face and the painting in the same shot. Pulling a silly grin, I nailed it and pressed send.

Standing up on the bed, I threw the duvet off and managed to make it land on the side table, knocking off both the lamp and the tea which I heard topple to the floor.

'Idiot!' I yelled.

Seeing the room was en-suite, I took a giant stride off the bed and entered the bathroom at speed. The door crashed against the wall and I put my arm out to stop it rebounding back onto me. Sunlight from the bedroom cascaded in and fell upon Sergio, who was unconscious in the bath with his wrists slit. The bathwater was a deep red.

Whenever I'd seen horror films, the girls always screamed, but this sucked the air right out of me. It was more like I'd been winded – I couldn't have screamed.

I stepped backwards in horror and unintentionally closed the door, which left me in the dark with this horrific scene etched upon my eyes. I turned around and pulled at the handle, but my hands seemed to have numbed and were about as useful as jelly. I kept thinking he was going to rise out of the bath like some kind of zombie, which made me panic even more and I managed to open the door with sheer will rather than any manual capability. Back in the bedroom, I panted like I'd been sprinting. I opened the door fractionally just to glance in at him again.

'Call an ambulance, CALL AN AMBULANCE!' I screamed at no-one. Pulling out my phone again, I managed to slap the numbers 118 for medical emergency.

I stared at him as I waited to be connected. Why hadn't I forced myself to endure the lectures at university? I might have been able to do something practical to save his life. He needed me now and I had nothing. The seconds ticked by as the phone connected and the person asked for my details. It all seemed to take a ludicrously long time and every second was precious, yet I was impotent to assist.

When someone did come on the line, I was fairly incoherent which didn't help. My brain seemed to have lost all my Italian and I jabbered in something that was neither that nor English. The woman on the phone eventually got the address and asked if he was still alive.

I hadn't even checked. Of course, he must be. He was

my dream love. Dream loves were like superheroes: they couldn't die. I walked back into the bathroom and struggled to force myself to press my fingers to his neck. I prayed, *Please, God, give him a pulse*. A flicker, not quite a beat, replied.

'Yes, yes, yes,' I shouted into the phone. 'He's alive.'

I couldn't bear to stay with him, but I needed to do something useful. CPR? But didn't you only do that if someone didn't have a pulse? I couldn't remember. Kissing him I'd imagined doing a lot. Giving him the kiss-of-life I had not.

I couldn't just sit and wait until the ambulance arrived. Propping the door open, I eyed the slashes on his wrists. Sergio usually had a golden tan, but now he looked as white as a marble sculpture. I decided to drain the water and set about drying him as best I could. The water was tepid. That meant that while I'd been messing around like an idiot in his bedroom, his life-force had been pouring into the bathtub.

I left dry towels over him to try and warm his body a little. There was no way I could lift him. When everything I could do was done, I knelt on the floor, put my arms around his neck and laid my head next to his. The adrenaline dropped and my tears fell onto his shoulders and ran down his torso.

'You're not allowed to die,' I told him. 'It's such a cliché. Rich party-boy artist dies young. You'd hate that.' Kneeling, I tried to hug him over the edge of the bath.

As I waited, I thought about how out of character this seemed for Sergio. He had been with me less than an hour ago and had shown no signs of depression or even distraction. In fact, I couldn't ever recall him being anything other than in the highest of spirits. I didn't know much about mental health problems, though. Maybe he'd hidden it well like Blake.

The ambulance came and I sat on the bed anxiously as the paramedics worked. It was the first time in my life I'd really considered that perhaps I should become a doctor. I rang Lorin and texted Blake to tell them the situation before the paramedics moved Sergio downstairs and we travelled together to the hospital in the ambulance. They let me hold his hand.

I sat in the waiting room while he was being assessed and treated, feeling completely exhausted. I must have been holding every muscle in my body tight since I'd found Sergio as I felt stiff from my calves to my shoulders, and cold, even though nowhere in Milan could be cold in summer.

A small, stocky male doctor came out from the treatment area. It was like looking at Friar Tuck and I had to concentrate really hard not to draw him in my head.

'Are you a relation?' he asked. I was tempted to lie, but seeing as I'd been bargaining with God about how good I'd be for the rest of my life, I resisted.

'I'm just a friend, but I did find him.'

'An excellent friend. He's fine.'

Relief and euphoria pirouetted through my veins.

'He's definitely okay? Can I see him?'

'His body will have to work through the pills he'd taken. He's unlikely to be conscious for several hours. Can you fill in some forms for us?'

The doctor was holding a clipboard in his hand. Being more than a foot taller than him, I reached down to take it from his hand, and at the same moment, he moved it up to give it to me. Perhaps my reactions were a little delayed from stress, or maybe it was my eagerness to be of use which provided the momentum, but my hand kept going and I grasped a little more than either of us had bargained for.

'Oh!' he spluttered and dropped the clipboard.

'I'm so sorry,' I said, horrified. 'I didn't mean to grab...'

Don't finish that sentence, Frankie! I thought.

He bobbed his head to pick up the clipboard as I was frozen to the spot in humiliation. 'I'll just leave it over here,' he said, stepping around me and putting it down on one of the waiting room chairs before making off to the safety of the non-public area.

'I am sorry,' I said again, this time to his back as he disappeared through the double doors.

'Sorry for what?' Lorin said, coming up behind me as I stared after the doctor. '*I'm* sorry it took so long for me to get here.'

I turned around and felt overwhelmed by thankfulness that he'd come. I leaned into his chest, burying my face there.

'I goosed the doctor,' I said in a muffled voice.

'I don't understand.' It was probably the first thing I'd ever said in English that Lorin hadn't understood.

'Never mind. There probably isn't a word for it in Italian because no-one in this country could be this stupid.'

He pushed me out of his chest. 'Frankie, I can't hear you at all.'

My skin felt hot with embarrassment. I went to sit down and fill in the forms. Lorin sat beside me while I babbled.

'He was with me this morning and perfectly fine. It doesn't make sense. I can't do these forms. Why did he give me these forms? I don't know who his next of kin is. And I'm sure Sergio loves himself too much to commit suicide and he's too selfish. None of it makes sense.'

I thrust the clipboard at Lorin, feeling tears spilling down my cheeks.

'It's a good job he didn't die with a eulogy like that

prepared for him.' He wiped away a tear that had just formed under my right eye with his thumb. 'These things never make sense to those on the outside.'

'I could just as easily have not gone there, you know. Then...'

The probability of this scenario made me feel sick. He put his arm around my shoulders.

'Don't think about it. His parents are on their way. They can finish the forms. Let me take you home. It's been a traumatising couple of days.'

You have no idea, I thought. Going home feels pretty traumatising too.

Chapter 19

Re-entering the room I'd left ravaged that afternoon, I found it as immaculate as any first class hotel which brought back the fears I had temporarily set aside with Sergio's emergency. Slipping out of my clothes, I walked into the enormous shower which I turned on full blast. I touched the cool ceramic tiles and leaned into the initial bite of the cold water, needing it to unfog my brain.

My mum would definitely say I'd lost the passport, and now I was a bit calmer, it seemed the most likely explanation. I had arrived that first day in a total state, and I didn't exactly have the best record in the keeping track-of-things department. I didn't like to admit, even to myself, how many times I'd been sure I had my keys before I'd realised I'd lost them. I would have to go to the British Embassy and see if they could help me.

I switched off the shower and stood with my arms

open in the full body drier until my hair stood straight up like I'd been electrocuted - *again*.

'I miss towels,' I sighed. On the back of the bathroom door hung three varieties of robe. I selected a silk kimono in a bright pattern. Not having the patience to deal with my hair, I tied it back.

Sitting on the bed, I texted Dad to tell him I wasn't going to the party at the opera house. Lorin had told me Dad would visit Sergio tomorrow, but I was surprised he was still in the mood to go to a party.

I grabbed my phone and headphones from my bag and moved over to my desk. Turning the music up loud, I blocked out the world and began to draw. First, the body in the bath, but this was no cartoon. I drew the long lines of Sergio's figure, neck tilted back, throat exposed, one arm along the side of the bath with blood falling in sheets from the wrist. Next, I drew him from above, featuring his sculpted torso, but not his head. This sketch was all about the blood in the bath, the swirls as the water mixed with the darker pools.

When I felt fingers trail across my neck, there was only a half-beat of surprise before the same fears surfaced which had had me sprinting through reception at Marchione Street earlier that day. Lorin shushed and steadied me by settling his hands on my shoulders. I pulled off my headphones.

'Hey! You frightened me!'

He almost smiled.

'Chef wanted to know if you were hungry. You weren't answering.' He nodded at the wall phone. 'I'm in awe of your talent,' and he really sounded like he was. He strummed a finger against my skin. 'Your dad asked me to arrange to rent a studio for you today. Maybe we could view some together.'

I turned around, tugging the kimono up which had dropped from my shoulders and was barely covering my chest. I mounted my chair, laying my arms along his shoulders, I placed my head into the crook of his neck and breathed in his clean scent.

'You've just described my favourite dream of all time. Wish I didn't feel so ... scared.'

He pulled away from me a fraction, forcing me to lift my head and look at him. Tugging a tendril of hair out from behind my ear, he said, 'Don't be scared. Neither your father nor I will let anything happen to you, I promise you that.'

'Have you seen my passport anywhere? I can't find it. I must have been in such a mess the day I arrived that I lost it.'

'No, I haven't, but I'll ask the house staff if they have.'

Perhaps to distract me, he dropped his hands and slid them beneath my kimono, encircling my waist so that his fingers nearly touched. Excitement and attraction swirled around us in a heady mixture. Our breathing mirrored one another's: shallow. I looked into his eyes, which were silver in the light. Could you trust a man with wolf's eyes? There was a hint of something else I couldn't immediately translate there too. I knew if I drew them, I'd tease out their meaning.

'Tell the chef I'm starving. I don't think I've eaten since breakfast.' He nodded and turned to go. I held on to the hand I already had. 'Will you come back after you finish?'

'No.'

The vibe between us evaporated. I felt my confidence retreat.

'Uh, okay,' I said, dropping his hand and stepping off the chair to turn back to my sketch. The back of my throat stung with the tang of humiliation.

He caught my waist with both his hands. 'I don't want to be disturbed this time. Tonight, you can come to mine,' he whispered in my ear.

***

The chef did not disappoint me. He had two trays sent up with a starter of crab spaghetti, a main course of Sicilian chicken with green beans, and a dessert of praline mousse-cake. Although the food was worthy of high praise, I debased it slightly by watching TV while I ate.

A text arrived from Lorin as I was lying on the bed thinking I might not be able to move off it unless a fire broke out.

Am going home, Apartment A, 68 Frankfurt Street

Going out shouldn't be hard as Dad was still out, but I wasn't quite sure how I'd explain my absence if it was noticed. Being at university for a year – or, to be precise, not at university – had given me a taste for the freedom of living on my own terms. Having to explain my movements again was a hard pill to swallow. I intended to be at the hospital to see Sergio as early as I could, so I'd probably be able to make an excuse about meeting some English people in a bar and then deciding to sketch until it was light. Dad wouldn't believe me, but what could he do? Lock me up? Well, he might do that anyway. I felt a twinge of anxiety – it was too soon to joke about that.

My heart spun like a Catherine wheel when I thought about Lorin. What made me like him so much? He was beautiful with those unusual eyes, and his army physique was not too shabby either. The artist in me was drawn to beautiful things. It was one of the reasons I'd fallen so fully for Sergio, but it was like Lorin was two people. There was the one who was serious and worked like a robot for my dad, then a glimpse of the other person occasionally broke out: the one whose smile burst out the day we went to Peck's; the one who liked art; the one who had been wounded by trauma.

I straightened my hair and put on more make-up than I usually wore, finishing the look by brightening my lips with a strong red and dressing in my prettiest black underwear. I laced my skin with lotion and put up my hair. One lock of hair wouldn't be bound and fell down around my face. Wearing jeans and boots and a camisole top, I left my room and slipped out through the small side door which led from the courtyard, along the side of the house and into the street.

My phone showed Frankfurt Street to be no more than five minutes away. In Milan, one tall, imposing building leads on to another without breaking formation, and they cast uninterrupted shadows on the pavement. I'd never felt nervous in Milan before, but the loneliness of the street caused goose-bumps to rise on my arms as Terry, my personal bogeyman, was conjured up in my head. Was he in prison? I suppose I could have found that out if I'd set my mind to it, but what if he wasn't? Maybe he'd only been cautioned, in which case my sudden fear of the dark had some foundation, but there was also that gunshot – it had sounded so final.

I was glad to arrive at Lorin's door and buzz the apartment. The building was traditional in style, faced with a solid surface of limestone bricks, carved ornamental details added on for good measure. Apartment A was on the first floor and I chose to walk the stairs, which was a stupid decision because it meant that when I arrived at his front door, I was panting and slightly dizzy from the exertion.

He answered the door wearing glasses and I liked the change immediately. They looked right on him, like I was seeing the real Lorin. He opened the door wide enough for me to view the most enormous apartment I'd ever seen. I couldn't close my mouth or step inside as I was so taken aback. I wasn't sure quite what I had been expecting – perhaps a flat like the one I'd found Sergio in with small, serviceable rooms, but not this. The ceilings were at least as tall as in my dad's house, and this room must be the same scale as our ballroom.

'Are you coming in?'

He was holding a glass of red wine, looking amused. I nodded. The room was lit with chunky candles on various surfaces.

'Are we having a séance or ritualistic sacrifice?' I said, stepping into the dramatic, dark room. At the far end was a large window, the surround of which was carved so ornately it would have fitted in at Versailles. There was a large black L-shaped sofa on a rug with a coffee table in front of it. I walked towards it in a trance-like state.

The rest of the room was almost bare. The wooden floor, which made our footsteps echo as we walked, added to the empty feeling of the place. The vast proportions and uncluttered living area allowed the original features of the room to speak. There was a bookcase and some books out on the floor near the sofa. Jazz was playing on invisible speakers, but there was no television. Lorin either didn't own things or perhaps didn't need them. I suspected the latter.

Lorin stood still at the door, watching me as I walked the room shaking my head in wonder.

'Is this my dad's place?'

'No, it's mine.'

'Really?' I asked, my voice all amazement. He actually laughed as he walked over to me and stood very close.

'Would you like some wine?' I nodded. 'You don't usually wear lipstick; I like it.' He dipped his head and kissed me lightly, teasingly. 'Don't want to rub too much off,' he said as he walked towards another room.

'Yeah,' I said, pivoting to take in a view of the whole

room again. 'My lipstick is a big surprise.'

I walked across to a wall where a photograph was mounted and switched on a small lamp on a neat computer desk just below it. Lorin must have been aged around seventeen. He stood on a golden beach, his arms slung around the necks of a blond boy and dark haired girl. Their skins were bronzed by regular contact with the sun. All three looked as if they'd been on the beach all day with sand stuck to their bodies and windswept hair. Lorin was grinning madly, as were the other two. Their happiness was infectious and I found myself smiling too. That was the Lorin I'd glimpsed. He was who I wanted to find.

'My brother and sister,' Lorin said, as close to me as my shadow. I turned into him, and he dropped his head at just the right moment so that our mouths met momentarily, giving me my first taste of the bold, fruity wine. He held both arms wide with a glass in each hand to stop the wine spilling.

'You look happy there,' I said, taking my glass and tossing my gaze in the direction of the photograph.

'I was,' he said, stepping back and studying my lips. His focused gaze was heating me up as much as the kiss had. I could sense the shape of his thoughts, none of which were pure, and every hair on my body stood to attention. I wanted to bolt, but was hemmed in by the desk behind me.

I lost control of my mouth. 'If you are independently wealthy, then why are you working for my dad?'

The dynamic changed. His gaze fell from my lips to the floor.

'Is a personal assistant not a good job?' he said to my feet and then turned away.

'I don't mean that,' I said, swigging my wine in the hope of finding diplomacy in it. 'It's just with this kind of money you could probably run your own business, or have a less demanding job at the very least. You finished at nine o'clock tonight, which I know isn't unusual, and my dad is challenging in other ways too. It doesn't give you much time for a life of your own.'

He walked across to the masculine couch and I followed. He sat down, and I chose to kneel in front of him to regain his eye contact. He breathed in as I did this and made a low noise in the back of his throat.

'My family is rich, but I am not,' he said, giving a slight shrug. 'Something else that we have in common.'

I took a slug of wine and put my glass next to his on the floor. *Excellent way to undermine him, Frankie, well done. Mayday, Mayday!* Lifting myself up, I reached forward and plucked at his T-shirt.

'Can you take this off?' His surprise made me laugh, but in an instant he reared up and pulled his T-shirt over his head, dropping it to the floor revealing hard, muscular shoulders, narrow waist, flat stomach and a small tattoo. I gasped at his outline and he allowed me to admire him in the flickering candlelight.

'I'm very obliging, you see. I think that's what makes me an excellent assistant. And now your turn?'

His brows dropped and he looked at me in expectation.

'I think you mistake my intention,' I said, gaining my feet and walking to my bag. 'I only want to draw you.' I lifted my sketch pad and pencils out. 'Get a book and lie down in front of the coffee table so that the candles are behind you. I can't let such a fine specimen pass me by.'

I was enjoying taking control of our dynamic. He picked up a book that lay next to the sofa while I sat on the wooden floor cross-legged. Grabbing a cushion from the sofa, he threw it over with the eye of a sniper and hit me square on the forehead. There was no way to maintain the upper hand when my expression was so dazed. His laughter echoed around the room; I would have to

216

draw that rare and delicious smile. The pillow having shaken my carefully constructed hairstyle, I released the pins and shook it so that it tumbled down.

'Better,' he commented.

I sat on the cushion with my legs stretched out in front of me. He lay on the rug, taking a few minutes to settle himself with his wine. I stood up and moved a few candles in front of him to gain more definition on his face.

'Stretch out with your body facing me if you can.' He obeyed and we fell silent, though instead of reading his book, he studied my lips and then his eyes met mine, asking. I denied him and continued to sketch the landscape of his torso, teasing him by taking hold of his gaze and then casting it loose when it became too intense. The heat was building between us; my head was humming with it.

'What did you choose to read?' I asked, just to remind him he had a book to distract himself with.

'William Blake.'

'A truth that's told with bad intent beats all the lies you can invent,' I quoted.

The candlelight danced in his eyes and they widened slightly.

He said in a soft voice, 'And his dark secret love does thy life destroy.'

As my pencil left the undulations of his shoulders to capture those spirited shapes cutting across his irises, he swallowed, looked down and took a mouthful of wine. When his eyes came back up, guilt was at their forefront and my stomach back-flipped.

'Frankie, I need to tell you something.'

'Don't.' My pencil stilled. 'This is definitely the most fun I've had since I've come to Milan. Don't spoil it.'

'Do you trust me?'

Oh no! All the fears that had chased me that day rose

217

like spectres.

'If this is the guild's way of capturing me, then at least let me enjoy the perks of the plan.'

I laughed, hearing the nerves jangle in my voice. He moved across the floor as quickly as a cat stalking a bird. His heat met me a fraction of a second before his arms. He slid one hand around my waist, our mouths so close they almost touched. Now that there was no candlelight in his eyes, they were as dark as ink.

'It wasn't the Society, but I was asked to seduce you.'

I closed my eyes and dropped my head, feeling a tightness expand across my sternum like someone had pressed pause on my lungs. The disappointment seemed to push every ounce of my euphoric mood out of my body. Then an even more awful thought struck me. I looked up at him, pleadingly.

'Please don't tell me my dad orchestrated this to gain information for the Society.'

He shook his head, forming the words no-no on his lips. I tensed and pushed him further from me.

'It wasn't your father, it was mine.' Sensing I was about to ignite, he continued quickly, 'Our fathers are the closest of friends. They are very similar in many ways except that my father is a little more conventional than yours, having a wife and three children. I am the middle child. They were at university together, have both gone into business and gained more wealth on top of their inheritance, and both have ancestral roots in the guild. Though this is where they differ in particular.

'Domenico is the head of the Society as it stands and has worked tirelessly to bring about a renaissance of it. Through Abigail, he hopes to achieve his ambition. My father also wants to be head of the Society, but his viewpoint is quite different. He wants it to modernise. He believes the search and enslavement of alchemists should be relegated to the past and that we should honour and protect the secrets of alchemy which have founded the family fortunes of all the members. He believes that the Society should have new goals which relate to cooperation and benefit to members' businesses.'

Now I knew that Dad was definitely not helping Abigail for the altruistic reasons that he claimed.

'So I'm collateral damage.'

He didn't meet my eyes.

'Whichever one wins, I am a pawn in their chess game. I was encouraged to take the assistant job to feed my father information about what Domenico is planning for Abigail so that it might be derailed somehow.'

'And me?' I looked up into his eyes, searching for truth within them.

'And then my father asked me to make a play for you, and I agreed.'

Heat rippled through me, but not in the sexy way which it had moments ago. This was more like the kind of spike in temperature you get right before you realise you have norovirus.

'So it's all been fake, all under instruction?' I struggled against him to get to my feet, but his body pinned me. My muscles screamed at his as they pushed against his restraint.

'Think about it, Frankie – if it had been, would I have told you? I'm giving you the truth because I want us to have a chance. I was asked to do it, but I didn't know you when I agreed to it. Since the day I saw you drawing by the Duomo, you've stayed with me. It wasn't about being asked, I swear it.

I wanted to believe him, but had he told me or had I discovered it? His body heat was encircling me. It was hard to think clearly when my desire for this man was spinning a cocktail in my brain. Had his disclosure changed anything? It made him more vulnerable. He knew I had a weapon if I wanted to use it.

I was so busy thinking, his kiss took me by surprise. He kissed me with real need: an adult kiss, the way I used to fantasise about Sergio kissing me, but there had been safety in that because it wouldn't actually happen.

I pulled away. 'I think I need to go.' This time when I pushed against him, he didn't resist. He remained on the floor, leaning over his legs.

'Haven't you ever made a decision that you've regretted, Frankie? Has your life really been so spotless?'

He threw this at me: a grenade of bitterness. I didn't answer him immediately, but went to fetch my bag. Tearing off the unfinished sketch, I put the rest of the sketch pad in my bag and bent down to where he sat on the floor. I knelt so that I was above him and ran my fingertips through his hair and down his neck.

'I'm not angry, but I don't want to wake up tomorrow and find that I am. Better to let tonight go and return to this with no regrets.'

He lifted his lips and mine tingled in anticipation. I brought them down on his and felt the fire within me which had burned down to heated embers rekindle. One of his hands lifted to my waist and he slipped it into the tiny gap above my jeans, stroking the skin and strumming my stomach, sending all manner of vibrations downwards.

'You don't feel the same way about me as I do about you,' he said and I felt the guilt strike me.

'I don't know how I feel. None of this has been easy.'

He smiled at me in a knowing way and reached up with his hand to stroke my neck.

'If you felt the way I do, you'd know. Please stay.'

He trailed his fingers down my arm and clasped my hand, his lips touching my shoulder. The way my body was singing to his, I almost did stay. It took immense effort to force myself to stand and walk towards the door.

Looking at me from the floor, he wore a wry expression.

'I'm quitting poetry. It's bad for my sex life,' he said.

Chapter 20

The next morning I was feeling pretty low, slumped in the corner of a taxi on the way to visit Sergio. It was still early enough for there to be little traffic on the roads. We drove north along Corso Buenos Aires, one of Milan's wide boulevards where you could almost imagine yourself in Paris as the street-style had been mimicked so accurately during the city's short history under Napoleonic rule.

My head felt like there were dodgems bashing around inside, but for once it was not from a migraine. I'd been right not to stay with Lorin, though it hadn't been easy to go. His revelation about his father's hand in our relationship had been like finding a fly in my cupcake, but that seemed nothing when compared to the new double-headed dilemma that I now found myself stepping around gingerly: either my dad was a crazed, lying fanatic, or Lorin, my secret-liaison, was scheming with his own father to turn me against my own flesh and blood. I took a deep breath and wished for a simpler life.

I turned away from that thought to the equally awful one of Sergio severing his desire to live, the man of my fantasies draining away with the blood-rich water. How long had he been battling with depression? Had something happened on the way home from being with me? Had Luca broken up with him?

Asking at reception, I was directed to Sergio's ward. Early hours must be the routine here as the whole ward was buzzing with activity. Sergio had a private room. I knocked lightly on the door. He was sitting up in bed and reading from his phone. I waved, he scowled.

I pushed the door open, feeling a little unconfident. He turned away from me to face the opposite wall.

'I don't want to see you. Go away.'

I wasn't quite sure what to do. The word *Hi* teetered unsteadily in the air. I walked over to him and perched on the side of the bed, putting a hand on his shoulder. 'How are you feeling?'

'I'd be better if you left,' he said in an unsteady voice.

I didn't want to pressure him if he couldn't face me. He stayed silent, which was something I'd never known him manage for more than about ten seconds. Unsure whether to go as asked or foist my support on him, I spoke shakily.

'Is it because I found you? You didn't want to be ... saved?'

He turned to look at me and his colouring was all wrong. I'd invested much time in analysing Sergio and what it was about him that so appealed to me. It was a lot to do with the vibrancy he radiated. Today, he was out of juice and there was exhaustion even in his expression. He opened his mouth to say something and then changed his mind and shook his head. I felt completely

223

ill-equipped to say the right thing. I knew little about depression, only that it was an oubliette people could become lost within, never finding a way out. I shuddered at the thought.

'I could get us a cup of coffee?' I offered. He didn't respond. Where had this silence come from? It was like a sticky glue that was stopping our words coming out. Our friendship had never suffered from this. 'You must have been feeling pretty desperate. I wish you'd told me.'

It was like I'd lit a fuse. The vibe in the room, which had been hostile but stable, exploded. He turned on me and his eyes flashed.

'Go! Get out! Go!' he shouted. I stumbled backwards like he'd slapped me. Pulling the door wide, I was part way out when he sent his parting shot. 'You'll never make an artist if you can't see the whole picture.'

The door shut on the tail end of his words. I stood outside the room in confusion. A pretty blonde nurse smiled at me kindly. I walked away, my head down, his words ringing in my ears.

'Ciao, Giraffa.'

I looked up to see my dad looking fresh and immaculate in a tailored blue suit. Taking me by surprise, he came forward and gave me a squeeze, pouring sympathy, love and parental strength into his arms, making my heart swell. Tears sprang to my eyes and fell down my cheeks. *I don't want my dad to be a fiend.* My arms seemed to act of their own accord. I found them rising and wrapping around his broad body. I really did need a hug. The tears turned into deeper sobs.

'Shh, it's alright,' Dad crooned. 'He will be better in a few days, I promise.' He held me in his arms until the tears passed and then encouraged me towards Sergio's room. I felt myself pushing back.

'I was going to get coffee for me and Sergio.' My heart began a drum roll. I didn't want to go back in to see Sergio yet. At the same moment, the pretty nurse moved back towards her nurse's station and this time smiled at my dad. Twinkly blue eyes; in her twenties with a smile that revealed very becoming dimples; petite yet curvaceous with slender calves. Dad would never pass her by – this was an angel sent from heaven to save me.

'*Permesso, signorina.*' Dad took the opportunity immediately to introduce himself while I made an excuse and fled to the bathroom. I gave it enough time to make sure he would definitely go in to see Sergio ahead of me. I knew Sergio didn't want me there, so I slid back into the room and stayed close to the door. Dad was sitting at the end of the bed. Sergio was looking at him with wide eyes; I wondered if the nurses had him on some kind of medication.

A knock made me jump and the smiley nurse entered holding a tray of coffees. Dad must have sent her out like a waitress for us, but her dimples were out in force so she didn't seem to mind. My dad thanked her. I went to pick up a cup, stirred some sugar in and moved back to my chair.

'Pretty,' Dad commented as she left. 'Would make any man feel better just looking at her.'

'Not my type,' said Sergio firmly. 'I prefer Lorin.'

I couldn't help it. I sprayed my mouthful of coffee all over the back of Dad's immaculate suit.

'Dear me, Frankie, have you no manners?' Dad said, stroking his suit down in disgust.

'I'm sorry,' I choked. 'The coffee is very strong. I usually drink tea.' Some ran down my chin and neck. Going over to a small table under the window where there was a box of tissues, I dabbed at Dad's back, but the material seemed to have soaked all the coffee up so my effort was futile. I caught Sergio's eye over Dad's shoulder and thought I detected a glimmer of a smile.

Why had he said that? We all knew he was gay.

Dad was trying to dissuade Sergio from returning to Florence immediately. I moved to the side of his bed and listened, lifting a hand up to rest it on his shoulder. He reacted like I'd burned him, actually leaping out of the bed and standing there facing me and my dad in a hospital gown.

'Whoa,' I said like he was a spooked horse. 'It's okay.' I put my hands up surrender-style and backed away from the bed into the corner of the room.

When I was at a safe distance, he inched back into bed.

'As I was saying,' Dad continued, 'Florence is certainly the best place for you after you have fulfilled your obligations here. I can see why you'd want to go home – there are lots of temptations in Milan.'

Sergio's jaw was rigid with tension and his breathing was uneven as if he didn't dare relax.

'And, it's much more dangerous than I'd imagined,' he said, looking at me like I was a lion sitting in the corner.

I gave him a look to try and say, '*I don't get it.*'

'Well, I'm glad you have the measure of the situation now. It will prevent such an unfortunate thing happening again, I'm sure. Your public are expecting more magnificent artworks; you couldn't possibly disappoint them. Frankie will miss you.'

'I don't think so. It's not like we've really spent much time together.'

I opened my eyes and mouth wide in shock, the word *Liar!* forming in my mouth.

Dad's phone rang. 'Excuse me,' he said, standing and leaving the pair of us together.

As soon as he was outside, my curiosity burst. I took a step towards Sergio, but it looked like he might jump out of bed again so I stopped.

'Obviously to attempt suicide you must have been pretty desperate and any weirdness should be completely explained by that fact, but am I missing something else?'

'I wish I'd known I was suicidal!' he said, anger roaring out of him.

'So do I,' I said in a regretful tone, shaking my head.

'It came on so quickly, you see, when I was grabbed outside my flat, had pills forced down my throat in my own hallway, had my phone taken, told to strip naked and sit on my bed for fifteen minutes. Only when I could hardly keep my eyes open was I forced into a bath and held while my wrists were being cut.'

'What?' My voice was so loud he shushed me. 'You're saying someone tried to murder you? Why?'

'A case of mistaken identity, I imagine. Or maybe I upset someone,' he said, glancing at the door and then back at me with a knowing stare.

'Are you suggesting it was Dad? That's ridiculous! Blake is actually jealous because he treats you more like a son than he does him.'

'Well, Blake better look out because this is how he treats his son when he's angry!' Sergio said, shaking his dressed wrists. 'He thinks I have been indulging your not-so-secret fantasies. Have you been indiscreet?'

'I don't think so. I've sent a few texts about someone, but they weren't about you anyway.'

Sergio gave me a look that said, '*There you go then*'.

'But he knows you're gay.'

'Men like your father don't believe in the gay preference. They think we wouldn't turn down first-class female pickings.'

I suddenly felt really tired. My body and brain were taxed to the max. If this was true, it did make my dad evil. Putting the whodunnit to one side, though, I realised it was a more realistic explanation than Sergio being suicidal. Could my fledgling relationship with

Lorin have nearly caused Sergio to be murdered?

'Are you sure it was Dad?' At that moment, my father put his head around the door and made us both jump in fright.

'I'm sorry, Sergio. I have to go – something has come up.' Dad came through the door towards Sergio to say goodbye. I saw Sergio tense as Dad squeezed him. 'A new beginning, I hope.'

In the context of Sergio's revelation, every phrase seemed to have more than one meaning.

'Francesca, come,' Dad barked. I followed him along to the lift, playing with what Sergio had told me in my mind. Dad screening my phone and emails seemed unlikely, but if it was true, Sergio's flirtatious and touchy-feely behaviour might have cemented the idea in his head.

The lift doors opened, and the little blonde nurse appeared and ran after us. She reached my dad and blushed becomingly and pressed a piece of paper into his hand. He smiled a wolfish smile. If I'd had my pencil, I'd have drawn her as Little Red Riding Hood and Dad with a nice long tongue coming out of his mouth, licking his sharp teeth.

***

Dad asked Lorin to drop him at Marchione Street then take me home. As soon as Lorin had pulled into the next street, I insisted he stop the car so I could climb in the front next to him.

'I'm levelling the social hierarchy,' I told him, but really it was because it was harder to talk to him in the back seat.

I could feel a good vibe coming from him. His energy was definitely up.

'Sergio told me something bizarre.'

'It's no wonder that boy gets in trouble. He doesn't know when to keep his mouth shut or when to behave.'

I exhaled and leaned my head against the glass, closing my eyes. 'Please don't tell me you were involved in hurting him.' I couldn't even look at him as I spoke.

Seeing my distress, he took hold of my hand. 'No, of course not.'

'But you did know. Don't you feel bad? It happened because Dad thought he was fooling around with me.'

'Why should I feel bad? Anyway, it wasn't just about you. He's been pretty stupid recently.'

'They left him to die!'

'It was just to scare him,' he scoffed. 'I understand they barely scratched his wrists. He'd have woken up in some cold water a few hours later if you hadn't found him.'

I felt bile rise in my throat. 'How can you be so heartless? He's my friend and you have no idea what you're talking about. I saw it. There was a lot of blood.'

'Not his, pig's blood. You can't really expect me to share your love of that particular friend considering the way he behaves around you.'

His face lit momentarily with humour. Unbelievable! This man couldn't crack a smile on a sunny day, but a suicide prank amused him. I huffed and released my seatbelt, turning round ninety degrees to face him.

'And you said nothing to me yesterday about this?'

'I didn't think Sergio would be stupid enough to share with you, of all people, the truth about why he ended up in hospital. It was a warning to moderate his behaviour in several ways, but particularly around you. He's had plenty of advice that he should do that before, but he's chosen to ignore it. He's very lucky your father likes him so much.'

I turned back round, unable to credit what I was hearing. Ridiculously, I felt more annoyed with Lorin than with my dad, which wasn't fair.

'So why are you taking such a risk?' I couldn't hide the annoyance in my own voice.

Lorin turned to me. 'The win is worth it.' He moved his hand to my thigh, and I stared at it in the same way I might if I found a snake settled there.

We were silent for a short while.

'There's a guild event happening at Marchione Street in two days' time, isn't there? I overheard something about it. Is it going to involve Abigail?' I was thinking particularly of the making of a cage.

'Are you taking advantage of me for information?' he asked teasingly, but seeing my stern face, he answered the question. 'It's an annual event, but she will be there.'

'Why?'

Swerving the car to the side of the road, he pulled up sharply. A couple of horns blared. He turned to me and took hold of my hand again.

'It's good news, Frankie. Since your results were revealed, your father has been very reflective. He has visited my family home and consulted with several other Society members who are known to be modernisers. This morning he informed me that he will be making a big announcement at tomorrow's event. I am sure he is changing sides and I think he wants to wash his hands of her and lead the Society towards a new era.'

His eyes were blazing, zealot-like, with the passion of his proclamation.

'Again, why?'

'Because of you. It's all because of you. I knew from the first time I saw you at the airport that you were the key.'

'At the airport?' I said sceptically. 'I was more mess than messiah.'

'Your father will protect you, but he can't do that if he continues to uphold the Society's old ways of enslaving people like Abigail. If he did, he'd be accused of hypocrisy and the Society might call a vote of no confidence. It might be a more difficult decision for him if Abigail had shown any sign of being a real alchemist. So far, there has been nothing other than her psychic ability that makes her unusual, and this will strengthen his argument to leave the past in the past.'

I leaned my head back against the headrest and looked at the leather-clad ceiling. 'Did my dad tell you he was changing positions?'

'He said that he came to discuss it.'

We fell silent and Lorin set off again. 'I need to ring and check if your father needs me after I've dropped you off,' he said, pressing a button on the phone which was held on the dashboard. I watched the shadows play across his face and saw the sketches I would draw of him that night. As my eye found the characteristics that would make the sketches authentic, I gasped at something I hadn't seen there before: triumph.

As he came off the phone, I attacked him, slapping him hard first on the arm and next across his ear, managing one blow to his shoulder before he took his hand off the steering wheel to defend himself. I saw my rage bewilder him.

'I'm such a little idiot,' I shouted, tears clawing at my voice and stinging my eyes. 'Me, who prides myself on being observant! I assumed it was Abigail who told him I could see her, but it was you. You found me in the office on the floor that night the way you'd seen Abigail behave when she'd projected. Dad wouldn't have known any of that if you hadn't told him. It was you using me to push your father's agenda, banking on the fact that my dad wouldn't allow his own daughter to be imprisoned. You weren't just here to be your father's eyes and ears, you were here to make it come about.'

'And I was right.' He lifted his chin a little and his

voice sounded unrepentant.

'You couldn't have been sure. You risked me, used me, and what's more despicable is I wasn't a stranger to you.'

We'd arrived at home and he pulled up outside the house. He looked across at me warily.

'You have to understand. This practice of taking people has been going on for hundreds of years. It's barbaric, and for what? None of these men needs the money. It's about tradition and rarity: a vanity project. Look at Abigail – do you think she shouldn't be out living her own life? It was an opportunity and I took it. What else could have stopped your father?'

I opened the car door and got out. All my insecurities were clamouring for attention. I felt like a fool. Of course Lorin hadn't wanted me. He was handsome, worldly, educated, and I was barely twenty and a dropout. The tears were trying to barge out of my eyes and I knew I wouldn't manage to hold them for much longer.

I moved around the car to his side and he opened his door slightly. He made a grab at my wrist, but I stepped away.

'I'm sorry I didn't tell you everything. I didn't think…'

I cut him off. 'You didn't think I'd sleep with you if you did.'

This was like flicking a match onto a petrol-doused rag. His anger ignited and he sprang out of the car, making me back away. We faced each other on the pavement, and he was so angry he could hardly form words.

'It had nothing to do with that. I'm trying to do something to end this barbarism.' I looked around, aware that we shouldn't be discussing this here. '*I'm* not scared of making decisions.'

232

Instead of riling me up, this comment took my breath away because it was so near the mark. I took a couple of seconds and then managed to speak in a controlled voice.

'If you ever want to be in a real relationship with someone then you can't use people you care about, whatever the justification.' The tears had arrived and I couldn't keep them back. I wiped them away with the back of my hand in annoyance and turned towards the house. As I did, I heard a loud smash and spun. Lorin must have thrown a punch that would have felled a tree. The glass in the car's side window looked like a million fragments of ice all held in suspension before he withdrew his arm and it fell out in great clumps around his feet. His hand, and some of the glass, was covered in blood. Without looking at me, he got into the driving seat, tiny fragments of glass falling from his arm as he did so, and drove off at speed.

I couldn't help stare at the fragments of glass which were all that remained of the scene. Even my tears were stilled by witnessing his calm persona annihilated in that one act. I didn't know him at all, and yet some part of him had connected with me.

I trudged up the staircase and straight to my drawing desk. The tears, the anger, the hurt spun into a cyclone and exited through my hand with the same level of violence as Lorin's. The pencil moved across the paper; swirls and shapes fell, accompanied by my tears. I was engraving the paper rather than drawing. Page after page I covered and tore off in such rapid succession that a small hill grew beside my desk.

When my hand began to spasm from clenching the pencil and my head ached from the strain of containing so many emotions, then the tears dried and so did the creativity. My back and neck were stiff from holding my body so tightly as I drew. I flicked the electronic blinds into motion, and as the room darkened, I crawled over to the bed, curled up and fell into the kind of deep, disturbed sleep that only daytime can provide.

Chapter 21

I woke in a suffocating sweat. I hadn't switched on the air conditioning before falling asleep and I was basting in my own juices as the room cooked me slowly. With a heavy head, I rolled off the bed and stepped across the room to open my balcony door and gain some relief from the air outside. The sweet scent of the warm jasmine and clematis climbers in the courtyard encircled me and the mature tones of the setting sun stole through my eyelids, insisting on admiration.

The roof! I could watch the sun's swansong from there and dangle my feet into the cool water of the pool. Walking the stairs was hard, but when I was met by the sun hovering just above the outline of the Milan rooftops, it was worth traipsing up for. The crystal coloured water in the pool was still. It couldn't have been more alien compared to the pulsing, ripe sun which looked as if it was about to burst at any moment. Feeling hypnotised by it, I responded to the tug which took me over to the rooftop's small wall and railings.

My head was beginning to throb from all the drama of the day. I didn't want a migraine, and now I knew there was a way to escape it. I closed my eyes. The previous times that I'd left my body, the passage had been uncontrolled. This time I was calm and confident that I could do it. With a movement akin to a shiver, I shrugged off my body and let it drop to the ground.

Standing in perfect silence, shimmering in my own haze, I thought about Sergio's angel sculpture and threw my head back in imitation of the figure. I took a moment to enjoy the blissfulness of this golden out-of-body experience.

The sun looked different when I was in this state. No longer was it bound like a ball, but instead I could see thousands of threads of light reaching out in every direction. The lines of light came towards me, curling around me like ivy creepers. They wanted me, and I wanted them to help me escape from my father, my mother, Lorin, Sergio, the Society and Milan. I stood up on the little wall running around the terrace, and it felt right to put my legs over the railings too and stand on the ledge. It felt absolutely right to step off the roof of the palazzo and into the air.

I thought I would float, but instead I plummeted just like a corporeal body falling. The air pushed against my face, against my skin. What face? What skin? I was flailing rather than falling and the ground was too near, too fast, too solid.

Thoughts flashed through my head, *up* being the predominant one. Then, Abigail in her haze flashed into my mind, and a millisecond before I hit the street, I thought of the statue in the reception of Marchione Street. I didn't cannon into the floor even though I closed my eyes. When I opened them I was in the reception at

Marchione Street, standing next to the Gormley sculpture: the artist's version of my actual state. How was I here? Why was I here?

This statue had been my last thought. Had I had been falling because I thought I was falling? If that was the case, I didn't need to walk anywhere when I was like this. I just had to think of where I was going. So why hadn't *up* worked? Too abstract? Maybe I needed a place to anchor myself to.

I should find Abigail. I thought about her and then opened my eyes. Nothing – I was still in reception. *Annoying.* I didn't know where she was so I couldn't send myself there. I'd have to do it the old fashioned way, starting in the basement where we'd both been in the glass chambers. She'd arrived from a doorway at the far side of the room. I could start there.

I closed my eyes. I probably didn't have to, but it seemed the right way to do things and it had worked last time. When I opened them, I was in the basement, but this wasn't the basement I remembered with the extensive laboratory and the glass test chambers. There was no lab, no people, no boxes, just an enormous draughty basement. Where had it all gone? Lorin would say this was good news, that it was more evidence that my dad was disentangling himself from the whole scheme, but I felt butterflies in my virtual chest.

I walked the floor, checking for any signs that the lab had been there, but every trace had been eradicated. Could they also eradicate Abigail's existence so thoroughly? How about me who'd witnessed it, and would they forget about my *markers*? Apprehension swept through me. Leaving my body in such a vulnerable place had been a stupid thing to do.

I walked towards the door at the far end of the room. She'd been escorted through it the day that we'd done the *exercise*. Peering through a small square window with gridded glass, I could see a staircase and was about to think myself there when I paused. I should check on my body before going to see Abigail.

I closed my eyes and thought myself back to the roof. It was dark now. The sun had gone, but my body was still on the ground. My legs were curled under me. Closing my eyes again, I returned to the stairs I'd seen through the glass. This was so cool! As I moved up the milky-white terrazzo stairs, I wondered why Abigail hadn't told me how to do this. She'd had other stuff to worry about, I suppose, and she'd always seemed to move like she was still in her body.

Above me was a landing, and instead of walking the stairs, I thought myself up them. It wasn't necessary as walking wasn't tiring like it would have been in my body, but why walk when you don't have to? Then I felt guilty. Abigail was trapped in here and God only knew what might be happening to her. Perhaps the lab had been moved to where she was. I felt my mood dip – was I prepared for what I might find here?

Moving higher up the building, I went against all my instincts. Surely, she couldn't be being detained along-side the offices? The answer seemed to be that she was. The first set of doors I found must have been on the twelfth floor, at least. They were the same as the doors in the basement with glass rectangles. I steeled myself before looking through. What was I about to see: a modern day torture chamber or a cell with Abigail clamped to a bed?

What I did see resembled an upmarket hotel suite: a deep bed with unwrinkled and crisp white pillows and sheets, a flat screen TV, a writing desk. The lighting was soft. Abigail was reading in an armchair with her legs tucked under her. I slipped through the door. I thought she glanced my way, but then she dropped her gaze, returning her attention to the book.

Had she not seen me? She lifted her hands to her mouth and yawned in an exaggerated way, stretching her arms up and out to the side. Tilting her neck one way and then the other, she stood. I waved with both hands to get her to see me. Her eyes flickered, but she did not react. Walking over to the bed, she picked up a pencil and wrote.

They are watching.

She shook her wrist. There was a heavy electronic bracelet on it. She rubbed around the skin as if it was sore. I beckoned for her to come out of her body.

She wrote *if my heart rate drops for more than a few minutes, they'll come to check on me*. Then she scored out what she'd written so it was truly obliterated and poured herself a glass of water from the jug at the side of her bed. After taking a few sips, she set it next to the pad and let herself fall back onto the bed, knocking against the glass so that it fell across the pad, soaking it.

She jumped up and ran to the bathroom, returning more slowly and taking her time to let the water soak into the paper fully. Then she picked up the pad, pulled at the sodden top sheets so pieces broke off and dropped the pieces into the bin.

Lying on the bed, she ignored me and picked up the remote control and pointed it, switching on the TV. I stood at the edge of her bed, feeling stupid and staring at her. As soon as the TV was on, she slid out of her body and lifted her finger to start writing a message in the air, but I thought my words.

'Your eyes are still open.' I pointed at her body on the bed.

'How are you doing that?' she said, shaking her head like she had water in her ears.

'Don't you know?'

'I've never had anyone else to speak to.'

The answer to why she hadn't told me I could move

by thinking came to me – she hadn't known that either.

'Wait,' she said and slipped back into her body. She fidgeted around on the bed, pummelling her pillows, then she was out again. 'How did you get here?'

'Sort of accidentally. I figured out how this works. You can travel anywhere if you think yourself to a place.'

'I can't go anywhere. They have me figured out too.'

'What do they do when you sleep? Then your heart rate must drop.'

'They drug me. When I'm drugged, I can't do this. It's like they've put glue in my veins.'

She moved back to her body, lifted the remote control and changed the channel a few times.

'Lorin says they are dropping this programme. That you're going to be moved away from here.' To my surprise, fear spread into her every feature. 'He says it's a good thing.'

'That depends where I get sent to.' She looked up and her eyes widened. I turned my head to see two men enter the room, one in a white coat. 'Frankie, please, get me a weapon – something to protect myself with. God knows where they'll take me. Please!' Distress made her words quake in my head.

She phased back into her body and I saw her prop herself up on her elbows and talk to the men. She looked annoyed and was shaking her head, pointing at the TV. The one in a white coat took out a small syringe from his pocket and the other guy held her arm and pulled up her sleeve. She didn't fight them. She turned her head to me and her eyes beseeched me. *Please*.

I thought myself back to my body. The rooftop was lit by garden lanterns, but I could hardly see my body over by the wall. Standing next to it, I realised something very significant. I'd never been in control of the return to my own body – someone had always woken me. Abigail made it look pretty easy, but I had no idea how to do it.

Trying to climb back in didn't work. I was still outside myself even though technically I was in myself. The golden haze remained all around me. I closed my eyes and tried to think my way in. That didn't work either.

With a jittery feeling in my chest, I sat up in frustration. I couldn't even go back and ask Abigail how to do it as she would be in a drugged stupor by now. *Damn, I need to get back in!*

I tried to relax. My body looked uncomfortable. What had I been thinking, dropping it like it was an old rag? Quieting my mind, I thought about what I had done when I'd left my body. I looked for light. In this state, my mind was all light, so I looked for dark instead. I thought about darkness the way I'd thought about the statue at Marchione Street or getting back to the roof.

When I opened my eyes, I no longer saw the golden haze around me. The relief that my mind had re-tethered to my body was so welcome that I got a whole second's delay before it felt like I was inside the world's largest bell and the clock had just struck twelve. My head rang and my body was being shaken without respite. Coldness was in every cell and my legs were unresponsive. I tried to move my torso, but the muscles spasmed and I screamed in pain, breathing as shallowly as possibly.

I directed all my attention to straightening out my legs without moving my back, and doing this recommenced the circulation which must have been cut off by my position. The firing of the blood moving through the vessels set off pins and needles on steroids.

'Ahhh,' I moaned.

The terrace door slammed. I turned my head and saw a skinny man, almost bald and fairly short, wearing a white chef's coat come out onto the terrace. He walked over to a section of the wall at the far side of the garden beneath a lamp and pulled out a packet of cigarettes.

'Do you think you could help me?' I said in Italian.

The man's body went rigid. He scanned the terrace, but as I was in the dark and below his eye line, he couldn't see me. His cigarette drooped low and he peered around his vicinity with an expression of confusion. I managed to lift one arm. It couldn't be called waving, but I flapped in his direction and my floppy fingers caught his eye.

He ran over to me, and kneeling down, asked, 'Do you need an ambulance?' Without waiting for an answer, he lifted his phone to his ear to get one.

'No, no, no. I'm fine, I have just hurt my back. Do you think you could carry me to my room?'

He looked even more startled than he had when he'd heard my voice in the dark. I suppose I wasn't the kind of petite girl most men could pick up with ease, though Lorin had managed fine. I didn't have the nickname Giraffe for nothing.

My legs were buzzing and my back felt like it had solidified into steel.

'Perhaps you could just help me get up and to the room? That would be fine.'

He nodded and put his arms underneath mine to hoist me to my feet. My body was a dead weight, and the poor man couldn't help but utter a few of Naples's choicest swear words with a muttered apology tagged on to each one as we pitched left and right. My legs kept bending like they were made of rubber. I clung to him, almost dragging him down to the floor several times.

Taking a brief pause to regroup, I decided it seemed rude not to know anything about him when he was doing me such a favour. He was too focused on the situation to give me anything apart from his name, Carlo, as he described for me, in serious tones, the best way to proceed, which however you dressed it came down to him piggybacking me into the house. By the time we got to the first floor where my room was, the poor man was panting like he was in danger of an asthma attack.

Lorin happened to be crossing the hallway just as my grunting saviour hauled me the last few yards to my bedroom door. Sitting on his back, I was about a couple of feet higher than the banister rail. As Lorin watched me ride one of the chefs along the corridor, he stopped his progress, his brow turning down into a V-shape and his lower jaw opening slightly as if he was about to make a remark. I stared back at him, face as still as a sculpture, trying to cling on to a modicum of self-respect, but I knew I'd failed when Lorin's serious expression twitched and he smothered his smile with his hand.

Back in my room, I thanked Carlo several dozen times and promised to come and visit him in the kitchen when I'd made a recovery. He didn't look keen to see me again, but was polite. As he mopped his head, I wondered if I should comment that he looked dishevelled, but decided against it. Instead I swallowed down Ibuprofen, crawled into the bathroom and fell down the hole of my sunken bath to soak my aching limbs in hot water.

***

The next morning, I dialled Blake's number. My calf muscles had gone into spasm during the night at three different times, causing me to sit up in bed and howl in pain. My body ached all over, but it was functioning again.

'It's 10.30am – bit early for you, isn't it?' he quipped as he answered.

'Very funny. Did you get that bag of superiority free when you joined the world of work? Just to inflate your head a little more, I'm actually calling for some advice. Can I come and meet you?'

'Well, I'm not at Marchione Street. I'm collecting something that Dad has reserved at Nonostante Marras, do you know it?'

'No.'

He gave a brief snort of laughter. 'You have to see it. It's the fashion designer Antonio Marras's concept store. It has some of his clothes, shoes and accessories for sale, but also other weird and wonderful pieces. Come and meet me. I'll text you the address.'

When I arrived in the taxi, Blake looked like an advert for Antonio Marras in his designer suit, hair tousled, leaning casually against the flaky wall at the entrance to a courtyard on Via Cola di Rienzo. Cascades of flowers decorated the courtyard, adding to the splashes of colour given by brightly coloured parasols; tables and chairs gathered between batches of blooms in groups of galvanised buckets and rusting half drums.

'What are we collecting?'

'Some ruby earrings for one of Papa's conquests,' said Blake.

The shop space had an open beamed ceiling and the walls were textured with patches of whitewash next to more exposed masonry. It was laid out like an apartment that blended shabby chic with curiosity shop; I definitely wanted to meet the imaginary person who lived there.

As Blake talked to the assistant, I sat down on a mismatched chair in a seating area designed for conversation and looked at the tower of wooden boxes of varying sizes that housed books in the centre of the room. Strung from the ceiling was an elaborate display of foliage and flowers: a kind of upside down garden.

Blake strolled over and slammed down into a battered leather chair. 'She doesn't know anything about the earrings.' He shrugged. 'I told her she'd better investigate – I can't see Papa being very happy if I come back empty-handed. Tell me about Sergio. Good job you happened to go round there. It must have been terrifying.'

He leaned forward in anticipation of some gruesome details. I was about to tell him what Lorin had told me that it had all been about teaching Sergio a lesson, but stopped myself just in time. Blake might become suspicious about confidences being passed between me and Lorin.

'Should I go and visit him do you think? Comfort him in his hour of need?' His eyes twinkled with devilment.

With enormous effort, I put away the desire to snipe at him and tried to close down a rerun of that awful moment when I'd found Sergio in the bath. What was the point in reliving the pain of that when he'd been in no danger at all?

'You don't look much like a student any more. You'll hardly fit in at university when you're back.'

Blake looked down at his feet and twisted his mouth. 'I thought if I looked the part, Papa might give me some weightier assignments. I'm not really being challenged at the moment, but I'm thinking about transferring my final year at university to Milan. It makes sense as I could work around my studies then.'

'I thought you liked Bologna. Transferring will be disruptive and you'll miss all your friends. I wouldn't turn your life upside down to please Dad. He'll welcome you back as soon as you've finished, I'm sure.'

Blake didn't meet my eyes.

'Dad must be giving you *some* interesting assignments,' I said slyly, knowing he'd been in the meeting that I'd overheard.

'Yes, but he still hasn't looked in on me once. I just get messages about when I'm being moved around.'

'The fact you are being moved around means he is thinking of you.'

He gave a small shrug, stood up and wandered across to a linen cabinet to peer in. I followed. Inside there were some cut-glass bottles with silver caps; ivory hair combs; vintage wines; old diaries with silk covers, the pages of which had foxed; a divine bronze of a fawn sitting on a log.

'Do you think Antonella would like the hair combs?' he asked.

'I like them more than the dresses,' I whispered, nodding to the rail of designer dresses hanging adjacent to a speckled mirror.

The assistant returned. 'I've found them,' she said, lifting a small packet of paper above her head.

Blake and I walked over to look at them. 'Nice,' said Blake in awe as he stared at two generous ruby orbs encircled with diamond daisies.

'Designed in the 1950s by Jean Schlumberger,' said the assistant, folding them back into the paper and handing them over to Blake.

I escorted him to the exit, then stopped.

'Have you heard anything more about Abigail? Lorin says that Dad intends to make some changes with regards to her.'

'I don't think Papa would be too pleased if he thought Lorin, or I, was talking to you about such things.'

'Please. I'm just worried about her.'

He rubbed his mouth and chin. 'She's been staying on the twelfth floor. About a third of the office space was decommissioned, but now they are moving out all the other departments on that floor. Yesterday afternoon, I helped to move computers and printers from there down to the ninth.'

'I was hoping Dad might have confided in you.'

Blake gave a short blast of derisive laughter. 'Don't be ridiculous.'

'There's a big function tomorrow night at Marchione Street. I know you know about it.' I didn't want to say *because I was in the meeting too.* 'Can you help to get me in?'

'You'll need an invitation.'

I wrinkled my nose. 'I'll figure something out, but will you help me if I need it?'

He sighed, theatrically. 'If I must, but now I'm going back to work.'

I gave a joyful jump and he moved off into the court-yard.

'I'm going to stay and look around some more. I'll see you tomorrow.'

He lifted his hand without turning around.

After another lap of the shop, I was drawn back to the linen cabinet which contained the small bronze statue. It was quite fine, a deep chestnut colour with a few specks of green on the base, around eighteen inches high. The assistant, seeing she had some interest, encouraged me to open the cabinet and take it out, saying something about the quality of the casting and its substantial weight. I turned it over to see if it was solid or not. The bronze was about half an inch thick inside, but the statue was hollow apart from that. Wide at the base and tapering, it reminded me of a hood from underneath.

'I'm sure that statue has a marble base somewhere,' she said. 'Where did it go?' She flitted around the shop, looking underneath other items and eventually locating it being used as a coaster for a copper kettle. 'If you wanted it, there would be no extra cost.' The base was a simple piece of white marble. It was cut into a circle and could be fixed from the bottom up into the rim of the statue with some small screws.

It must have been my subconscious that spotted it. I

couldn't believe my luck. I paid the heavily inflated price without haggling so much as a penny. How I'd get a weapon to Abigail had been gnawing away at me during the night, and this statue offered the perfect solution.

Chapter 22

Action was good – it stopped me dwelling on the Lorin mess. I returned home and took the statue directly into my bathroom, placing it in the wide rectangular marble sink. I was about to commit an act of vandalism and I was in the perfect mood for it.

The patina looked beautiful in this light, but it wasn't a very valuable object so it was no good being sentimental. I'd made up my mind. I took some toothpaste, squirted it on the surface and rubbed it in with my finger. At first, nothing much happened. There were no cleaning cloths in here, but I had a flannel. I rubbed the toothpaste haphazardly into the bronze. This seemed to work better; I could see where I'd spread the toothpaste as it looked different from the darker surface. The harder I scrubbed, the more the colour came away, but it was quite slow progress.

I looked around the bathroom. Inside a cupboard was

a toilet brush and toilet cleaner product. Grabbing this, I read, *With Added Limescale Remover*. That sounded good. I poured it liberally all over the fawn's head and then rubbed it in with my flannel. This time more happened, and quickly. The colour disappeared, and this statue seemed to have a yellow skin rather than the pink one I'd seen on Sergio's angel.

After about five minutes, I ran the tap over it. My aim had been to mess it up and I had done that royally. It looked gruesome now: the face and body were disfigured and streaked; it looked more like a ghoul than a fawn. My flannel looked pretty bad too so that went in the bin. I had to dry the sculpture with the hand dryer. Carrying it back to my room, I then stowed it in the wardrobe.

The next stage would be harder. I'd done a film props workshop one weekend last Easter, run by St Martin's School of Art in London, and what I'd learned there was about to come in very useful. I intended to make a replica of my dad's Roman dagger – the one Abigail had grabbed the day Terry had barged in. It would need to be good enough to convince from a few feet away. I would swap the replica for the real one, which I would send to Abigail inside the cavity of the sculpture.

I looked inside my art desk drawers. They were bursting with brand new art materials. The third drawer down had sculpting materials: clay, plaster and all types of tools. Opening a plastic bag of unused clay, I cut big silvery soft chunks into two pieces using a cheese wire. Batching sections together, I rolled out two nice solid rectangles on my desk. From the bathroom, I soaked one of my T-shirts in hot water and laid it over the clay so it could absorb the warmth and help keep the rectangles malleable. Taking out one of the large-scale hardback books from my shelves, I used it as a tray to transport the two slices of clay down to the ballroom. Covering them with my jumper, I carried them downstairs and laid them on the floor along with my sketchbook.

Taking down Dad's Roman dagger, I laid it on the wooden floor and sat cross-legged on the floor to sketch it. I knew Dad and Lorin were in and there could be security cameras on too. I hadn't seen Dad since Lorin had told me about his tasteless prank on Sergio, and I would have to watch my behaviour around him as I knew so much that I shouldn't. True to form, I hadn't made a decision about my dad yet. The evidence was not in his favour, but I still had a glimmer of hope that somehow there would be an explanation to prove him to be the man I'd always known. For now, I was focusing on getting Abigail her weapon, which meant I needed to play nice with Dad.

Within half an hour of me settling down, he came in to visit.

'*Ciao, Giraffa,* I'm about to go out. What are you doing?'

'I have an idea for a large sketch, but the detail of the dagger is the focal point so I need to get it just right.'

He patted me on the head like I was an obedient mongrel and paid several compliments, even though I'd only drawn the odd line. He seemed in tremendous spirits. I thought I'd cash in on his upbeat mood.

'Oh, I nearly forgot. I bought a nice statue today, but its colour is a mess. I really like it, though. I wondered if Abigail might recolour it for me.'

'I don't see why not. If you take it to Marchione Street in the morning and get them to call my assistant, Micala, she'll authorise them to take it to her. Where did you find it?'

'At Nonostante Marras – what a great place.'

'Hmm, I like it there too.' His voice told me that he was there in his head. I was desperate to know who the ruby earrings were for.

'Who are you seeing tonight?' I swivelled to look at him and he gave his eyebrows a flick. 'Not the lady from last night? Dad, you don't want her to think you really like her,' I said, adding in as much sarcasm as I could.

Giving me the smile of a schoolboy caught doing something he oughtn't, he said, 'I have a date with the nurse.'

'Dad, you're awful. She's far too young for you.'

'Oh, I wouldn't say that,' he said, his heels clicking on the wooden floor as he left the room with a definite strut.

I pulled across the clay and placed it directly in front of me and pushed one side of the dagger into one of the squares until it was exactly half way submerged. Removing it without disfiguring the clay took some gentle manoeuvring, but I managed it. The delicate leaf-shape and fine grooved lines were perfectly replicated in the silky grey-brown clay.

I repeated the process for the other segment. When I'd finished, I used the now cool T-shirt to clean the clay off the dagger and ensured it was dry by rubbing it hard with my jumper. I continued the sketch for another ten minutes and then returned the dagger to its original position.

Back in my room, I mixed up a small bowl of plaster with some lukewarm water and poured it directly into the clay impressions. Annoyingly, I didn't have any sandpaper and would need to pare down the contours so that when I fitted the two sections together they would meet perfectly. A knife would do, but it did mean visiting the kitchen to beg for one. The replica dagger wouldn't be perfect, but I reckoned I could make one that would pass at a glance.

I picked up my drawing pad and looked at the sketches of the dagger's evil tip. Junk food would be a good excuse to go to the kitchen. I was so involved in thinking through the steps of my plan, I didn't realised I'd carried the pad with me until I was at the bottom of the main stairs.

As I went down the final flight, the first person I saw, and last person I wanted to see, was Lorin. He was sitting in the kitchen on a bar stool, having a slice of cake and a coffee and talking to the head chef. The chef had his back to me and was leaning against the granite island in the middle of the kitchen. Lorin looked at me, eyes solemn. It took every fibre of my willpower not to slam into reverse and haul myself back up those stairs.

The chef turned around and looked at me in surprise. 'Can I help you, *signorina*?' I knew him better than many of my dad's other staff as it wasn't uncommon for my father to have him brought up after a particularly fine meal and invite him to take a glass of wine with us.

'I just wanted a cup of tea, English tea, if one was available. I don't mind making it.' The chef tutted and barked at one of his assistants. 'And some biscotti,' I added.

The chef frowned. 'It is very close to dinner,' he re-marked.

I'm not three years old, I wanted to snap. I will eat my dinner.

'I missed lunch,' I stated, not dropping his gaze. 'Oh, and do you have a knife I can borrow? I'm making something in my room.'

The chef's eyebrows disappeared out of sight in his hairline at this request. Clearly, using a knife for anything unrelated to cooking or eating was not very Italian.

Lorin was staring at me with his eyebrows slightly raised. I felt the creeping-crawling of his suspicion run across my skin.

Ignore him, I told myself. *Mind your own business*, I wanted to say, but it would have been too familiar. I stared back at him unrepentantly for a minute or two, but then I thought about his hands on my neck the night before last and lost the game, lowering my eyes.

While waiting for my tea, I sat down at the island and tried not to watch Lorin eat, which was nearly impossible. Though I was hurt and furious with this man, I could still feel every atom in my body wanting to move towards him like iron filings to a magnet. I didn't want him to sense his advantage and so I directed my attention elsewhere. Spotting a pen on a shelf at knee level on the island, I turned over a page in my pad and scribbled a particularly mean sketch. I made Lorin much fatter than he really was, pushing a big piece of apple pie into an enlarged mouth. Lorin's character was all in his forehead, eyebrows and wayward hair, meaning I could practically do anything else with the face and body and you'd still know it was him. I gave him a few rolls of fat around his middle for good measure, and made the filling of the pie squelch out from the pastry and drip in large droplets down either side of his face.

The chef brought across my cup of tea, presenting it to me, and I showed him my sketch. He laughed so loudly I had to put my hand over my ear. His was one of those laughs that used his whole diaphragm. Lorin, his mouth full of pie, raised himself slightly off his stool to see. Furious, he made a sound like an annoyed cow. Despite my aim of ignoring him, this made me laugh and the chef boomed again. Lorin grabbed at the pad, pulling the page out and looking at it in shock before screwing it up and throwing it towards the bin. The chef was too quick. He grabbed the balled up piece of paper and straightened it out. Folding it, he inserted into his top pocket and gave it a little pat.

Carlo brought me over a plate of biscuits. '*Ciao!*' I said, pleased to see him. He gave me a wary smile. I wasn't about to ask him to carry me back to my room again, but he acted like I might. I nodded my thanks and stood to leave. My work was done here.

'I do need a knife. I'll bring it back later,' I told the chef.

'Please do, I don't like to lose a good knife. It's always the one you don't have that you need,' he said in Italian. He must have been quoting the Tao of the kitchen.

He showed me a selection that looked more like an armoury than a cluster of cooking utensils. I chose a small bladed sharp one, perfect for carving. The chef took Lorin's depiction from his pocket, smoothed it out and stared at it, laughing again. He fixed it to one of his fridges and I thanked him and went up to my room to tidy up my plaster model. As I walked the stairs, I looked at my biscuits. I had been hoping for a Mars bar, but shortbread and rose-infused almond amaretti wisps would have to do. I was turning into my mother. Her socialism would have bristled at these first class biscuits.

***

After dinner, which I ate in front of the TV, the plaster was solid enough for me to cut away the clay. I dried off both clammy halves with a hairdryer. Putting them together, I found they were not far from being a good match. I buttered some more plaster between them and used the hairdryer again. Fairly soon, they were strong.

There wasn't much to straighten up, just a few edges to tidy. I painted it over in a white acrylic and left it to dry while I fished for the right combination of colours for the next step. It needed a metallic bronze, but nothing too glaring. I had a metallic bronze, but it was very glitzy. I painted out some samples on a card: glitzy bronze with a wash of umber didn't look too bad. I allowed it to dry and then stippled over the top, first with flat brown acrylic, then with a darker hue which was almost black. This looked great with the metallic paint coming through only here and there.

I repeated it larger scale with the plaster dagger and used the photos I'd taken on my phone to compare. Not perfect, but a good imitation. I placed it out of the way on the top shelf of my wardrobe.

I texted Sergio a couple of times and WhatsApped Kristin a tonne of times, then watched a film until about 11pm, at which point the house seemed at its quietest. I peeped out of my room: the hallway was dark and I couldn't see any other lights on. Taking down my plaster-and-paint weapon from the wardrobe, I walked downstairs as quietly as I could. There were only patches of moonlight in squares leading down the carpeted steps to guide me. I did my best to stay in the shadows.

Slipping into the ballroom, I moved to the wall where the weapons were displayed. The dark had no interruption as the shutters had been closed. I stood on tiptoes and ran my hands along the wall to locate the bronze dagger. I came across two or three other items first, but they were the wrong shape or length. Finding it, I clasped the cold metal. Flashes of Abigail cutting her hands took me by surprise. I had to concentrate hard not to drop the weighty dagger when lifting it away from its clasps, and manoeuvring the plaster replica into its place wasn't made easier by replays in my head of Terry pushing me through the ballroom door. I checked three times to make sure I hadn't put it the wrong way up. If I did, that would be an immediate giveaway.

With the dagger in my hand, I spun and felt the darkness press in on me. A shiver of deep terror ran through me of what might lay in the dense darkness – I hadn't experienced this since I was a small child. I ran the run of nightmares where something evil is chasing you. Every minute I expected someone to put out a hand and grab me or drag me backwards down the stairs by my hair. When I dived on the bed in my own room, burying the dagger below my pillow, I lay across it panting and gasping for breath, my heart hammering from make-believe terror.

That's when I heard a knock on my door. I was off my bed in a trice, looking at the back of the door like it might reveal who was on the other side. Could it be Lorin? Unlikely. My heart was thumping as I walked towards the door, and the knock came again, louder this time.

I turned on my light and opened the door only a little. It was Dad's head chef.

'I'm here for the knife,' he said and put out his hand, palm up.

Humiliation crawled over my skin like insects. I dropped my eyes and blushed. How awful to be caught stealing something from my own father. He must have seen me running up the stairs in the moonlight.

'I'm sorry,' I stammered. 'I just – oh, please don't tell my dad.' My voice cracked with pathetic despera-tion. He looked confused and then concerned. Inclining his head to one side, he tried to catch my eye.

'Have you not finished with it yet?' he said, very gently.

Only then did a drop of brain activity begin to trickle through. He didn't mean the dagger.

'Yes! I've finished with it!' I said, rapturously. This bizarre change in my behaviour made him take a step back. 'I'll get it for you.'

I ran to my desk and snatched up the small knife he'd loaned me earlier, presenting it to him with the most delighted face. He cast a wary look my way and left.

'Thanks for dinner,' I called after him and added a wave.

Closing the door, I leaned against it and slid down to the floor. What would he have thought if I'd gone and got the Roman dagger from under my pillow and presented it to him? The fact it had so nearly happened and his astonished face when I'd said yes made me laugh so much that I tipped into the kind of hysteria which made my eyes wet with tears. Gasping for breath, I realised that I was laughing uncontrollably on my own and this sobered me a little. My life was a mess.

Once I'd calmed down, I wrapped the dagger in one of my vest tops and concealed it inside the statue. The inside cavern was slender, but the dagger was a fairly good fit and there wasn't a lot of space for movement with the vest top padding. I tightened up the base and left the statue by the bed ready to deliver to Abigail.

.

Chapter 23

I sat in a cleaning cupboard on the seventh floor of Marchione Street at 7.45pm the next evening. Though I had no invitation, I was not going to miss out on the Society's big event. I wanted to hear from Dad what he had planned for the Society and Abigail. Lorin was sure I was safe, but hundreds of years of history might be an unwieldy ship to steer. I'd been thinking over these things for much of the afternoon and my anxiety was becoming so acute that I had to keep swallowing to relieve it.

What would I do if Lorin was wrong? Would I run, hide out in Milan and apply for a new passport? Lorin had said that if the Society wanted me, they'd take me whether I was in the UK or Milan, and his words kept floating back to me. I had to know my position tonight, and I wanted to know what would happen to Abigail.

My bum was numb from sitting on the terrazzo floor

and I shifted to allow some more blood to the area. My stomach felt like there was a diver inside doing the Twister on a continuous loop. I picked up the little rectangular art-deco mirror from my bedroom and checked my disguise for the hundredth time. The mirror shook in my hand.

I did look so different. I'd spent the early part of the morning shopping for wigs and had found one in a cropped elfin style in black. I'd put on fake tan last night and this morning to warm the shade of my usually cool skin tone. On top of this, I'd used a translucent pearly foundation which blended well with the tan to soften the shade. I had plucked my eyebrows earlier and had used a brow pencil to lengthen them out. My eyes were naturally quite large, but I'd emphasised their horizontal lines which made them look more sleepy and sexy than usual. With my lips I'd gone for a plum red, a colour I normally could never wear, but it went well with the dark hair and skin tone. I filled out the lips, making them rounder than was natural. The final addition had been dark rectangular-framed glasses which I'd picked up in a department store.

I was wearing a black cocktail dress with a low waist, very 1920s inspired, heavily beaded in patterns of fans and stopping above the knee. I added plain patent leather ballet pumps too as I certainly didn't need to be any taller. I stared at myself. It really was a shocking transformation. The make-up made me look sultry and cool: nothing like my usual self. I had a good chance of not being recognised by Dad at the event. The disguise was good, and he would be very busy being the most important man there, but I wasn't so sure about getting past security. At least Blake was on my team.

Earlier today, we'd met on the top floor of Dad's building. As Blake got me a coffee from the cart in the corner, I admired the space. The roof was made from slanting glass rectangles of differing colours. The space was open plan, and the theme was one of an indoor garden with extras. There were raised vegetable and flower beds, interspersed with freestanding library shelves stocked with classics, bestsellers and magazines. How could Dad be an evil man when he had such concern for the welfare of his staff? The more I considered it, the less likely it seemed. It was a puzzle piece that didn't fit with raising millions for charity or the many individuals I'd met over the years who'd thanked him for help he'd given them in some area of their lives.

As he passed me a cappuccino, I scolded Blake for not taking me there sooner. We sat below trees housed in pots and clustered to form an indoor orchard where the staff could read, nap or relax during their breaks. The climate was heavily controlled, making the space pleasant rather than stifling.

'Please. Please – I'm only asking for a small thing.' I looked at him with as much hope and desperation as I could cram into my expression.

'Can't you just be the kind of sister who asks me to cover while she sneaks out to meet her boyfriend?'

'This is kind of the same thing. It's no big deal. All you need to do is leave the building using my electronic pass so that on the computer, I am signed out. If your card won't let you back in, then just make a fuss at reception about your pass being faulty. Please, Dad will never know.'

'I'm warning you, Frankie, he probably will find out. I don't know how he does it, but if Beth in accounts sneezes, he seems to hear about it.'

'He's probably sleeping with Beth in accounts,' I said, which made us both laugh.

After Blake went back to work, I'd gone in search of a cupboard to hide myself in. I had only one more mission to complete before settling in to get ready for the party. I'd gone to check on Abigail and ensure she had my statue. Once I was locked in the cupboard, I was able to project myself to the bedside I'd left her at the previous night.

The room was filled with people. Abigail was sitting at a dressing table in front of a mirror with a particularly sour expression while a small man was painting a gel onto her hair. Another girl was giving her a manicure. There was a make-up artist with a trestle table who was lifting items out of her kit, and on the bed was a large bag obviously holding a dress.

Abigail saw me in the reflection of the glass. She tried not to react, but I could see it was hard for her. I held my hands apart to indicate to her roughly the size of the statue. She didn't understand.

For some seconds, I stood making incoherent shapes with my hands. It wasn't easy to mime a fawn sitting on a log. Beginning to get desperate, I considered whether to canter around the room in a fawn-like caper.

Abigail stood up and spoke to the others in the room. They nodded and she walked towards the door. I followed.

Doors led off, left and right, from the corridor outside, but instead of clear glass meeting rooms, as there were on the other corridors, each room was frosted to obscure the inside. One door was held open with a chair. Abigail paused and said something to someone inside. I moved ahead of her and looked in. There were two men dressed as security guards inside, sitting behind a fleet of CCTV screens. Each screen showed different angles of every room.

She walked on to the last room in the corridor and entered. Inside was a laboratory-style room, or perhaps a very tidy art studio. Every surface was gleaming and there were cupboards floor to ceiling. On one of the benches, in the centre of the room, stood the statue I'd mauled with limescale remover.

I smiled in relief that we'd found it. She didn't look at me, but circled it as if assessing its merit. I then did the worst mime of a knife that anyone has probably ever done. I pointed up inside the sculpture, pretending to cut my hands as I'd seen her do when Terry had held me hostage. This she understood, but she didn't look pleased. She looked up to the ceiling and around the room. I followed her gaze and saw three cameras.

I shrugged. I had no idea how she would be able to access the statue without being seen, but I would have to leave that to her. Hopefully, she wouldn't need to access it so the solution wouldn't need to be found.

At almost eight o'clock, I decided to leave my cupboard. Blake had told me that entry was from 7pm so I felt sure that there would be sufficient people in the room for me to blend in with by now. I stood up and felt light headed. Leaning against the wall, I contemplated ducking out of my body and attending as a projection, but I wouldn't be able to hear anything. No, this way was the better way if I could control my nerves.

Moving up the staircase, I got to the eighteenth floor. I was breathless as I pushed open the swing doors leading from the staircase. I'd had to stop on every landing from about the fifteenth floor onward to regain my breath.

I found a beefy security guard with headphones directly inside. My heart jumped in my chest. I smiled and tried to move past him.

'Are you with the catering staff, madam?' he asked in Italian.

I shook my head. 'I can't use lifts, I'm claustrophobic. I'm here for the...event.' My voice echoed in my throat – *I needed to control my nerves*. 'That is a lot of stairs,' I said, concentrating on lengthening my breathing. My eyes darted along the corridor and I could see two more security guards at the other end.

'Have you been stamped?' His eyes bored into me. It seemed his radar was well tuned.

'No, should I have been?' I smiled at him as innocently as possible.

'Yes, at reception.'

'You can't really be asking me to walk nearly forty flights down and up again?' I added a slight laugh. 'You've probably never walked them, but there are two flights per floor.'

He looked at me and I could tell he was thinking it over. I didn't want to make too big a fuss, but my name wouldn't be on any list at reception.

'I'm sorry, miss – I can't let you in,' he said, shrugging.

I pouted, sighed heavily and stepped back into the stairwell. Pulling out my phone, I called Blake.

He answered on the third ring. 'I need your help!' I yelled down the phone.

'Already? I thought you had a plan.'

'I did, for hair and make-up, but it turns out not much else. The security guard won't let me in – he says I need a stamp!' I could see the security guard watching me through the glass. I lowered my voice. *He's definitely suspicious.* I waved at him.

'What the hell can I do? I don't have a stamp,' Blake said.

'Can't you come and vouch for me or something? I'm in the stairwell on the eighteenth floor.'

He sighed. 'Give me ten minutes.'

I waited anxiously, pacing up and down the landing and glancing at the security guard now and then, chewing my index finger's nail. Then I saw Blake through the glass, talking to the security guard. He was holding an iPad. I stared and then shot forward and opened the door.

I wish I could have drawn him at the instant he saw

me. He couldn't have looked more like a cartoon character if he'd tried: his eyes actually bulged and his jaw dropped down as he took in my appearance, then he pulled himself together and scrolled down a long spreadsheet.

'Are *you* Miss Sylvia Valentino?'

'Yes, yes.' I nodded furiously.

'I'm from reception.' Blake showed me his security pass which was around his neck. He was in character. 'They said you couldn't use the lifts?' The security guard was looking closely at Blake's pass. 'I'm also Signor Milliardo's son.' The guard took a step back.

'I'm just a bag of nerves,' I said, holding up my chewed nail for inspection. Both men looked at it. I wish I could have drawn the tough security guard's expression of disgust. It was worthy of committing to posterity.

'She's on the list,' Blake confirmed in a bored voice. 'Come with me,' he added formally. The security guard just looked pleased I was someone else's problem.

Following Blake and struggling not to giggle as I looked at his back, I leaned forward and whispered, 'You missed your calling – you should have been an actor.'

Blake half turned. I just caught the side of his smile before I froze in horror as I realised too late that my dad was about three steps in front of us and walking our way. If he stopped to talk to Blake, we would all be in very close proximity in the corridor.

I dropped my clutch handbag and scrabbled about on the floor with my head bent down.

'Ah, there you are. I want you to speak to the bar staff,' Dad said to Blake in Italian. He took Blake's arm and steered him inside the main room, whispering in his ear as he did so. I stood slowly and peered after them.

Even though it was early in the evening by Italian standards, the room was heaving, and despite the air

265

conditioning, it felt tropical. The noise also took some adjusting to. People spilled out from the room, filling the corridor and the lobby space in front of the lifts. I slipped inside. You couldn't even see the rows of display cases because people were so tightly packed around them, and I imagined Vero, Blake's mum, would be horrified as they were using them to stand their drinks on.

The room was fairly dark, lit predominantly by the display cases. I entered at about the middle part of the room and my eye was immediately caught by the brightness at one end where there was a stage. As my eyes found her, I felt my throat constrict.

Abigail sat inside an ornately gilded cage. It looked just like the type of cage that Victorian ladies would keep small birds inside, with tapered bars narrowly spaced which met at the top forming a scroll. She was styled in the most incredible outfit: a bodice with a narrow waist and full skirt entirely in the brightest gold. Her hair had been dyed platinum blonde, and was styled off her face with a rose-gold collar. Her eyeshadow, lipstick and nails were all in gold too, and she even had false eyelashes which had had the tips dipped in gold. The effect was hugely theatrical.

Abigail had her head resting against the bars and was staring into space, seemingly unaware of the jam of people in the room. She looked medicated. I tore my eyes from the indisputable evidence that my dad had lied and he was the very monster that, a few hours ago, I'd convinced myself he couldn't be. My heart felt like it was shrinking as the love I had for my dad seemed to be leaking out. *How could he do such a thing?*

On the other side of the stage stood Sergio's incredible sculpture which had undergone a transformation of its own. Instead of the coloured surface that I'd seen last time, it now glowed in the staged lighting, showing off a perfect gold surface. People were gathering around it and discussing it intensely. It must be gilded. Abigail hadn't done that. At least, I hoped she hadn't – if she had then there was no way they would let her go, or me either.

My phone buzzed. It was Blake. *Papa had it cast in gold*, the text said. I looked across the room to where he was standing talking to one of the bar staff. Nodding my acknowledgment, I smiled at him.

I turned away and surveyed the room, looking for my father. He was at the far corner in the centre of a group. Waiters with canapés were trying to push themselves through the crowd, but they were struggling to gain any ground. Glasses of champagne were being handed through the crowd and empty glasses returned the same way because of the lack of space to circulate. This was useful as it meant my dad couldn't take me by surprise again by moving across the room too quickly.

I was so busy people-watching that that when Lorin whispered in my ear, 'What are you doing here, Francesca?' I jumped.

He was looking even more stellar than normal in a tux. His hair still looked slightly wet from the shower and was coaxed off his face. The strength in his body seemed even more on display than usual, though he was entirely covered up. I had to remind myself of his betrayal to stop myself gushing.

We stood side by side, him facing one direction and me the other.

'You're not supposed to be able to recognise me,' I said, slightly annoyed that he had.

'I know the back of your neck better than most people.'

'I didn't believe you when you told me the reason why Dad was holding Abigail. I didn't want to believe it so I came to see for myself.'

'Understandable.'

'Why is she dressed like that, and the statue too? Rather misconstruing the situation, isn't it?'

'She's an exhibit – along with the rest of the items in the cases. By the way, I found your passport.'

'You didn't!' My heart gave a double bounce. 'Where?'

'Your dad's safe.' My heart steadied again.

'I can't stay in Milan now that I know about this.'

'Don't make assumptions. You don't know what will happen yet.'

I allowed myself a moment's thought saturated in selfishness where I enjoyed a magnificent art career with Lorin at my side and my father at the helm, ignoring all that I'd discovered tonight.

'I'm not happy here anyway. I seem to be in touching distance of so many possibilities, but they all keep receding instead of coming closer.'

He turned his blue-grey eyes upon me. 'You're still angry.'

I took a deep breath and turned to look at Abigail. 'Not really. I understand your motives, but they're still not palatable to me.'

'Please stay,' he whispered. I turned my head to him and he slipped his hand into mine. I tried to suppress the ripple of happiness that ran over my skin. 'Stay for me. You're a glimmer of light in my life.'

I'm more of a golden haze, I thought.

'I swear I won't let anything happen to you.'

'How can you say that to me when I'm in potential danger because of you? What chance do we have? We both have alpha-male fathers who won't like the match at all, and we mustn't forget the psychopathic Society that has its sights set on me, but that would be nothing if I was sure I could trust you.'

Lorin shushed me. 'Careful. I am sorry.'

'But you'd do it again, if you had your time over,

wouldn't you?'

He swallowed and looked up. His eyes said, *Don't ask me that*. Seeming to sense that we had come to a conclusion, he turned so that he was looking in the same direction as me. There was no need to hide our intimacy now; it had evaporated. Even his tone of voice changed, becoming more conversational.

'My father's standing next to yours.'

He was much taller than my dad with broad shoulders like Lorin's, but straight silver hair rather than Lorin's curls. He was animated and laughing. It reminded me of the way Lorin had laughed in the picture with his siblings.

'He's on the move,' Lorin said, gently pushing me out of my dad's path and behind him. I melded into the crowd. With Blake following, my dad was parting the crowd as he walked towards toward the stage. He shook hands with people as he passed them, and leaned in to whisper brief comments to one or two, giving a wry smile or a pat on the shoulder before he moved on. Reaching the front of the room, just in front of Abigail's cage, he stepped on to the stage and was handed a microphone. Blake joined him like his lieutenant, looking proud.

The lights were lowered so that only the stage was lit. 'If I can have your attention, please,' my dad began in Italian. 'I'm delighted you're all here this evening. This is the first annual meeting of our Society, as far back as records have been kept, that every member has accepted their invitation. I can only imagine this is because I have upgraded the champagne.'

He flicked his eyebrows upwards and the crowd laughed.

When the room stilled, he continued. 'Of course, I do know that you are all here to see our most recent subject: Argent.' The spotlight moved on to the cage as he said

Abigail's name and the crowd buzzed. Abigail stared at the ground.

I ran my eyes along the rows of people in front of me, enjoying the differing outlines of their shoulders and heads – fodder for a great line drawing later – until a solid white-haired figure stopped my eyes in their tracks. The hairs on the back of my neck flexed.

My dad's voice echoed around the room. 'She is certainly an incredible young woman,' he continued. 'And I believe she has a great deal of potential. Tonight I will be speaking about the future. In my own businesses and as leader of this Society, I believe that members' voices should be heard.'

It's hard to be sure of a person's identity from behind, but Terry Gerrard's heavyweight boxer's physique made him distinctive and took me straight back to the day in the ballroom when he was compressing my neck between iron bicep and forearm as he held a gun to my head. I dropped my head forward almost onto my chest as the memory slapped my stomach.

Lorin squeezed my arm. 'Are you okay?' he whispered.

I felt breathless and couldn't lift my head in that moment. My dad's speech filled my ears.

'There can be no-one here who is not aware that our group has become divided into those who believe in the Society's current manifesto and those who do not. I have been to visit some of those who have the strongest objections to the status quo and engaged in a considered dialogue with them.'

Feeling Lorin cup my hand, I lifted my head to look at Terry again. *What was he doing here? What was he planning?*

'The argument is that the ethos of our Society should change to reflect the era in which we live and that we can go on protecting the real history of alchemy without the need for living subjects. Many of these voices are my most esteemed and trusted friends and business colleagues, people whose opinions I value.'

There were murmurs in the crowd.

'It's Terry Gerrard. He's near the front row,' I said to Lorin, pointing to where he stood. 'We have to tell my dad, now!'

Lorin shook his head. His expression was conflicted.

'Not now – this is the pinnacle of his speech. He won't thank you for it. I'll alert security.'

He started tapping out a message on his phone. I couldn't just stand there so I pushed past the person in front of me, who tutted. Lorin caught my arm and drew me back.

'Listen.' He gestured to my dad. 'This is the moment we've been waiting for. He's going to free her.'

Dad's voice became louder. 'My conclusion is that protecting the real history of alchemy, as we have done for hundreds of years, is not about a treasure trove of artefacts.' He lifted his hand, moving it horizontally to indicate the rows of display cases. 'It is about understanding the gift. To find subjects in this era where we have unprecedented analysis and technology may prove to shape the world in ways that many of our ancestors predicted. Argent, and others, could be the key to so many new discoveries about the human brain's capabilities.'

It was as if I'd been hosed down and left to stand in a draught. 'Argent *and others*,' rang in my head. Dad had chosen the Society over me. There was no disputing it. I felt the final fragments of faith I'd had in him fall one by one. Lorin, who I hadn't realised had been holding my hand, dropped it. He was shaking his head slightly like he had water in his ears and wasn't hearing correctly.

There was a shout from the other side of the room where Lorin's father stood. Everyone's head turned like

271

they were following an ace flying down the centre line at Wimbledon.

'A surprising conclusion, Domenico, but do tell us all how successful an alchemist Abigail has proven herself so far. The gold cage and gold statue are very fitting decorations for our event, but I understand that she has shown herself to have achieved nothing more exceptional than colouring a piece of bronze. Detainment for such a talent seems desperate.'

Everyone's heads swivelled back.

'She has other markers, as I'm sure you know,' Dad said and swivelled his head to look directly at Lorin with an expression of fury. I looked down at my feet and tried to shuffle to my right, out of his eye line. He turned back and continued to speak, but I'd stopped hearing him. Questions were shooting through my brain like darts.

Had Abigail even murdered Pierro? Had Dad murdered Terry's wife? Had Abigail had an affair with Terry?

I looked around at the crowd. Many of them were nodding and clapping. My heart felt like it was curling up to protect itself. I glanced at Abigail, who was now standing as if she'd woken from her sleep. She pressed her face against the bars and tried to form words which didn't come out clearly. They were jumbled like her tongue was leaden. She sounded like me when I suffered with migraine auras.

Dad acted quickly, not wanting a scene where she might plead with the audience. He gave a nod to the two security guards at the room's entrance, who had a hard job moving through the crowd as they were not slight men. Dad removed a large gilded key from his pocket and opened the cage door. He offered his hand to assist her to step out. Abigail stared at it like it might bite her and instead chose to steady herself by placing both hands on the bars, bending her head to go through the small door.

From the corner of my eye, I saw Terry make his move. He didn't have far to go, having placed himself perfectly. I didn't stop to think.

'Dad! It's Terry!'

My voice rent the air and a few faces turned to me with looks of disgust at my behaviour, but it was enough to jolt Dad's attention and make him aware of Terry who was about to cannon into him. In Terry's hand, I saw a flash of something metallic, and the recognition of the blade that I had armed Abigail with was an ugly moment. I could see how it was about to kill my dad before it even happened. Super-strength seemed to burst from my body and I was shoving through the crowd in front of me. A shout came from my throat and met somebody else's, ricocheting off one another.

I gained the front just in time to see Blake's arm snaking around my dad's chest, pushing him off balance so that he crashed to the floor. Blake was travelling forward and met Terry's blade at maximum impact, ensuring it rammed through his throat from hilt to tip.

There was a moment where no-one moved or spoke and Blake's body came down to meet the floor with nothing to break its fall. The impact forced blood to shoot out of his throat and land in tiny pools across the floor. Then he started to gasp and choke. My dad was over to him in a second. An icy-coldness spread through my veins and into my brain, stopping my thoughts.

Lorin appeared at my side. 'The doctors are coming from the hospital wing. We need to keep the oxygen flowing to his brain. Any doctors here?' he shouted to the crowd. Two men moved forward and began to administer help.

I could only stare at the hilt of the Roman dagger that butted up against Blake's neck and poked out the other side.

Security had hold of Terry, who wasn't showing any signs of a struggle. Our eyes met and my mouth watered as I felt a wave of sickness. I lifted my hand to my mouth and that's when I began to cry choking tears that stabbed the throat.

'It wasn't for you,' I screamed at him. 'It wasn't meant for you!'

People around us were staring. Lorin shushed me.

'Don't say anything else,' he whispered and turned my body to his chest. I cried into it. He put his arms around me.

Blake was making horrible noises, his eyes flickering. The blood was leaving his body at an increased pace. Dad, and now Vero too, were bending over him, both crying while the doctors tried to slow the speed with which his blood was sprinting away.

Lorin knelt and spoke to them both. Dad's eyes were unseeing; he wasn't taking anything in.

'The doctors will be here in a minute. I've called an ambulance too as I doubt they have the facilities on-site to deal with this. I will take Abigail back,' he said, but got no reply from my father.

He led Abigail, who was standing as still as Sergio's statue just in front of the cage, across the room. Lorin was known to most in the room and people parted as they walked through. I watched her leave. From behind, the dress had a ridiculous train like the feathers of a golden peacock.

My heart and head were in a raging tangle. I forced myself to look down again at the hideous dagger exposed from Blake's neck.

What had I done? How had Terry got it? He must have had inside help.

I bent down, wanting to touch Blake, but my dad and Vero looked at me like I was an invader and turned their backs on me. I remembered I didn't look as I usually did and instead sat on the edge of the stage, allowing the pain to rip pieces from me. The medics arrived and Blake was completely cut off while they worked. I didn't even get to say goodbye when they were ready to move him.

Chapter 24

My father and Vero followed Blake and the room began to empty of people. I sat on the stage, staring into space, numb with the pain of what I'd done. Lorin returned. He placed his arm under my elbow and lifted me to my feet. Without asking where we were going, I allowed him to steer me towards the door and into the corridor. I didn't protest. I needed someone to take control.

We were moving towards the staircase, but a few metres before we reached the door, the two burly security guards, who had been speaking on their phones, spotted us and barged forward.

One stood a step in front of the other. 'Where is she, Lorin?' he said.

'I don't know what you mean,' Lorin replied, his face a mask.

'Where did you take her?'

'Excuse me, *signori*, this young lady has been separated from her party.'

The guard tried a more diplomatic approach.

'Lorin, I'm sure this is just a mistake, but Abigail is not in her rooms. All security is on high-alert until we locate her.'

When he got no answer from Lorin, he turned his face to one side to say something to the other guard. As his face moved into profile, Lorin shifted his weight on to his back foot. His right arm streaked through the air and he crunched into the guard's windpipe with the side of his hand.

The guard buckled, making a rattling noise as he clasped his throat in an attempt to breathe. The second guard came forward and Lorin twisted slightly and dealt a kick which turned into a stamp-down on the side of his knee, causing him to shout in pain and collapse. Lorin leaped over him, but as I attempted the same, the guard made a grab at me. In a movement so fluid it could have been ballet, Lorin back-kicked the man in the head, knocking him to the floor.

We were out of the corridor and sprinting down the stairs. There were a few other people on the staircase, moving down slowly and chatting amongst themselves about Blake. We accelerated past them. Lorin's urgency pulsed through his hands as he forced me to leap three and four steps at a time.

I was struggling to formulate thoughts, let alone speak at this pace, but I managed to garble, 'Why are they asking about Abigail?'

'She's out. I put her in a taxi, gave her my visa card. I just saw the opportunity.' His words tumbled over one another in his haste to explain.

You got her a taxi? whirled in my head, but I had no more time to question as a couple of guards ran on to the staircase two floors above us and their shouts echoed over us.

'Come on!' he yelled, shooting forward, though I'd never have thought it possible to go faster. As we went past another door, two more guards tried to exit from the corridor on to the landing. Lorin shoved the door shut until I was past and then sprang away. I seemed to be running and jumping into the air the way I did when I wasn't in my body. The guards were so close, they were treading on our shadows. As we hit the second floor, I realised I'd left my bag in the utility cupboard. For a second, I hesitated, and then one of the guards grabbed my collar. Lorin hit him with a punch that in a boxing ring would have been considered showboating, but the swing made it a world class knockout. He not only floored my assailant, but the man collapsed knocking over the other guard who was a pace behind him.

We made the ground floor and then ran headlong into a sea of guests who were backed up, clogging the reception area. They were being checked before they could leave the building by a line of security men, probably screening for us. We were absorbed into the crowd, forcing us to shuffle rather than run. Lorin lifted his hands to his hair and looked left and right, unsure how to get around this new obstacle.

Sucking in great gasping breaths, I saw that we had neither odds nor luck on our side. My chest felt tight, locked up by nerves. We were being crushed together by the crowd. I glanced at Lorin for guidance, and he looked down at me, regret spreading across his expression like a shadow. He slipped his fingers into mine and lifted them to his lips.

'Francesca, it's time to say goodbye. They don't know it's you. The best way I can protect you is by giving you time to get away. Separate from me and go!'

Of all the times it could have happened, it was at this crazy, dangerous, inconvenient moment that I fell in love with him. A firework sparked in the pit of my stomach and soared up, screaming like a banshee, to explode over my heart in a cascade of twinkling stars.

I looked at Lorin's perfect profile. It was wide-eyed, like he must be able to see through me to what was happening on the inside, but he had slipped my hand and was watching the guards. He tried to part a few people and push past them, putting space between us, but the further he got, the more fireworks blasted off. I yelped at the pain of the separation and bounded after him.

There was a shout, and then three guards were pointing at Lorin. In total, seven moved into the crowd, snaking towards us. Lorin's face looked strained and he mouthed, 'Move away from me!' I shook my head. In less than a minute, the guards surrounded us and we were corralled into the side area of reception where my favourite statue stood. People were staring. The guards hadn't taken hold of Lorin yet. Understanding completely what my father was capable of, I began to shake with panic. Lorin was being backed against a corner and his stance was poised to fight, but there were too many of them.

He erupted from the corner. Spinning at blurring speed and yet with the precision of an archer, he took two men down. His agility as he swung high kicks that crunched down on bones and jabs that must have split jaws had me gawping rather than thinking of any way to help, but more security guards were leaving the entrance and moving in on Lorin. He would be badly beaten, if not worse.

Then a whistle blast rang out: a note that made even Lorin look as the guards changed their sights and turned away from him. There was a shimmer in the darkness. On the pavement, just outside the entrance of the building, I could see Abigail, and she was glowing.

'Get down!' I shouted at Lorin, whose expression was uncomprehending. He saw me dive to the floor and followed suit at the same instant that her power hit us all. A blinding light and blast as if from a bomb felled everyone in the reception area. I rolled as I tried to regain the air that had been punched out of my lungs, but I had an advantage over the others around me as I could see when they could not. The golden haze hung in the air like a dense mist and the cacophony of noise that had been sewn together from the voices in the crowd was ripped apart, leaving a blank silence hovering. Knowing I couldn't let a grain of this precious time slip through my fingers, I was on my feet and over to Lorin before anyone else had even raised their heads from the floor. Feeling my hands upon him, he grabbed at me in panic, nearly dragging me down too.

Tugging wildly at him until he found his feet, I picked my way with him over people. His movements had lost the nimbleness that had characterised them minutes before. He fell over people rather than stepped. Guards, in the dark uniforms, were beginning to twitch, looking like beetles flipped on their backs. It was moments before we were through the entrance doors and out on to the street.

Abigail had collapsed, her golden dress consuming her. Lorin bent, but his own balance was still upset and he fell to the pavement clumsily on one hip. I swung my head around and saw the security guards stirring.

'Come on!' I shouted.

Shaking his head, Lorin scooped Abigail up, revealing the bare feet of an urchin, and we ran up Marchione Street. As we gained the corner, Lorin surged forward. His eyes were focused ahead of us and his coordination seemed to be returning. I was already breathless before our pace increased and now I struggled to stay close to him. Carrying Abigail's body seemed to make no difference to him. I lagged behind as he twisted and turned down smaller streets and then slowed as he shifted Abigail over his shoulder and groped inside his pockets. In front of us was a black Alfa Romeo, and this was the direction in which Lorin was heading.

He laid Abigail out on the back seat, her dress nearly filling the whole space. The engine roared into life, but our collective gasping almost drowned it out. As he hit fifty miles an hour in only a couple of seconds, his expression was one of fixed concentration. From nowhere, I felt the wave of love come over me again, as sensuous as a warm breeze blown over naked skin. *What was wrong with me? My life had just crashed on jagged rocks and I was swooning over my boyfriend.*

Lorin's lips were moving; I battled with myself to focus.

'Take the batteries out of our phones.' He tugged his own out of his pocket and threw it at me. 'The first thing they'll do is track us.'

The arrow on the speed dial was up to eighty miles per hour and he dodged around other cars in a way that under normal circumstances would have been terrifying, but today just blended in with my other fears. I sat silently, trying to think and let him concentrate on getting us away.

His body was stiff, a determined look in his eyes. Occasionally, he would say, 'No-one following us, yet.'

I glanced at Abigail in the back seat; she was still unconscious. As Lorin gained the main road leading out of Milan, his chest began to rise and fall more evenly. I tried to force mine to do the same. Little twinkling lights were dancing on the periphery of my vision. I laid my head in my hands and the tears arrived, unchecked by the curtain of my palms. Blake's hideous injury filled my mind. Lorin put his hand on my shoulder. The early migraine sickness churned in my stomach and I groaned. Lorin slipped his hand on to my knee.

'Try not to focus on your dad or Blake right now.

None of this is your fault.'

His kindness felt like another lash of a whip that had already done ninety-nine. On top of losing Blake, my dad, my art career, potentially my freedom, I felt losing Lorin when my heart had just opened up to him to be like the work of a sadist.

We were travelling at a speed far above any legal limit, but there was little on the road. I turned my head away from him and let my tears continue to expel the pain.

***

When Abigail rose up and appeared in the windscreen mirror, both Lorin and I started. We stared at her with twin expressions of surprise, having let go of her presence while lost in our own thoughts. She ran her hands through her hair in an attempt to make it lie down. Having been styled with a great deal of hairspray, it was sticking out in a structured way as if offering platforms for something to sit.

'I hate blonde hair,' she said.

I turned around to look at her fully. 'Thanks.'

'I mean on me.' She sighed and sat back, defeated by the state of her hair. This made me lift my hand to my wig, which was still held in place with clips, but askew, and I pulled it off.

'Why did you come back?' Lorin said in his growly voice, which now played a melodic scale up and down my insides as he spoke.

She shrugged. 'You both helped me. I knew you'd be in trouble. Besides, I've been taken twice now by the Society. I need allies.'

'What about the police? Surely there's a chance now that the Society will be exposed. There'll be a lot of questions raised about what happened tonight.'

I looked at Lorin with hope. He shook his head.

'Everyone who was in that room is committed to protecting the Society's secrets. No-one there will mention having ever seen Abigail to the police.'

'Even when something so evil has just happened, they will still protect the Society?'

'What your father has done to me and Terry – that was evil,' Abigail said defiantly.

I turned on her. 'Whatever he's done doesn't justify murdering Blake. You know that knife wasn't meant for that! How did he even get it?'

'Terry didn't go for the boy,' snapped Abigail.

Lorin interrupted us. 'What am I missing?'

Both Abigail and I looked at each other, and I felt the same sensation as I had when I'd jumped from the balcony after my fight with Lorin – like I was hurtling towards the ground at speed, anticipating the crash.

Abigail answered for me. 'Terry has been working undercover in that building since the end of the summer last year. Ironically, he got a job working for security without much difficulty.'

'And the knife?' Lorin pressed.

I took a deep breath. 'That was my doing, my mistake.' I looked up at him and winced as I caught his eye. 'Abigail was scared about where she might be moved to. I sent her the knife inside a statue.'

Lorin formed the word '*Oh*' on his lips, but didn't speak. The explosion of love I'd felt for him earlier melded into something more solid and forged a lump in my throat. He concentrated on the road, and I observed with dread the dazzling lights beginning to crowd my vision.

'Tonight's events will be reported as having nothing to do with the Society,' he said. 'I'm sure they will say that Terry attempted to murder your father because he believed he was responsible for the disappearance of his

283

wife, but your brother intervened. There is even footage of Terry holding you hostage only a few weeks ago.'

'But Terry will tell the police everything, surely?' I turned in my seat, giving Abigail an enquiring expression. She shrugged.

'The police will have been incentivised for years to be on your father's side in many matters – you're not in England now,' Lorin said, gruffly.

'Also, a man wailing about alchemists will get short shrift from the police, I imagine,' Abigail added.

I tried to force the lights away by rubbing my temples. 'Have you got any Ibuprofen? I'm getting a migraine.' I pulled open the glove compartment and rooted through, but found only a hand gun ... *great.*

Lorin stayed silent, but moved lanes and took the slip road leading off the main road. I felt like I was spinning in a whirlpool of desolation. I could feel his energy withdrawing from me as every second slipped past. He must be thinking what I was thinking. *How could I have given her a knife and not expected someone to get hurt?* As he came to a stop in a side road, I looked at him with wild eyes, considering that he might be about to drop me off and drive away.

He turned to Abigail. 'Can you wait here for a few minutes?'

He got out of the car and walked around to my side. My heart was hammering in my chest as he opened my door. He didn't offer his hand. I scrambled up, trying to meet his eye and predict his intentions, but read nothing from his Vulcan-stare of no emotion.

The silky night air calmed the dazzling a little. We stood on a narrow residential street with tall apartment blocks leaning in on each other. This wasn't a picturesque historic Milan street. It was a gritty, contemporary suburb with graffiti and grime in equal amounts. Many of the windows were open and lights glowed from them, showing washing strung between the buildings. The sounds of chatter and clinking of cutlery being handled echoed in the sky. I felt the chasm between where we were and the small happinesses of normal life.

Lorin turned and walked slightly ahead of me along the pavement. I wanted to reach out to him and claim his hand. I'd fallen in love with this man, and despite what he thought of me now, I needed to own it. I reached forward, but we'd come to the end of the block and he turned into a small community garden.

Darkness offered only the outline of the flowers and shrubs that had been carefully cultivated around the perimeter. In the centre of the gravelly path was a small stone drinking fountain with bronze *putti* dancing above the outlet.

'No Ibuprofen, but water,' he said, holding the button down for me so that a cascade of water fell. As I leaned forward to drink, he added, 'A friend of my family used to live in that building.' He pointed across the road. 'We would come and sit here when I visited.' The water was very cold, and although it wasn't an *awesome* pill, it was soothing.

As I pulled away, droplets hovering on my lips, he took my hand. 'It's not your fault. None of this is your fault. You did not kill him, do you understand me? All this is because of the Society. You made a mistake, that's all.'

The moonlight was not strong enough to give colour to his eyes, but earnestness was in every feature. The fireworks were exploding in my chest again.

'Nothing can change how I feel about you. With you, I see a glimmer of hope: a way out of the darkness that I've been facing into for too long. You offer a different future – one with laughter and art and happiness. I know there are a lot of complications, but I have this sense that we need each other,' he said.

He sought my lips, slipping his hand behind my neck and running his lips along mine before kissing me with a hunger that made me forget the mess our lives were in.

'Will you guys hurry up?' Abigail's voice pulled us out of our moment. 'There will be plenty of time for that after we've exposed the Society!'

'We'll be there in a minute,' Lorin snapped, which made me smile. We *were* always getting interrupted.

I tugged his hand. 'Come on, she's right. They might not be that far behind us. Where were you driving us to?'

'Rome. I know a place we can stay and be safe for a while.'

As we walked back along the street, some realities began to elbow my tender head.

Abigail was leaning against the car. Her dress reflected the yellow glow of the street lamp making her figure shimmer.

'I don't want to be on the run for the rest of my life,' I said as we reached her.

'Well, that's fine by me. I'm tired of running,' she said. 'So the only thing left to do is to bring the ugly truth about alchemy into the light.'

The End

Acknowledgments

I would like to acknowledge my parents who have always had boundless faith in me and have encouraged my efforts with practical assistance and enthusiasm. I would like to thank my husband who has been encouraging when I really needed it. Hugs to Catherine Bower – a true friend and champion. Sincere thanks to Alison and Jim McLean who continue to support me in every way. Thanks to my editor, Alison Jack, proofreader Rachel Phillipson and cover designer Debbie Cassidy. To my beta-readers – I couldn't have done it without you! Particular thanks to Helen Winstanley, Catherine Bower, Siân Fletcher and Rachel Phillipson

If you enjoyed this book, please review it. Reviews make a really big difference to small presses like ours.

Want to know the truth about Abigail? Want to know who Terry really is? Or if Abigail is a murderer?

Read

A RARER GIFT THAN GOLD

Lucy Branch loves hearing from her readers so if you would like to drop her a line – please do!

Email *lucy@antiquebronze.co.uk* or go to Lucy's website *www.lucybranch.com* where you can become a member of her Readers' Group. Being part of Lucy's Readers' Group gives you a chance to receive free copies of her new novels, hear about other authors' promotions and have a chance to share your passion for reading.

Twitter and Facebook are Lucy's favourite places to hang out so find Lucy *@lucyBranch11* or *https://www.facebook.com/lucybranchauthor*

18996118R00163

Printed in Great Britain
by Amazon